I hope my first will become a loyal reader!

Antonio

First Published 2016
Paperback Edition first published 2016

© Antonio Spaccapietra

Antonio Spaccapietra has asserted his right under the Copyright, Designs and Patents Act, 1988, to be identified as the author of this work.

All rights reserved. No part of this publication may be reproduced or transmitted in any form or by any means, electronic or mechanical, including photocopying, recording or any information storage or retrieval system, without prior permission in writing from the author.

ISBN: 978-1530264384

PREFACE

This book is about the *all-embracing art form*; what others have called the *Gesamtkunstwerk*. How may all of the arts merge? Do you ever wander what the fusion of the arts looks like?

If you do, I want you to think about the following: fusions are liquid are they not? If I smelt gold and silver together it will be liquid; if I mix oil paints, the same applies. If I make an exquisite smoothie that combines all the fruits imaginable, what is the effect? A juicy pulp.

As you scour through this book I want you to remember that the all-embracing art form will be a liquid. Return to this page when you have read the last.

Why *must* the fusion of all the senses, of all the arts, be watery? The objects of greatest beauty in this world are all aqueous; think of perfumes, of wine, baptisms, the sexual experience, to tears to ink or sea, or even of the rain.

Chapter 1.

He had always seen the garden as the place that most closely expressed the fragility of his own mind. It was the indoors without clocks, where time was gone and differences between history forgotten. Between the house and the garden where the seconds in-between his timeless escape from the 21st century to the years before.

As a gardener he believed it his duty, by the orange stained birches, and the working aprons flecked in green, to nurse what language had called a wild woman: "Flora". Thomas had devoted his life to this philosophy of flowers. But he had not been very successful. A third rate competition in Surrey had been his only accolade in his bountyless bouquet of feats. He had wooed Flora all his life here in his house of flowers much like a brothel, with lace-petal blouses by the windowsills and forgotten pink lady's slippers by the doormat. His heart, like a Russian doll, would forever contain this warp of woman.

Now at the age of sixty-four he was due to retire. He was exhausted. If only he could just loosen up a little. He had always believed in the beauty of flowers, but not so much in anything else. He had only really cared for Flora, up until he had replaced her for someone new – someone real.

Life as a pensioner for Thomas would be like a long Sunday, and every Sunday would find him exploring the marshes of a nearby lake, picking plums, or arranging those pots like beds, where Flora slept nude.

Yet there was another woman he thought about; one that had left him, unlike Flora, someone far younger.

With her terrible and lovely legs she had walked out of his life, without any notice at all, leaving him somewhat confused and again, exhausted. His second love! Their separation had been dolorous, some might even say even poetic. She had left him on his birthday. Even if she had made a fool of him, he would remember her, religiously.

Here is our gardener by the window of his home. He is in his studio, with his head resting on a desk like an altar. He is thinking about this woman, Flora's successor, amongst the reverie of books on his pivoting bookshelf. The quaint candelabrum only intensifies the colour of the fawn divan behind him, where he has stirred and pressed the tube of a pomade near the Pembroke table. His hands are always dry when he is anxious. It is this tube on the table that reminds him of things half full. He remembers her rejection, and then his raw animal craving for company.

He has just returned from the town-centre and the crowds of the street just witnessed remind him of his solitude. He lifts the newest plant he has brought home from the market on to his desk. With all the grains of soil falling, flickering in a ripe ember violet, here is the *Astrantia*.

Who was the botanist that named this plant?

"Astrantia".

He cannot remember. It does correspond well to the image however: "flowers like stars". But what about stars like flowers? He only knows that the type he holds in his hands now is called "ruby wedding".

Thomas places the astrantia plant upon a teal-dressed porcelain plate that places the stems in a contrast of delight, and fondles one of the tools that is positioned across the picture symmetrically, in a slow movement. He cuts the stem of the flower with a vertical and fabulous jerk. With a knife tied to a protractor mechanically he dismembers each petal from the flower, in a clockwork cut that must not falter, otherwise he must start again. He tremors at all the shine of purple, as if he has just dismembered an amethyst outer space, as if he were a jeweller of the skies.

The petals become unbound and fall upon the plate. The bracts are in his quivering hands. He is holding the stars. The gardener emits a sigh that inflates his eyes like tissue-paste that soon might burst. His glistening iris is a new entry of the constellation. He offers the blessing for the second time, "Amen" and the astrantia becomes his type of Eucharist. Taking it, believing it, madly he eats, and a purple flake of the sky flowers in his chest. Here is his purple mass!

You look at him and you think you know everything about him, but let us begin with the times before these; before Thomas had started eating flowers and before his second love, second only to Flora, had left him for money.

Chapter 2.

He could live nowhere else than Surrey, England. The place where his life had become like a ubiquitous garden, and he could be surrounded by his art, wherever he went. He could stroll here amongst foxes and stags to the frequency of dandy gentlemen. "Slowly dilating glimpses of green" was what he saw pressed under his eyelids whenever he fell asleep by his balcony. His home was just behind the Guildford chantries, and almost every day, he would observe the valleys, the bushes he pruned, or the voluptuous violet cherry blossoms he planted. Surrey was one great garden. If ever a man should tire of the office, then it should be he.

But Thomas did not tire easily. In his youth he had worked hard, but now he was in charge of planning and designing gardens. He designed gardens with grass like green velvet or minimalist things Scandinavian. And it was in Scandinavia, where he had travelled a few times, that he had heard the words, "less is more"; a motto he had rejected. Beauty, as a flower that flounders, was florid.

"I really have to get started" he said to himself in his house of flowers, where there were so many variegated incarnations of Flora, the wild woman, that he might have been a melancholy man in a brothel.

The *Chelsea Flower Show* in September would be his last and best work. At these types of shows he would have to design gardens for the public to admire and then a jury would select a winner. The RHS Chelsea Flower Show, formally known as the Great Spring Show, was a garden show held for five days in May by the Royal

Horticultural Society in the grounds of the Royal Hospital. Held at Chelsea since 1912, it was the most famous flower show in the United Kingdom, and perhaps in the world, attracting visitors from all continents. This year it was going to place in September, to add an autumnal twist to the competition, never seen before. It was late May, but he needed to already start thinking and planning to come up with some ideas.

He wanted his work to be classic but at the same time modern. He knew that flowers, however common, however banal, would never go out of fashion. They would be printed upon dresses and shirts; and they would be given as gifts to people of all centuries. Whilst this last flower show at Chelsea would need to be his best work, every show to him was unforgettable. He had captured them all in a picture book which he now took in his arms.

"A Bouquet of Flowers: A VICTORIAN PHOTOGRAPH ALBUM" read the front cover of the picture book. The famous illustrator, Dorne Wright, had decorated the book with rare drawings of butterflies. Thomas undid the chlorine-green ribbon and began reading. The picture book's first page had some descriptions of gardens.

In one paragraph of this book, every time, he would read how *"the Victorian artist was not only a craftsperson, but also a scientist, a poet and an explorer. In this respect Dorne was a latter Victorian artist, though her exploration often took her no further than her own garden or the fields which surrounded her cottage in Nottinghamshire".*

These lines of the picture book that murmured of a totality of art, "science", "exploration" and "poetry" would be the beginning of his work. Totality? The idea inspired him. Dorne Wright the illustrator was supposedly the complete person that knew how to do everything. But the real all-encompassing and extraordinary man in the world of art was Wagner. The German composer. Thomas would soon discover his ideal. That would become his chief aim before retiring. To go out in style! To do everything!

"Your last work must include everything."
Alles!

But Thomas would not understand whom or what had spoken. He was yet to discover that his last show at Chelsea, would require of him a "total work of art".

Unlike Dorne the illustrator, Thomas was a character loathe to activity but prostitute to working hard. He was always contradictory. For this he adored a static flower. But for this he also desired to move and dance. Making music with the soles of his shoes dusting on the floor, and walking towards his desk, he tapped into the signals of creativity. All he needed was an idea. All he wanted was just some inspiration. He deposited the picture book on the desk and fingered the pages. Looked at all the shows he had made so far in his gardening career.

Flicking through the pages, there seemed to be a common motif in all of them. Shimmering narcissus flowers reflected him best. Or so he thought, even if he was not inwardly in love, if not only with Flora, his phenomenal Flora. He had posed with her around the world. Where the picture books of others were filled by persons, his was solely filled by flowers: Lily, Jasmine and Marigold to name a few.

There was one other picture of the show that perhaps he was most proud of. It was a tribute to Lewis Carroll's Alice. Carroll was actually buried in Guildford, not too far from the chantries. In lauding gesture Thomas had arranged a mirror's glass made of Narcissus flowers, with vitrified glossy petals. Looking at the picture again, his senses began to fuse by the rose-bush he had used to imitate porcelain. The mirror's glass he had made, looked like a sheet of white with blotches of amber. The mirror permitted him three pleasures. A reflection, a fragrance, and a chance to put one's hand through its glass, just as Alice had done in Carroll's story, to make fingers come out on the other side.

When he put his hand there, when he considered the heavy and thick incantation of the tuberose slowly creeping inside, his fingers felt soft as a gauze. His spine tingled. But he did have one last desire for this mirror. He wanted to scratch his name in the glass, like lovers used to do in pleasure homes. He had heard that lovers of Victorian times used to write their names on mirrors with their jewellery. Now he too wanted to scratch his name here with a ring, *Thomas*!, all over, with the scrawl of goblins and guinea. But he could not. He could only echo slippery fantasies. Was far too ambitious.

He was so lost in looking at these pictures that he did not hear the first *Ring*! at his door. On the second *Ring*! he was shaken into reality. *Ring*! *Ring*! *Ring*! There was a visitor at his door. Put down the picture book and go downstairs to open the door.

The postman and then the stamps on the letters he carried; there were thousands collected in the guestroom opposite the studio. He did not like this fellow however because whenever he would come into his driveway, he would jump through the hedges, and then spoil all the plants he had laboured to order. The post-man would also show off his youth; was just twenty and had effeminate mannerisms that Thomas did not like on a man.

"If you could sign here."

Signed his name and took the letters. There were two of them.

"These stamps are so ugly" he said as he tore open the first envelope. It was just the bills. The second and last letter he opened was written in hand-writing that he recognised. The post stamp was foreign. It came from Tuscany. Turning the letter on its head, he saw the sender. It was his godmother.

Dear Thomas,

This is the third time I've tried writing you this letter today. It's the nostalgia that gets me every time. Do you remember? The time passes but still I think of our days in England, of you and my daughter. Do you ever see her in Guildford? Do you travel much to London? Do you ever return to Hampton court?

I still have those photographs of your birthdays at Hampton. I must send them to you. They are on my desk and just now as I scribble, the photo of a boy with his Godmother and her daughter stares back at me. You were so terribly disobedient. Always have been. I still think about the fright you gave me when you got lost in the maze and we had to look for you. Or what about that time you almost drowned in the pool?

I know that you are competing a last time at the Chelsea Flower show over there in England. You've won it before haven't you? I wish I could come see you. But you know I can't. You know I can't travel anymore.

I am writing this letter to you because I am soon going about writing my will.

I have three things that may be of interest to you. My house here, the flat in Guildford and my portrait we got done by that artist. I know you already have the picture and I would like you to keep it.

I want to leave you the house in Tuscany. It's not worth much but it can be yours. I remember how much you liked the vista that looks out over the hill. I'm getting the agent to come and evaluate it tomorrow.

The lawyer should be sending some letters to you. Expect these to arrive, in Italian, in the next weeks. You shouldn't have trouble translating them. You must sign these to claim the insurance and all this.

You don't have to reply to me, I know you're stubborn like that, but in some way let me know. You're always in my thoughts.

Lots of love,
Flora

She was trying to repair a broken relationship. He needed to check again the sender. Yes. It really was *Flora*. His godmother. He had not heard from her since she had left Guildford permanently, several years ago. Every Christmas he had sent greeting cards but had received no answer back. Why was she writing now? Turning the envelope he noticed something that seemed wrong; the address of the sender and the house that he would presumably inherit.

Via Winspear 23 Magliano Toscana Italia

It did not correspond to the address he knew and had sent all his letters to. Italian names were difficult to remember but he was sure of the mistake.

"That address Eleanor gave me was false."

"Who is Eleanor?" recoiled the other flowers in a gemmed jealousy. A topaz tulip was furious.

"How cheap is she?"

"Ah Eleanor… Eleanor, Eleanor, Eleanor."

Eleanor was Flora's daughter. He had been infatuated with her when they were children. But Eleanor had always been rude with him. Even now they would sometimes bump into each other in Guildford and she would always pretend not to see him.

"Oh come here Thomas, I am thirsty and I long for you" whispered an enormous vase of Lilies that emitted a barrage of its scent.

He went to take the watering-can to satisfy his loves, but all the while he thought of someone else; Eleanor. A woman knows when she is second in the heart of man and severed by thoughts of jealously, the lilies moved their heads away to pretend they did not know, that they were oblivious to his divided love as he bestowed his balm upon them, in delightful ejaculations. When the thirsty flowers had all received their fluid, and he had finished, Thomas deposited the watering-can in the utility room and ascended the stairs in a pensive daze. Nude. Exhausted.

Caught in an identity crisis – was he Thomas or Flower? - he too felt the need to be watered. He went upstairs and began running a warm bath. It was only midday but he tumbled in the bathtub as if it were his bed, with the curtains blowing open and the sun casting its cerise beam into the room.

Flora. And Eleanor? What had happened to her? These two people had always pretended to be kind and hospitable. Yes, his godmother had written now, but for years she had been a stranger. He would take the house in Tuscany, but then he would try to never think about her again. Sliding down in the bathtub, soon after he fell asleep. Out of his pigeon-chest came jays, waxwings and passerines of all kind.

Chapter 3.

Sometime after Thomas awoke in the bathtub. He had slept far too long, and opened his eyes whilst still saying the name, "Eleanor". No need to think about her however, nor his godmother; it was more important to move on in his life and to forget those people.

Before getting dressed he began thinking about his work and remembered that he needed to go into town. A burgundy & blue shawl wrapped itself around his neck seductively as he left the house. Pilgrim's road and then Shalford road. Guildford town-centre was just a short fifteen minute walk away and he needed some new notebooks to start designing his project.

As he walked a jet flew over him as if it were a pencil falling. He observed the sky as a large desk and watched this streak of white dribble down its design. Charmed until he reached the town and crossed the road, ignoring the traffic lights, he reached the part of the pavement that led one out to the high-street. There was a statue of a scholar that danced in glee that he always admired but for now his elusive memory misplaced every street and shop. *Whibleys* was much further up the road, and the bank somewhere else entirely, but no! The town had not changed. It was only his demented mind. But where was Waterstone's?

Rearranging the tangle of streets in his memory, just after the post office, he found it and entered. He began to walk around the bookstore and wasted time by the stationary. There was a magazine to find out how to stop foxes from urinating on the grass; many men and women browsing through the books in search of something to read for the summer. Some music books. Perhaps he could include music too at the Chelsea show. After all, what difference was there between writer and musician, florist or gardener? Everyone creates from nothing.

He took in his hands different books all binded with the same extravagant style. Vignettes showed figures in evening-dresses who lived in a box of gold and white; guilty of ornament, charm and luxury. As he put the books back he considered that he too wanted to be bound in white pages, to be mummified in a marvellous front cover. Then they could sprinkle talc over him and no rust would corrode him. Then he could truly retire; do and be whatever he wanted in superficial appearances and facades.

Came the relief of impermissible desires. He left Waterstone's and paid for the books with an agonising sum of coins. The man at the till frowned at him when he saw all the coins emerge from his hands.

Thomas came out on the high-street and felt his body humming. At last! It's so warm today; continued on with the shawl. On the high-street, amongst the windows of fashion and women of Surrey, he was envied and admired, at times condescended. When he arrived further up the road, he gave the change in his pockets to some beggars on the street. His look was altogether so bohemian, that some people mistook him for one of them.

When he had run out of change and he had received the glares of many men and women, he gave to the high-street his curious and rather bizarre ballerino walk. He had tried dancing once after his birthday at

Hampton Court, when he had seen the recreation of a Tudor ball; actors pretending to the play of a harp. He had told his godmother Flora of his desire to dance and she had welcomed it. So he had taken up lessons of dance, paid for by his godmother, in the days when their relationship had not been severed by time. The dances had ended quickly and abruptly. He had given up long ago. But he still carried dusty traces of ballet upon cobblestone; added already to the traces of sugar that a zephyr chanced to spread over from the cafe tables.

He walked amongst the other crowds of the street, shepherded by the glittered currents of desire. Then he also succumbed to an irresistible liver sausage sandwich. Bending over the sweet and sour sauces he finished the salad and then the jam doughnuts. Holding palms amorously with the plastic bag, he decided to stay in the town a while longer. There was a glassware shop down the road he wanted to see.

"Hello" said the owner when he entered.

A "just browsing" which never reached his lips and he was lolling amongst the pieces on display. In the centre of the room was a divisive bookshelf-like structure. He began to walk around its perimeters. The first side was crowned with collections of American art nouveau; Aurene Ware that emitted a blue and gold lustre and here and there some Tyrian glass which only intensified the effect of being in a petrified sea. He turned the corner of the shelf to inspect the other side and here were examples of Polish and Czech Glass.

"These ones come from *Loetz* and are made from burning *treez*" spoke the owner.

"Italians do it better" he heard Flora's voice again. Besides dance, besides music, Italians could craft better glass too, he remembered the Venetian vase which had rested on Flora's cabinet. What was it's name? Ah yes, murano, the same sound of the word - murano! - carried its movement of furnace dust; shaped to an artist's desire like a breast or a palm. He began to see Flora, his Godmother, in all things. In a vase, in a reflection of a toucan, or even in the "strange coincidence" that the owner, like Flora, was a foreigner. Worst of all he didn't even want to be here, the window had seduced him in. He was alike to an old telephone call; bound by cables to the same receiver. *Yes? Hello?* He kept thinking about Flora, telephoning her, and the narrative of his thoughts stumbled terribly. Repetition was everywhere. Flora was everywhere and it was nauseating. He had seen such a type of mind once before. When he had gardened the fields of a wealthy woman on Chantry View Road many years ago. What was that woman's name? Bertha?

Bertha's husband had cheated on her.

"Can you believe it?!" said Bertha all those years ago, as he was mowing the lawn.

"That cheater! That filthy cheater!"

The roar of the lawnmower then disguised what she said next, until she began to weep.

"Oh but I love him! I still love him!" - to which Thomas said nothing. And turned off the lawnmower. Flora also loved this sentimentality. She was classic and professorial but also contemporary.

Later he would understand the beauty of the water which flows upon a woman's cheeks, as the pump that nourishes grass, something ancient that echoed the caveman.

"And the worst thing!" she continued, "is that I can't help not thinking about him!"".

"Give me one thing and I bet it will make think of him" she said in the rhetorical command of the decade.

He looked at her unsure what to say. Not caring very much at all, he thought how lacking in salt his liver sausage sandwich had been that morning. So, utterly serious, he had said:

"Salt".

"Ah! she cried. "Salt!"

"Salt… like the salt of the sea in the tropical island where he's staying! Oh- that bastard!".

He was actually impressed. Perhaps she could go on one of those programmes on television when the eventual divorce would rip apart her life, bejewelled in horns, cornute, she could prize away a fortune. Without thinking he tapped her on the shoulder in a spontaneous congratulation. Bertha thought that perhaps he was being promiscuous at last, like all gardeners. Heather the neighbour had had her own midsummer flirtation with a florist tumble in an ill-advised but pleasurable disaster. Why shouldn't she concede herself this cheap pleasure? Ah yes – she hated cheap things. When Thomas took the car and had left with stuttering starts and stops, she had glared at him in the window. Full of tears. Moist in both extremes of the body. Then Bertha thought how stupid and blind all men really were.

Back in the glassware shop, Thomas lingered a few moments longer in his telephone call to memory. He had begun to stare at a bowl on the shelf. A woman on the other side began to think he was staring at her. Thomas met the corner. He had seen all of the items, except for the one which two men were carrying through the door. *Crash*! - went the stained glass.

The owner stood up from his stool and put his hands in his hair. Thomas looked at the collision he had caused. "I'm so sorry" said Thomas at last, half-heartedly. The other customers of the glass shop were very embarrassed. Some sympathised with Thomas, others with the owner. Whose fault was it? But Thomas could not care to convince anybody of his innocence. He was just looking at the woman who was leaving the store.

"Eleanor?" he called out to her.

The woman stopped.

"Is it really you?"

"Thomas…"

"Do you know this guy?!" said the owner.

"Yes… he is…"

(Reluctantly): Family…

"She's leaving me the house in Tuscany, all of it" he said abruptly.

"I'm sorry?" said Eleanor, although she had understood perfectly.

"Flora, my *Godmother*" he stressed, "is leaving me the house in Italy, she wrote to me in her will".

"It can't be."

"Oh but it can."

Eleanor's mouth opened to breathe out a floral mist of antipathy. Meanwhile the owner interpreted Thomas' last remark as a provocation; with this house in

Tuscany, he didn't have any excuses to refuse a timely and generous reimbursement.

"You're just crazy."

"*Ding!*" the doorbell rang to her dismissal.

He looked again at the owner.

"I'm sorry but you're going to have to repay me, all of it".

"I don't have any money here."

"But tomorrow" he said.

"I will come back."

"Then you're going to have to leave me your details."

Walking back home Thomas' head became ballooned with thoughts: the bills to pay, Flora's sudden return and his last work at Chelsea. When he closed the door of his home, he threw all his things on the floor and put his feet up. He unbuttoned his shirt. He took off his socks and untightened his belt that pressed on his belly. Had it really been Eleanor in the shop earlier? He had become so used to bumping into her like that in Guildford that it became inconsequential.

Having not eaten dinner, he squeezed some pomegranate juice into a jar. He took out the knife and cut out the pomegranate seeds. As he was squeezing the juice with his palms, he saw the fox was in his garden. It was urinating on the grass. Holding the juice he paced out towards the patio, unlocking the sliding-door.

"I'll get you eventually!" he cried out to the fox.

"I will catch you sooner or later" he repeated.

The hunger-stricken fox emitted a hideous and tenuous growl, stealing off in the distance with a smirk resting on its fangs. Regrettably he would have to sow new seeds in the place where the fox had urinated. He looked out to the neighbours' fence and sighed with his lips tainted pomegranate red. As he closed the patio's door he thought that he might even come to miss the fox if he ever were to trap it. If gardens were stages they were ever so desolate and without actors.

He closed the sliding-door and then went to lock all the other doors of the house before ascending upstairs. In the studio he hung his shawl on the chair and then put the new journals on the desk and sat down; closed his eyes for a few moments and then sighed from the boredom. Not knowing what to do, Thomas began tidying his studio. There were some shirts left to dry on the radiator and he folded them and put them in the drawers.

In the centre of the mahogany desk was still the picture book with all his life's work, just as he had left it. Earlier he had been looking at a picture of Alice in wonderland. But this was not the photograph in front of him. When he had gone downstairs to the mailman, a page of the picture book had turned by itself. Here was another page of the picture book he had earmarked.

He looked at the picture of an opera house. "*The Richard-Wagner-Festspielhaus*" was the titled he had given it, when he had been in Germany several months ago. The Festspielhaus was one of the opera houses Wagner, the German composer, had designed and Thomas had visited it.

"Richard Wagner…" he read, remembering the days he had passed in Germany. Underneath the title he had written another word, with an arrow:

GESAMKUNTSWERK

It felt like he had never seen this word before. He took out his magnifying glass to inspect it better. The word became intelligible. Translated in English it read:

THE ALL EMBRACING ART FORM

The *all-embracing art form*? Could there ever be such a creation? He had forgotten entirely about having taken this picture and having written this word next to it. At the time he had written it here in the picture book because the idea had inspired him for one of his shows. Sitting in the arms of his chair, as if lazing in the glow of the page, he inhaled the beauty of these words, "all-embracing art form", with a narcotic necromancy. He was allured by the supple reward that dramatism of art such as this might promise in a bottle or a needle or the pursuit of something dangerously bohemian and grotesque.

He had read about Wagner in scintillating books, in one of his trips to the library. When he sought to acquire new material for his gardens or to further his understanding of culture. He'd been enamoured by how deranged that man was - overpowering - the bolts of thunder in his songs and the brute bell that echoed in triumphs his own instrumental body. Now tuned to old age, at times he was lyricized in this staccato, in other instances legato – bound to the chair.

But now he could not remember the Wagnerian ideal entirely. Why had he written it here? Wagner had written about art but what was the *Gesamtkunstwerk*? And what did it have to do with his work as a gardener? Wagner had dreamt of fusing all the arts together, music, painting and writing and now he thought it would be a good idea to do the same, for his last show at Chelsea.

He took the picture book and his person towards the divan, lying down in a pensive stretch of aspiration and ingenuity. This could be the theme that he could treat in his last work. Wagner's work, Wagner's dream, it inspired him. He couldn't think of anything more orangely occult, yet enlightening, than this for his last project. Surely it would be successful and everyone would like it. But Wagner had failed in realising it. He knew that he, as Wagner, had failed, in his relations to society, Eleanor and then his solitude. But wasn't failure necessary in the arm form?

His godmother's house in Tuscany would be his only consolation prize. He, Thomas Haller, could be the unlikely prodigy; the ugly man ushering this promiscuity of all the arts. Enchanted by the thought of failure, he became closer to the great show he imagined. "This is going to be fantastic" he said alone in his room.

Chapter 4.

The next morning would be less fantastic. Thomas rose at seven o'clock and then went out towards the kitchen to see the grass was turning a pale colour. He sighed loudly in frustration but then revelled in the plums at the end of the garden. By the neighbour's fence they levitated delectably as nipples. The gloomy morning was redeemed by this flutter of his fancies. Thomas put his hand on the windowpane and slowly began to salivate.

"*Riiiiiing*"

"The mailman? At this hour?" he thought as he opened the door.

"Eleanor?"

Eleanor, his godmother's daughter, was on his doorstep with her husband Bradley. Her husband was a well-known lawyer. So it had been her he'd met in the glass shop after all.

Without asking they had parked in his stone driveway. How annoying when people parked in the driveway. The car's warm laced wheels made one shudder.

"We're here" began the lawyer, "because as a family, we thought we could reach an agreement".

"Now if you could please let me see this letter Flora sent to you... we can fix this really quickly."

He almost entertained the idea.

"The matters to resolve are equal in number to the hairs on a bald man's head – zero."

"Now if you may please move the car out of the driveway."

"Enough" interrupted Eleanor.

"Let's just say it how it is."

"Flora, my mother, is leaving the house in Tuscany to me."

(Mirroring her): Flora, my *Godmother*, is leaving the house in Tuscany to me.

"Urgh!" she cried.

The lawyer tried to defend his wife, even thought about pushing Thomas for having disrespected her, but then he saw him stand in the doorway, with his enormous shoulders. He stepped back.

"Come on, we're just going to need you to sign some papers… testifying that the house is Eleanor's."

"The house is mine and that's that" he finished his last sentence and bade them goodbye with the door still open. He ascended upstairs but over the ring of the doorbell he could still hear them argue. He opened one of the draws in the studio and took his chequebook; he was a man of his word and he would reimburse the owner of the glassware shop. When he returned downstairs he unfastened the keys from the latch and found Eleanor and Bradley still accusing each other. They looked at him and directed their breath towards Thomas, his own mouth laced with the foul scents of morning dew, a line of white hanging upon the contours of his cupid's brow. No love or admiration could he conjure up in them.

"Get out of my way, I'm going out now."

Their bodies danced around him as two marionettes asking him a thousand questions. When Thomas had sealed his door shut, to leave for the town of Guildford, Eleanor had cried out:

"There is no chance that you're going to inherit my mother's house."

He looked at her from his porch and noticed how Eleanor had become fat. Perhaps his nickname for her didn't suit her anymore at all. She had stopped applying that serum in her hair that he liked. Bradley wrapped his arms around Eleanor and she took him in her arms. Together they looked at Thomas helplessly. Holding each other so closely, they humiliated him. Thomas felt himself like a lover caught in a triangle and wanted to be as far away from them as possible.

On that great long road that led to Guildford and passed by the canal, a boat piping smoke emerged on the water as Thomas walked in parallel on the pavement. In a game of perspective this boat became like a cigar in his mouth. Further down; walked arrogantly like a smoking Lieutenant by the green marshlands and then passed by Debenhams. The long building rested as a lazy arm in the ground and smacked of old age just as much as he did.

In the town centre, this time *Whibleys* and the Bank felt compassion for Thomas. They did not relocate address to mock him. He refused the *Big Issue* as he refused to acknowledge his poor choice of clothes; in a sweltering heat his skin began to moisten to the gasps of summer. He continued to walk in a peach-orange glare of naked light and every shop window seemed to be glossy, like a piece of paper.

The comic books he owned were similar to this avenue. The high-street could be observed in part, and could be observed in its entirety. Thomas noticed he could look at a part of the street by itself, or by the entire scene surrounding it, and it would change the impression. A man's shoe was different when looked at it by itself; was different again when compared to other people's ankles passing by. Observing one item in each window, his mind became a great miniature. He absorbed dollar snippets of denim, moccasins, watches, perfumes, magazines, a shower of bricks and at last one enormous clock tower crushing his scalp with a crevice.

When he came further up the road, he passed by the glassware shop and paid the sum of money he owed. He lingered in the store and tried making meaningless small talk with the owner. But he didn't want to speak to Thomas.

Out on the street again, Thomas saw the face of a familiar man; a man who worked in *Castle Street* that had been one of his own apprentices. How the years had passed. He had grown a beard and had a big dog beside him. The old apprentice carried boxes in his arms and turned the corner of the street without greeting him.

Even at his hour men and women fluttered amongst pigeons by the shop windows. He was also guilty of being seduced by clever marketing. Just the day before he had entered the antique store. But he had never gone so far as these people. Now he could see men and women positioned so closely to the shop-windows that they could melt into the glass, as if falling into a pool. At this noon hour charm seemed the order of the day. Behind those windows desire blew dust-red.

In one shop window he observed a strange thing. There were real people and not mannequins inside. Two models were in the window, with arrogant expressions, pretending to be statues. Never before had Thomas seen such clothes and such inspiring material for his *Chelsea Show*. In a geometrical floral dress one of the models was adorned with fine silks and moving life. Kaleidoscopic patterns sparkled in the turn of a revolution as Thomas spun his head in a wrap of scrutiny. A lump gripped his throat as he observed all the real-life mannequins in the window.

Yellow common madia with a blotch of blue in their iris were sown upon the blazer of the male mannequin and together they strode about the window with a fan blowing white rose petals here and there. What retailer was this? He looked at the sign. *Ted*. Here was a world similar to everything he considered to be noble. Here was an irresistible persuasion. Regrettably the shop window had done enough to lure him. Looking at those petals blowing in the window, crisp and caramelised as if in an oven, his mouth began to salivate and he entered.

"I have to speak with the person who made the window outside" he said whilst stumbling into *Ted*.

"Sir I'm afraid she's serving a customer at the moment."

"She?"

"Yes, she" said the shop assistant.

'Oh. Are you the regional manager due for the visit? From the head office?

"No."

"I'm just a gardener" said Thomas.

He looked around the shop and noticed that he was hungry. He reached into his pockets to produce a small pouch. He pulled out a green sphere that resembled a fig, the same one he had eaten yesterday, with a gauze of white leaking from its seems. He dropped the ball gloriously into his mouth, crushing it hard with his teeth.

(Frowning): Stella! Someone here wants to speak to you.

Behind a rack of fallen clothes, a carcass the retailers called them, emerged a woman of stellar appearance, the coil of her curls passing a current of sandstorm yellow into the extremity of her locks – her face infused with the stamp of lipstick - and behind that consciousness a neon glow of eyes which shed a bulbed incandescence, with every electric ripple.

"Hello, did you call for me? – I'm Stella. How may I help you?"

"I wanted to speak to you about the window outside" he began.

"Oh do you like it?!" she bellowed. She folded her hands upon her chest and leant back. One could have easily mistaken her extravagance for stupidity.

"Yes – I like it very much" he admitted. "What's the name of that dress in the window – the same dress you're wearing now?"

"Oh this one's called *Friyo*."

"Friyo…" he repeated clumsily.

"Would you like to buy one for your wife? It's on sale."

"No" he said and held his stomach.

"I'm not married. I'm a Gardener" he repeated.

"And I'm entering the Chelsea flower show in September. I'm looking well, for ideas".

"So you thought you'd copy mine?"

"No, no" he said, misinterpreting.

"The window outside is the closest thing I've seen to… to everything one could want. You've combined everything in that window."

"Wagner wrote about this. I was reading all about it last night. Do you know Wagner?" he asked for the second time that day.

"Yes I should do. After all I went to music school."

Thomas was not the first to ask questions like this. Many men had come in to charm Stella; she was a type of head-turner. Customers young and old would move their necks to look at her as she sashayed across the shop floor. In a delicious exercise of power; in a Vulcan desire, Stella could turn all those sinuous necks looking at her into brazened Mobius strips. The less clever men had tried to impress her with money but she had rejected them all. They did not know that Stella was out of place in this store. Whilst she stood proudly dressed in these silks, these dresses, her interests were in other things. Stella was a graduate of drama. She hadn't told anybody about her degree, nobody had asked. Except this man.

"I've recently been doing some research in the arts for my show. Do you know about the *Gesamtkunstwerk?*"

"The what?"

"The *Gesamtkunstwerk?*"

"It's German. It's supposed to be the *all embracing art form.*"

"I am trying to make it…" he said.

"Well that is quite impossible my dear."

They looked at each other and held a short pause.

"But it's no coincidence I guess" she continued, "that you would look for it here in Ted".

"Why is that?"

"Because fashion is perhaps the best or only example of something that is all encompassing, something global, like money".

"Money's the real total work of art."

Stella's colleagues looked at her with envy. They were surprised. They hadn't a clue what they were on about. They had never heard Stella speak in this way.

"Yes maybe it's money."

Thomas tried coming closer to speak to her then began to clutch his stomach and collapsed to the floor. Stella tried catching him but it proved of no use. His dead weight proved much to heavy for her strength. Stella's colleagues began to come over to see what was happening. As she held him, she inherited one of his tendencies to think about superfluous things at the wrong times. She noticed how he had not shaven both sides of his face evenly, "You've missed a spot", she wanted to say.

"Somebody help". A sense of emergency began to gel. Thomas saw something in the outline of a door, as if closing his eyes were the sudden shut of a sarcophagus - where muses and dirty fantasies were sealed inside. A crowd gathered everywhere around him until there was only an intermittent black out.

Chapter 5.

The smell of hospital awoke him in bed sheets that were green and hideous, as ugly as the man they covered. He continued what he had been saying to Stella. But why was she dressed in white all of a sudden? Oh. It was the nurse.

Holding him at arm's length she deposited a glass of water by his bedside, then she broke the news. "You have renal dysfunction" she told him. She began to explain the conditions of Thomas' kidneys and then his terrible diet. He had nodded and had pretended to not be frightened, in case she thought he were too frail and unmanly. When the nurse left, he took what she had said quite personally. They were wrong to criticise his diet.

On the first and second day Thomas refused the nurse's meals; then on the third he began to barter for some pomegranate juice. The nurse frowned but then chose to satisfy him eventually. She brought the glass into the room and left it by the bedside before staring at him. His toes crept from under the bed sheets and he occupied the entire mattress. As he drank the juice, the nurse told him to recompose himself. He had a visitor. And immediately he knew that it could only be one person. His godmother's daughter.

"How nice of her to come visit me."

His godmother's daughter, Eleanor, hated Thomas. In seeing him at his weakest, perhaps she would laugh and mock him. The woman who was not Eleanor entered, without Eleanor's physique, without Eleanor's mannerisms, but with a box of chocolates in her hands which masked her face and made an impression still woven in the fabric of anonymity.

"These are for you."
"I thought I'd come see how you were" said Stella.
"Well… thank you."
"I like these" he said whilst taking the chocolates. His stomach grumbled.
"I thought you might."
"But tell me" she began.
"What's wrong? Why did you faint?"
"I've got renal dysfunction."
"I'm sorry I collapsed in front of you."
"That's alright!"
"Believe me it's not the first time" she joked.
"…"
"…"
"So Stella where are you from?"

He wanted to relieve himself of one of his curiosities.

"I'm Greek."
"I thought you might be Italian."
"I'm from Rhodes actually. During the war the Italians occupied the city. My grandpa is Italian."

Whilst Stella and Thomas spoke and passed through each other as buttons entering the fastenings of a shirt, coming undone in ugliness and then admiration, the nurses watched them. Through the window petty mother-in-law gossip rained upon them.

"Look at the way she watches him. She's disgusted but totally fascinated too."

"Does he have a chance?"

"None."

"And of living?"

"None at all" she concluded.

"What do you think they're saying?" said Stella.

"I don't have a clue."

"I don't really care what they're saying."

"I don't really care about anything" he continued abruptly.

"Why? Are you alright? Is something on your mind?

"Well… my show firstly, you know, the one I was telling you about? Then there are some problems in the family at the moment."

"Ah yes, your show… I wanted to speak to you about that."

"It's one of the reasons why I came" she admitted.

"Yes?"

"I have a really good idea" she began.

'I did some research and thought that you and Ted can come up with a business plan. You were saying about the Chelsea flower show and well, flowers are in all of Ted's designs. So what about if you could help us with marketing and help bring our label to the show?"

"I already spoke about the idea with my head of department."

Her sales pitch was well recited, unexpected and spontaneous.

"Oh right."

Disappointment, a languor that was lachrymose fell on him as she delivered her sales pitch. Was this the real reason for her visit? Had she been serious when she had said that money was the real total work of art?

"I suppose that would be possible" he attempted to disguise his disappointment but his voice broke off. He wanted her to speak about something else. It still felt like he was in the store and was just a customer. She stared at him until it became awkward and she realised it was time for her to leave; her shift would start again soon.

"I have to go now" she said trying to avoid the silence.

"It's been a pleasure."

"Stella?!"

"Yes?"

"Can I ask you a favour?"

"Tell me."

"Could you go water my plants? I've been away for three days and it hasn't rained."

"Um, where are they?"

"In my garden, here in Guildford. Do you know where the chantries are? I live in Tile road, 62."

"The back gate's always open, all you need to do is water the ones on the patio."

"I would really appreciate it if you could."

She nodded, not knowing what she would do.

"Also... if you could do the ones inside too."

"There's a key under the left of the doormat. I trust you..."

"Please? They're very expensive."

"How far do you live from here?"

"Not very far. I'll give you the post code. Here..."

"Okay…"

"But let me know about that idea I told you about!" she said before closing the door.

Solitude was his again. It had been strange to see Stella here. She seemed so clever but had probably come to see him to tell him about this business idea. They weren't friends.

The rest of the day in the hospital became monotonous and boring. In the evening he thought back to something Stella had said. He'd told her about the all-embracing art form and then had asked her what she thought it might look like. She had said that in her opinion the fusion of the arts would look like a liquid, because fusions always became liquids.

He considered this strange thing Stella said. The *all embracing art form* would require of itself a new type of self destruction. It needed to be like an explosive liquid, a fizz, but never compromise the tact; that marvellous sense that even eclipses sight. Reassurance passed through him and so returned his hunger. He looked at the lamp by his bedside and was tempted to devour it. Listening to the radio by the effluvial steam of a kettle, he retired to his hospital chamber and his cradled dreams of artistry.

Great is the suffering of inactivity and even greater is the suffering of the bedridden and the hospitalised. So Thomas passed his days in the teal-green hospital bed sheets. Through his chamber's window he observed the nurses and doctors dressed in a lunar white. These became his self-proclaimed moon. He missed the outdoors. He missed being outside. And by the crackle of the fading television, idealisation fell on Thomas.

It appeared to him that he knew Stella well and that he was still getting to know her better even if she was gone. Speaking with her had been charming. Stella had calmed him with those lips of hers and had made him feel less alone. He felt satisfied, as if he had just eaten. He almost wanted to place Stella's chattering lips on a long refectory table, for they stretched far whenever she smiled. Had it been a daft idea to trust her with the key of his home under the doormat? Who knew? The plants really needed watering –it was worth the risk.

But now he needed a distraction. He needed to lose himself in complicated and digressive thoughts.

"But what do I know about Stella?" he thought, and tried to gamble, as a mad croupier, about what she might like. Would he make up things that weren't true?

He had taken notice of her theatre and her drama – the first imagination was correct - Stella was a graduate of theatre and had cultivated her passion of imitation and shadows. Passion, that *flatus vocis* of this latter day and age, which men and women throw about with indecency, was in truth original; was in truth no faint voice at all but a sonorous cant of bar walls, plasmated to her racketeering but perfectly supple jazz tender voice. Stella sang! Stella liked music even more than theatre.

She would sing after long working hours at the bar on top of the high-street, at "Amora-Amora - just enjoy", partly because of her niche for leisure and partly because of this place's catchy slogan: "just enjoy". She had attracted envy here too; had attracted that powdered blush upon her in all instances, was dusty and full of it.

In Rhodes she had been the envy of the family; the only woman in the whole Mediterranean with eyes other than almond, and then the envy of the entire music school; when she had come first in the entry exams. It had seemed that she had always been predestined for greatness. Or at least thought so, just like Thomas. At *Ted* she was slowly trying to build a career. The idea to sponsor Thomas at the Chelsea flower show had not been her first. At meetings and celebrations she could always acquire new contacts with her hair's curled sandstorm charisma. In this regard she was utterly different to Thomas. Thomas was quite unfriendly.

So Stella and Thomas were different. He felt hurt. He felt their connection in his mind begin to break. More importantly Thomas wanted to know how Stella thought. Would she think in images as he did? Or did she have a phonetic memory? Later he would discover that her memory was not very memorable at all. She'd said how she "adored detail" but her memory was quite terrible.

He on the other hand could remember everything.

Ten days later and he was released from the hospital. He would return home at last, to his promiscuous solitude.

Note:

Before Thomas returns to his home behind the chantries, let us now stop for a moment to think about circumstance. What is circumstance? Circumstances are the conditions that cause events to happen. How many times have we heard the words: "we wanted to marry but circumstance didn't permit" or "circumstance threw them together".

The circumstances that unravelled before the gardener were these; he had come to the end of his career, he had come to learn of the Wagnerian ideal, the *all embracing art form*, and he had met this woman by the name of Stella by stumbling into Ted. Circumstance had been kind, perhaps even extravagant with him.

Thomas believed that circumstance was like a man in his life. A type of Parisian Flaneur. Thomas had an affectionate name for him. Monsieur Circumstance. Thomas was convinced that Monsieur Circumstance meddled in his every affair; was the waiter that spilt coffee on him, was the postman who brought him his letters. The most important things in his life could be attributed to Monsieur. The protagonist of extras.

Consider Monsieur as Thomas essays his body down the street, be suspicious of him, for he is everywhere. Look! Monsieur Circumstance stares at you now. With monocle and heavenly eye, he begins to crumple some old sketches...

Chapter 6.

With neither chauffeur nor family to escort him, Thomas walked from St. Luke's Hospital to the chantries alone. Exhausted, but also feeling a light jab of adrenaline, he arrived at his home that stood delectably in ruin. It was full of withering stuccos. There was no point in repairing these parts of the house.

He stared into the walls of his home to stare into a luminous soul, and there the building reflected back a pleasure stained chrome yellow. Or perhaps it was just the paint coming off. Ignoring it all, he walked by the sides of the driveway. He opened the door and the floorboard creaked. It was good to be home. There was a perfume of Camomile.

His women, Camomile and Lily, were sitting and smoking and making conversation in the living room. Lily was laughing hysterically until she became abruptly serious. As Thomas went to drop his keys in the drawer, he noticed the house was a mess. Camomile and Lily had their feet up and had thrown their shoes around.

"Thomas."

"Come and join us" Lily was calling him.

What was the matter? Thomas went to sit down to speak with Lily. She seemed to want to tell him something urgently and looked worried.

He looked at Camomile whose dimpled face wasn't worried at all; whose dress broke off in intermittence, yellow and white. Camomile just seethed gently; she was the calmest person he had ever met. She always made the home feel at peace. He sat in the armchair and looked at her, she was generous and young and full of life. She seemed to glow with the celestial pulse of a saint, but was sensual and sexy too. Thomas put his arms around these girls beside him and the three of them were cellophaned together in the deepest pleasure.

"I'm really, really worried about this" said Lily.

"Oh come on. What's the matter now?" said Thomas.

Camomile did not like Thomas' abrupt remark. She took her hand from her lap and gently stroked Thomas to calm him down. Her hair flew back, as a burst, or a wind, or a fountain. She kissed Thomas. He became wide-eyed and catatonic and began to relax.

"I'm sorry... I don't know what came over me. What were you saying?"

Camomile tried consoling Lily. She stood up. From there she showed off her tender body; she was a woman with a dress of duet colours, a madrigal material of yellow and white; lulling and singing all at the same time. She dried Lily's tears and caressed her. Then she moved closer to her cheeks. When Lily had dried her lips from all the kisses, she began to feel better.

Came for Thomas the beatitude of lolling amongst belle-femmes. His women, all by the name of Flora, ran amok in these sublime displays of nudity, in this immense house of flowers, corsets tied, skirts untied, at times revealing that throbbing sex between their legs, that vaginal velvet where he would always look in rapture. It was a type of pavonine pleasure; an iridescent glee, opening before him in the semi-circled sway of a hand fan.

After a while that Camomile had fallen asleep, Lily began to panic. Thomas was still under a quilt of tranquillity when Lily spoke; catatonic and semi-circled in a smile, he swayed his head to listen.

"Listen now" said Lily.

"As you can see the house is in a terrible mess."

"Oh did you meet Stella? Isn't she so charming?" interrupted Thomas.

"Who?"

"Stella! She was supposed to come here whilst I was gone"

"I met her in a place, have you heard of Ted?"

It was there that Thomas betrayed the fact that his mind was somewhere else entirely. He was thinking about this other woman he had met. Lily immediately hated Stella.

"I told her the back-gate was always open and she could come in. I also told her that the key to the house was under the doormat."

So sudden, his mad mind.

"Now that explains it."

"Explains what?"

"Someone broke in. Look."

"The person that broke in, it must have been this stranger you've met. What did you say her name was? Stella? She came in here you see; through the patio."

"No it can't have been."

"Was this person a man or a woman?" Lily asked.

"A woman."

"Then there's your answer."

"And what" he could not come to his words. "Did she take?"

"Oh I don't know."

So Stella had broken into his home. At once Thomas escaped from the ensnaring pull of the armchair and cast a panoramic inspection towards the parlour. Leaping unto the kitchen he saw the sprawl of cabinets and kitchen drawers pulled open. The long and slender room, that was like a cylinder with in it a mahogany dining table, Persian rugs and other darlings of ornament, had been toppled and spun upon its head. The lights in the shape of upside down tainted wine glasses, had been left in full beam –forcing him to drink the light to fill his neck, with goitrous swell.

What in the world was happening? It appeared that Stella had not taken anything. She had flung all the objects of the kitchen at random. Some of his cups had been thrown to the floor.

"What did she take?"

Chapter 7.

He ascended to the first floor with all the illegitimacy of passion and surprise still screaming in his ear. Erected unto the level ground his own attempts to painting passed him by. He emerged in his studio and found! Order? Nothing had been taken, it seemed. He almost laughed as he sat down in his burgundy chesterfield chair. The chair with no elbow restraints let his hands drop to the floor.

"Everything's alright. Right Flora?" he said whilst turning his head to look at his God-mother's painting to the right of the room. It had been strange to hear his own voice again. His own voice calmed him. Numbed his senses. Gave him a breath. Made him feel sleepy. And inattentive. He felt restored. And he looked at the painting dreamily.

But it was not there.

The melodramatic reaction of theatre was not the one that descended on the gardener. He experienced loss in an entirely different way that day.

"Stella has taste if she chose to steal that painting" he said almost laughing.

He was right. Stella had taken the best portrait in the house. There came to him a comical thought. A homeowner and his burglar probably have similar tastes. The two could strike an incomparable partnership in the business of home decor. The thought of this partnership, or of any partnership at all with a woman such as Stella, skinned his anger with a sweet and sugary peel. Was it really Stella's fault? Had she really stolen the painting?

Thomas went downstairs and threw himself in the armchair of the vast room that was both living room and kitchen and duplicated himself in the glare of the doors. He picked up the telephone quickly to call the Ted store, for speaking with Stella was urgent.

"Yes? Hello? How are you?" he said as if he knew Ted.

"I'm well... thank you. Who's speaking?"

"I'd like to speak to Stella."

"She's busy right now. But if you want I can pass on a message."

"No, no. No message" said Thomas, and he breathed heavily into the telephone.

The man on the other line perceived his disappointment. Thomas said nothing.

Before he was about to put down, the man on the other line said:

"Sir, if you really want to speak to her you know where to find her. Everyone knows. She sings in the evening. *Amora-Amora*".

The *Ted* employee put down the line. He knew where Amora Amora was. He knew where to find Stella.

"Who was it?" said Stella to her colleague after she saw that someone had called.

"Another one asking for you."

"Oh... Another one" Stella sighed.

Thomas was not just any ordinary "other one". He was firstly far older than the other men that had asked after Stella. In instances such as this Stella regretted her kindness. She knew that because of her politeness, she would often find herself in these awkward situations. She hoped to never hear from Thomas again, but for a moment she did think about what it would be like for them to be together. Stella sometimes entertained any possibility just for the thrill of doing so. Maybe he was rude or horrible or maybe he was charming.

Meanwhile, on the other side, Thomas was glad to have found a way to speak to Stella. He would go to the bar where she sang and talk things over. He needed to know that it had not been her to steal his painting. Was it her fault? He would soon find out. But first he needed to get ready.

Thomas raised himself from the armchair and beat a few sounds upon his home's parquet; to reappear upstairs in his bedroom; to then tabulate his image in the bathroom mirror. He cupped his hand by the basin's stream of water to drink. Looking into the mirror he distilled his own picture, to find a face full of wrinkles and stubble.

"I have to shave tonight" he thought as he opened a drawer. He wet his face with the shaving cream, before taking out the razor to garden the stubble on his cheeks. Moving to the sail of the blade, his chin drooped to let it pass. The razor went east, west, east again, south, north, and his face became creased and full of wounds. He made many strange faces as he shaved. Perhaps as an actress Stella could make many strange faces like this too?

Afterwards he dried his face with his palm and then applied some quaint patchouli, slapping himself in a fragrant masochism. More substance around the nape of the neck. Now he just needed to get dressed.

In the bedroom was another room; a gentleman's closet that harboured the style of an old man's fashion.

He came in here, where there were windows whose glass was stained. As he opened the wardrobe he thought about what Stella might think of his clothes. Had she liked them as much as the painting? Perhaps not, the wardrobe suggested; all his clothes had been left untouched. He browsed through the shirts in his wardrobe; each was a man of different feeling and fabric. Some were terribly eccentric, and others just cheap.

"This one's too simple!" he said as he put away a white shirt he had just taken out. He did not want to wear something so simple tonight. He pulled out another shirt, a vintage lemon yellow seersucker. In his right arm, then in his other, until he spun in this sallow weed of old age; knocking down with his elbow the cluttered heap of novels in one of the shelves of the dressing room. Yes, books were in his dressing room. He had discovered that reading when naked was a marvellous experience.

Chapter 8.

Thomas' closet looked out on the street and the hills behind. As he dressed himself, a young girl stopped by the pavement of his home to peer into his window. His closet's stained windows distorted the figure they showed; they deformed a perfect body into an ugly one, and an ugly body into a perfect one. The girl on the street began to admire Thomas as he put on his trousers and his watch.

But the voyeur leaves and so do we.

Yes! Thomas is leaving the gentleman's closet and a magenta bleach modulates the sky in one cry; communicating nature's vanity to be worshiped and written about. By the stairs is a white vase that fastens together a set of umbrellas. He takes one when he sees that it is raining outside. As he lifts his eyes from his rose-gold watch, coming from the stairs, he sees a toad is standing in the doorway. He freezes on the last step of the staircase to look at this improbable toad. How did it get here?

The toad croaks and Thomas trips on the stairs and falls. The quadrant of his rose-gold watch cracks. He looks at it and notices that he is late. Come on. Stella is waiting for him.

Thomas looks at the door. He needs to get out of here as soon as possible. He picks himself up and moves quickly to the exit. Closes the door behind him to be away! Now he must substitute monster for magic and go hear Stella sing.

He began his journey to the town, regretting not to have brought a scarf now that the wind was picking up. His shoes were also beginning to get dirty and he realised he had made an error to pass by the fields.

In the town, he felt himself a rich man. Some telephone lines and rain imitated wet latches of jewellery. He followed the lamppost lights whose continuity made a dangled parure, in a long collectable necklace of the night. All the shops were already closed except for the pawn shop near the scholar's statue. He saw the owner still locking the store; a volley of flesh slide down the owner's thigh as she brought down the iron grating. That leg seemed to be like Stella's; it fell down and umbrellad his desire like a parasol silk. What he was going to say to Stella when he arrived at the bar? The sole thought made him blush.

As he was walking by the high-street, he passed again by *Ted*. The window reminded him of two weeks ago, when he had first entered the store and had met this woman that was slowly changing his life. Look! the male mannequin; dressed in a burgundy blazer with vinous patterns and silk cushion buttons by the sleeves. With a bowtie too, a "nœud papillon". The bowtie made the mannequin acquire an elegant and charming maleficence. It reminded him of dandy gentlemen and French Monsieurs.

He continued to walk towards this bar where Stella was singing tonight. "Amora Amora". It was not far from where he was now. Walked and looked above, to notice a pattern of stars that formed a crevice in the sky. A silver varnish dripped from the sky's seams, and by and by Thomas opened his mouth to drink it, to sober up his confidence.

He dragged his umbrella on the pavement; just a few more minutes and he would be there! He tried imagining this umbrella as the mark of his great character, as he looked at these other shops of the high-street. Ten minutes after having passed Ted: "I'm finally here". He tried checking his appearance in the murky reflections of shop windows, to give himself confidence. Did these burgundy suspenders make him look like a fashionable person? Or did they just make him look fat?

Before entering the bar he considered that outside of the garden, he could not exercise his gusto. It was true that he was a gardener, but he could not prune people, or himself. He opened the door of the bar before looking at his watch. Oh, I am just on time.

Chapter 9.

When he entered *Amora-Amora* there raged an eternal party. At once he realised that he had not been in a bar for years. Did they still serve the same drinks; was it still possible to smoke inside? The girls were prettier, or perhaps it was just his age that had made him acquire a certain wisdom when it came to taste.

On this night that Thomas had stumbled into *Amora Amora*, the bar had arranged a jazz theme night. Everyone had come in costumes and was dressed for the occasion. He found this strange, because he had actually lived those times and felt himself at home.

Some men and women were queuing up at the bar in a meticulous file of chaos and infidelity. Outside taxicabs loitered and expelled guests blowed rhythmic puffs of smoke in jade cigarette holders. Here were guests as actors of the past that always wished to be in an era different than the one they were already in.

For this party's jazz theme everyone was wearing tortoiseshell sunglasses with royal-blue lenses. When Thomas came through the door, this small ocean of sunglasses turned to look at him. One young girl just by the entrance stared at Thomas, marvelled a little and said:

"Maybe he's a crazy singer that will come up on stage."

He looked at the stage that the bar's tables were pointed towards. The stage was a metre above the ground and a balustrade had been fitted around the perimeter to make it become like a terrace. All around him lamp heads dangled down from above. These lampshades were pierced decoratively in blue feathers and bow ties and the open lid of a pianoforte also seemed to release gentle inundations of style and music.

Everyone seemed to be staring at him as he walked past, as if he were a person that had truly emerged from the jazz era. Some drunk idiots began waving at him and Thomas felt charmed to receive all this attention.

After he went by the bar side because he was still thirsty. Over the bar's roar he found it impossible to hear what the barman was saying.

"What would you like?"

"Sorry?"

"I said what would you like?!"

"That one" Thomas said with skeletal finger pointing.

Just as the barman began pouring some Jägermeister, Thomas changed his mind and said: "No, No, actually, I want some pomegranate juice".

The barman sighed and stared at Thomas; the typical problematical customer. It was right when Thomas was about to take the pomegranate that his umbrella fell. As he bent down, a man came by, Monsieur, and swapped Thomas' drink with the whiskey that belonged to the person beside. This caused a reaction at the bar side: "Hey, who took my drink?".

Thomas got up without answering. He was really becoming deaf and wanted to go say hello to those people who were still waving and pointing at him. He sat down at a table by himself and felt that if any prizes would be given for the best outfit, he would certainly be a winner. He continued to drink without noticing he had taken the wrong glass; he was much too worried about what he would say to Stella. How would he introduce the fact that he thought she was a thief?

It was right when he felt that he could give an answer that Stella appeared on stage to sing. Some people began clapping and cheered her. Immediately he felt jealous and began banging his hands together to be louder than them. Stella, for the party's theme, had come dressed as Lady Day.

In grand entrances people normally observe the person first and then their accessories. Here the reverse was true. Thomas looked at the flapper dress that had come on stage, at the lachrymose pattern over the bodice, and then at the frills on the side of the shoulders accessorised by the tussore of her smile.

"Me, Myself and I, are all in love with you. We just think you're wonderful we do."

She began singing.

A blow of breath on the microphone and flapper dress is turned to Day.

Spectation sways to the sea of syllable.

"Me, Myself and I" was one of Thomas' favourite songs by Lady Day. He began blushing when he thought that Stella was singing it to him.

"Me, myself and I have just one point of view, we just think you're wonderful we do."

He looked at the stage and imagined there were three Stellas singing. Where religion once worshiped the father, son and holy spirit, here Thomas worshipped lady day, lady day and lady day. He drank and took himself far from where he was now; imagined himself outside of a bar, perhaps in the café of a great boulevard with these three women. A melodious note translated to words:

***

Here were Thomas and the Lady Days on a table outside a square, by a grand avenue splintered in myriad gold, as the myriad pleasure in his company. The foam of Macchiatos would stain three lips, and his agony too would be snippeted in three like in a cut-up-window. Men and women on this boulevard would pass by and stare at him, envy his "Lady Days" whose appearance covered the trident spectrums of joy. Now by this table in this great boulevard, with the radiant green of trees lamping over his head, he looked at one of his Lady days whom everyone seemed to admire. And then, he laughed as he let teaspoons play in his hands, he thought that if this was Lady Day, to his side was Lady Day and to her side too, was Lady Day. Oh Lady Day was soon his favourite! A gust passed them by, and picked up the traces of sugar left on the table. A sugary dust fell on the four of them and euphemised any skin they had bear. They were made more dulcet-like than all the persons strutting in this square with elegant hats.

All these women here, they had different personalities. Thomas put his hand on the red and white linen of the table to stroke one of them. With a needle of sunlight falling in agony upon her, he saw her pale and soppy and witty. And then he looked at the one beside her, who didn't take his hand at first, for she was abrupt and cruel and sometimes even treated him badly to make him feel a masochistic sting. And in this place, somewhere in a piazza, he forgot all together about Flora and was oiled by the resinous tan that slipped from the skin of his three women. At last he realised his dreams of promiscuity outside of? Of what? He couldn't remember.

Smiling at him, Lady Day took the lemon from her water and put it in her mouth. A streak of lemon juice fell from her mouth to her flapper dress, to continue its pattern of tears…

***

Thomas enjoyed this song until he was brought back to his senses. He left the square. He awoke. He was back in the bar. Oh it was much less fun here in the bar again! But at least Stella was still there on the stage.

Thomas began to clap to cheer her on. A woman on a table just beside put her hand to her mouth and stood up. Her husband began following her; "Darling!" the two got up after they saw Thomas' boisterous erection. He saw them leave and noticed how the couple left behind their sunglasses. "Wait! You forgot these" he said. But they didn't hear him. In the meantime Stella passed the microphone between her hands and began to sing a different song as more people in waistcoats continued to drink.

Thomas wants to invite more guests to his table and buy everyone a drink. But he doesn't have enough money. He starts joining in the song, not knowing it is Stella's last before a short break. One of the vocalists leaves her post and goes to smoke outside. Thomas puts on the sunglasses the couple left behind and looks all around the bar. He observes all the different tables and waiters passing by and then he looks at Stella again. A bath of mist fills the entire room; men transform into the boutonnieres they are wearing. He begins to throw drinks everywhere and then he drops the sunglasses.

Soon after Thomas is thrown out of the bar. "But I have to speak to Stella" he says as the bouncer begins dragging him out. He is thrown outside. He looks up and sees himself covered by ash. One of the vocalists on her break was smoking above him.

"You alright?"
"Yes, I'm alright."

It felt strange to be outside again. It felt quiet. It felt abrupt. He felt out of place.

"I just have to speak to Stella" he repeated again.
"What do you want from her?"
"I need to ask her something. Do you know who she is?"
"Yes I do."
"I sing with her."
"Obviously" she wanted to add.

Looking down at him Stella's colleague saw him hopeless. He would do anything to hear about Stella. And she could tell him whatever she wanted. He would believe her. Gullible. The vocalist held the cigarette in her mouth and enjoyed the thought of this power. He was so desperate and she was so powerful. Smoking cruelly she held the cigarette's fuming edge and some ash began burning between the beds of her fingers.

"I have to know if she stole something from me or not."
"I think she may be a thief."

Here was the vocalist's opportunity to become the star of the show. Would chance ever give her an another evening such as this; another chance at the microphone as it were, thought the vocalist? Now she could be the protagonist. She could say any grand thing and he would believe her.

Thomas was still lying on the pavement. He looked up at her. He saw her smoking. Puffed. His eyes filled with agony. He needed to know what had happened in his home.

"Stolen what?"

"A painting."

"Valuable?"

"Invaluable."

"So what's the problem then if it's not valuable?"

"No you don't understand, it is" he said whilst raising himself, showing to her the back of his scalp. It was this last remark of his that only intensified her desire to speak badly about Stella.

"Well that doesn't surprise me... Doesn't surprise me at all."

"How do you mean?"

"Well, you know... Stella certainly isn't one you can trust?"

"You see these earrings?" actually he hadn't noticed them, he was much too distracted.

"Well one time... in the dressing room, I found her going right through all my things."

"Look, I'm not one to make assumptions but the facts are the facts."

"The facts are the facts" he repeated.

"Suppose I left something valuable in the changing room... like this ring. I know she would take it."

He believed her. Just as she had imagined. He put out his hand for her to stop speaking.

"I understand."

When Thomas left, the vocalist decided to lie to Stella too. The doors of Amora Amora opened and a tired Stella emerged.

"What did that old man want?"

"Nothing."

"What do you mean nothing?"

"What I mean. Why do you know him?"

"He fainted in front of me at *Ted* the other day and I went to see him at the hospital."

"Give me a cigarette please."

"He called today at Ted too. Knows a lot about art but I think he's crazy."

"Is that so?"

Stella's colleague began to doubt her. By the way Stella's hands trembled, perhaps the old man was right.

"What?" retorted Stella when she noticed she was being stared at.

"Nothing."

How did Thomas and Stella and her colleague spend the rest of their evening? We can only make a wild guess how Stella's red heel graced the pavement as she walked home, and how Thomas' moccasin met the macadam too and how Stella's colleague's fat foot just trailed behind in an amateurish lag.

Even if they went about their evening separately, they all echoed one another. When each person arrived at their home, they all pushed something- now imagine! six palms doing the same movement for different reasons.

For Thomas it was the push of his murano vase to the floor, which he wanted to destroy in anger because of his terrible evening, for Stella the push of her house-door that creaked awkwardly, for the vocalist the push to keep away her boyfriend - who wanted to make love that evening.

As we look at these three people, we embrace a point of view whose precision fades, but whose master laughs – *Monsieur* is in his studio enjoying a cigar by a telegram's typewriter.

And so, as Thomas taps his forehead because he has a headache, and the vocalist does the same to fend off her boyfriend's kisses, Stella taps her own forehead with a shrivelled and wet tissue to remove her makeup. The tones of jet-black comes off, as *Monsieur* continues to smoke and type, and Thomas is still tapping his head, and the vocalist too, until the make-up remover is dirty, just as dirty as Thomas' toilet paper in the same moment.

At present the tissue is in Stella's hand and she drops it to the floor, as Monsieur begins to drop ash, Stella goes to bed. She is angry. That she should be molested by an old man such as this, given too much attention here and none in her true artistic talents, only went to show how chance was a madman without meter. And so she sighs, as her colleague's lover does the same after finally being satisfied, and Thomas – well he sighs too when the telegram ejects a new message. A small matter. Flora had died.

Chapter 10.

If the absurdity and old fashioned soul of death could be expressed in words, then for Thomas it would sound[*] like this:

Bereavement so passed through the corridors of the brothel; that great house so shook with tremors of mourn and blue-flame stings of old and forgotten days; for indeed, just as I had surmised, the flower's matron had forgotten, and so colour and life had been sucked dry – lost to Hade's zephyr that chanced and passed it on again. The shades of every flower and plant that were flecked by mint green silk hangings, and borrowed lights from Marigold, that apricot rose-bronze, peached by delicate wounds, so lost their memory to grey and ceil and thus began to fester.

The telegram, that terrible epitaph, Flora is dead!, seemed to have sucked to it all the colours of the house and become an overflowing art jar. Submerged in all these tones and cockled to a swollen form, it held a name and in it all its lovers – Flora! - in a scalloped pattern.

Grey so filled the house with a bathetic but pleasurable wane! - one whose light trapped in rotund whirls of grey, a leaden petal or bud, lithe but specked in a dying fluorescence, I might have so been in an undertone of ceil. Unlike other mornings, I did not descend downstairs for breakfast. My palate was seized by the remittance of melancholy, as if a wine had passed its spit upon the bowels of desire.

---

[*] It is best if the following is read out loud.

In the late afternoon, fondling through the drawers, I found a cross given to me by my godmother years ago. I found this symbol most true to the beauty of failure, that so assembled itself in grim but glistening pomp beads. For the first time in my life, like a Christian, I understood the beauty of imperfection; which so swayed in the crooked nail of the cross and misalignment of the two wooden planks. By the mote of fall and loss, I arranged the grey and withered flowers around the cross, whose petals were now so sagged, so triumphant, that they vitrified into a hemlock mesh of bronze.

Blessed be Flora!

Chapter 11.

The next day Thomas went to visit Stella at work. In the morning he enquired about some lawyers so he could sue Eleanor for Flora's house. He was excited to meet his lawyer and hoped that it would be another pretty girl.

On the walk to the town there were still traces of the terrible news he had heard. Even if it was summer he could not feel at peace. Was his godmother really dead?

As he walked down Shalford road the desire for summer was molested by the looming hand of death and decay. As he paced the football fields and conspired against the cyclists that swirled around him in vulgar droppings of speed and silver, he thought about his godmother. He ruminated in his mouth a golden and bistre brown leaf.

For Flora's sake he desired the autumn. To make a scupper for the trees and let their lucent hue wash overboard. For the trees to hang as incomplete busts of an illustrator's journal, with smudges around the hips and the nape of the neck. He walked but the autumn he desired was only a pessimist's exquisite conspiracy. Everything was stronger than him. The children on bicycles had bodies plump and strong, and the women's rowing society flexed muscles that he envied.

Where the pavement of Shalford road had always been his haunt, this time he took another path. After the river, trudging between a flight of cars like bumblebees, he took a path that passed by Guildford castle. In a staircase-like turn he was ushered to a street so narrow that he looked above into the skies in search of space; to find a salmon-pink flag undulate on top of the castle. His greatest regret was that the council had never permitted him the chance to arrange this public park where the castle stood. It was his only true love in Guildford, besides Eleanor, besides Stella and besides his soon-to-be lawyer friend. He was a faithful man after all.

He was seduced by this castle because at this hour he could not go inside. It was closed to the public at noon. A great lock wrapped itself around the building like a necklace - of joys secret and impermissible. The castle's differently shaded bricks also formed a gorgeous lithe V neck-line on the facade. The lawn in front was just as lightsome as a polished ballroom floor, and it seemed to beg him to dance to stereophonic beats coming from all directions.

A type of happiness was sealed in that castle; a sarcophagus of all emotions. Perhaps Flora could be buried there, or Eleanor, or Stella, or his soon-to-be lawyer friend or the deck of Queens in his home. They could call be buried there as those saints that rest in marvellous prisons above soil; even though he and his women were no admirable saints. But would Flora be buried or cremated? She had once said how cremation went against the Catholic belief but to him it seemed a way to go out in style. To go out in flames!

A wind moved him and farewell Guildford castle. His walk was as fragile as his affections; now both were on a path that edged towards the high-street with the gilt view of the clock-tower a few yards ahead.

The owners of every shop looked out to see Thomas pass in all the differently arranged windows. The owner of the glassware shop trembled when he saw him pass by; when he saw on Thomas' cheeks a chandelier of tears, tense by his suspending dimples. Thomas seemed to carry it so clumsily on his cheeks, just like when he had stumbled and fallen in his store a few days ago. For the pawnshop he looked a worthless man. For the lipstick makers instead he could have been a likely customer. He was so effeminate. Was he a cross-dresser? In the window of the music store, no was the answer; he was made dull and classical amongst violins and cellos, an old maestro that only dressed up in black and white at the most.

At last he was made himself in the canopy of flower patterns at Ted. He emerged where Stella watched the street by the shop's entrance. As he came, she judged him more severely than all three stores he had just passed. In this blend, the judgments of glass, lipstick and instrument sellers were hurled upon him. Glass met lipstick-wax, wax smeared wood, and Thomas Haller was looked at by Stella behind a transparent screen of hatred. When he finally stopped and looked at Ted's window, he saw the real-life mannequins again: the models.

Inside Ted's window he saw the "Velvet Pipper Blazer". It was on sale by twenty per cent. He became excited and threw all his love to it, as if throwing an anchor in the blazer's watery tinge. One could sink in the dark-blue fabric.

What would he wear at Flora's funeral? Never mind what Eleanor or the stuffed up old priest would think; he'd wear this velvet blazer. Now he was imagining himself there at the funeral, amongst the family. He would be perfectly dressed for the occasion. "Yes" he said as he looked closely at the blazer and then at the pocket square. "It's the perfect funeral outfit".

Thomas was rocked mid way through the high-street. Men and women passed through in festive stampede. He was interrupted rudely from his window-shopping. What was the occasion? Why were people celebrating? Ah, The 13th of June – he remembered. The Queen's birthday.

A crowd rippled around him, as a trumpet band played on; patriotic men adorned in British flags were made even more vile in the sight of his inimitable blazer. To and fro people celebrated and he mourned. People sang and he just thought perchance how much the outfit was going to cost him.

As this crowd passed by him, Thomas saw a great number of ears. Thomas was convinced of a very strange thing. He was convinced that thoughts were in a person's ears. Thomas often noticed this in public places: when he sat beside a man or woman in silence, he could hear echoes of thoughts in the lobe, as if thoughts slipped out from the mind.

Thomas crossed the road and immersed himself in the crowd. As he looked all around he felt an interference and all the minds of the people in the crowd began to signal:

I am as I am and sometimes
they think of me
an extraordinaire
They think me too perfumed
My patchouli slaps them and I
I
In a fragrant masochism
haven't forgotten
You are

my daughter
also Hits the tab.
Hurry up I'm late
Already?

He untangled himself from the crowd and entered Ted.

"Good morning."

He looked at the shop assistant that sounded much like the man he had spoken to on the telephone.

"Where's Stella?"

The shop assistant began to sweat when he recognised Thomas.

"I'm more than happy to help you."

Thomas walked on and ignored him. As he passed by the clothes, his eyes began to hurt. He looked further down the store and saw a table of merino-wool socks and somewhere in-between a dallying Stella. To his side were small crowds of people looking at the shirts on sale. Stumbled again into another crowd.

Stella
It feels as if I haven't seen you in ages
You were like three people yesterday
You were like a Lady
Maybe he will buy it for me, what do you think?
It would have been nice to just exchange a few words
I just needed to ask you, you see, someone came into my home

what's that smell? Patchouli
You were very good at singing
You were so very good
But

He still hasn't called me back
you are hurting me
I just need to tell you one thing
for me thing there is no one other
we should get her that old one she wanted
Stella
yesterday, the pizzicato
meshed
on the lobe of your ear
to flavour it

Thomas distanced himself from the small crowd in this store as soon as it became too much. He felt tired of his life as if he were tired of a style.

He looked for Stella but she seemed to be ignoring him. As he moved closer to her, Stella approached a young man who was choosing amongst a set of ties. When she asked if he needed help, and he had replied "Nah I'm okay", she had said, "I insist!", and so she brought from under the cabinet the striped and monochrome cravats. All the while she tried to ignore Thomas and gave so much attention to this young fool, that he thought himself flattered.

Thomas watched as Stella waved around the ties with fake enthusiasm; he watched as the silks passed between her hands like a cascade. As Stella spoke to this young man and ignored him, he saw all the imperfections of her face assemble; the soft tissue of a nose which began to droop already, but only by a hair, the dented cuts under the chin and a minuscule blotch of white under the eyelid that the sun's bronze had forgotten to melt.

"Look at this one for example, it's on sale."

Stepping forward Thomas moved and pushed Stella:

"The painting damn it. Where is it?!"

And everyone in Ted turned their eyes on him.

What Thomas did not know is that Stella's legs were unlike the fragile vases where Flora stood; vases he had at times kicked in anger and sprites of soil had fallen upon the ground like broken bones. As Stella glided backwards in her fall, she caught hold of Thomas' shirt and dragged him to her, so that that they joined in a falling arabesque, scrolling violently towards each other. This fall, which for Thomas seemed slow and retarded, for Stella was adrenaline-filled and instinctive. As they fell Stella slapped Thomas upon the cheek, so that he landed first upon his back and cushioned her own fall. He lay supine upon the floor; with his arms spread widely apart.

"What…" began Stella.

"… Do you want from me?!"

Everyone was staring at them and here was a scene similar to the one of two weeks ago. The old man was on the ground again, but this time he was joined by Stella. The young fellow who Stella had been entertaining was seized by an instinctive desire to protect her, and so he stood in-between the gardener proudly, with clenched fists. But this only made matters worse. For when Thomas awoke from his daze, he looked at them both, Stella and young man, as two lovers. He cried out again and beat out at the legs of this person in front of him:

"You've taken it you thief! You thief."

At this point he raised himself up and mustered his strength for a new encounter, but he hardly had a moment before the second slap came.

Some men and women around them cheered. It was clear that this petty brawl had aroused more attention than any collection of dresses or shirts that afternoon. From the slaps Thomas' cheeks had been plastered a new red, as he passed his hands on them Stella said:

"Taken what? I don't even know you! You're a lunatic... just a lunatic" as if saying it twice might hammer the point home.

A third man, who had seen well the danger of the situation, separated the two of them, until the manager of the store came.

"He's been following me it's all his fault" said Stella as a set of women attempted to restrain her. She was certainly one not to shy away from conflict. The two of them were being restrained now, but they shouted as if in a market brawl. The makeup on Stella's face was beginning to smudge, the frills of her dress also began to flutter, as she became angry.

"I know it was you. You thought you could take advantage of an old man. Well you were wrong."

"Says the one!" she retorted.

"Who's been stalking me and coming to see where I sing"

Oh how ugly and typical was hysteria. But Thomas did not think so. As the men of the crowd restrained him from sucker-punching the young cravat man, he smiled. He imagined himself in a passion-struck brawl with his wife-to-be Stella. Weren't arguments a symptom of love? Yes, he smiled, fell back, grew angry and smiled again, until the manager gathered his colleagues and evacuated everyone from the shop floor.

Miscommunication was a terrible thing. If only Stella had had the chance to explain herself, perhaps she might not have lost her job that afternoon. If only Thomas had had a chance to explain himself, perhaps he might have not stumbled so violently into Ted in want of conflict. Whilst men and women were evacuated out of the store, Stella stayed behind to speak to her superior. Thomas was dragged outside, but as he turned to look at the Greek, he saw her mouth inaudible words over the alarm-bell to her manager.

He was outside. The two had been separated. He had expelled his anger. Yet he felt guilty. Foolish even. The crowd that had witnessed his violent passion scrutinised him as he came out at last. The young man, the cause of it all really, was still outside and now his mother had reconvened with him too. She gave to Thomas a filthy stare until Thomas felt a sudden itch to tip-toe away; he felt the fear of hearing another crowd's thoughts whirl around him in riddles.

Giving his back to the store's entrance, whose bell was still ringing, he left; putting himself through the street's pantomime and judgement again: music store, lipstick and glassware shop. And he had not even had a chance to ask the price of his Piper blazer!

Chapter 12.

A viscous tenderness cajoled Thomas to admire all his failures up to that moment. He was safe at home behind the chantries again, but felt terrible. He had made a dreadful attempt to speak to Stella. Both at *Amora-Amora* and then at *Ted*.

Walking on the stair-head, he tried to shake his neck and was so terribly frightened as his scalp almost slumped and melted to the spring's heat. Essayed against his will he tried to think today. Where had he gone wrong? What did he feel like this? Like in a type of perverted sonata, utterly alone in his studio, he said three names:

"Oh Eleanor…"
"Oh Stella…"
"Oh Flora…"

And the corridors of his home were filled by sounds they had already heard before, but never altogether. Thomas could find nothing but failure in all three of these names. He felt that in some sense all three of these women had let him down. He blamed them all; blamed them for what he knew to be more poetically called "forsaking".

"Yes that's it, forsaken… forsaken" and he leapt unto the sprawl of the word. It was through language like this in his head, that he solved his problems. Unriddled life with a word. Just as he passed by his room, it was the cross he had nailed to the wall to make him say this. To make him say "forsaken" and not "abandoned". Forsaken was a much more spiritual word he felt he needed to exercise in this moment.

He had never had the type of family to pass unto him teachings of faith. The cross he had bought by chance in an old road show. But one incident of the bible he knew. And for this reason he had collected this old cross. He knew that at some point, on the cross, Christ had cried out:

"Father why have you forsaken me?"

And most people, members of his limited entourage, did not know about this. He had heard it years ago in a Christmas sermon. Now he too, whilst on the stair-head, wanted to cry out:

"Flora, why have you forsaken me?"

Thinking about what Jesus Christ had said upon the cross, he repeated in his mind the words: "Father why have you forsaken me? Father why have forsaken me?

And fell there fell upon him a spontaneous analytic doubt, which mixed with the moments of the day; his life here in Guildford, his Chelsea Flower Show and his soon-to-be court hearing.

Did these words not mean that even Jesus Christ in a moment of weakness had began to doubt God? What were deities and saviours to the gardener? They were nothing if not personable attempts to better reality; in this he understood them. But otherwise he was averse to them.

He thought that even he, as Christ, though he might love Flora, might doubt Flora too. So he began to doubt everything before him.

"Maybe Flora is no great thing" he said whilst watching the street piously from his window.

"Maybe Eleanor is no great thing either" he said as he withdraw from it.

And dropping himself on the divan in his room, he mused and lounged and smirked cruelly, with his head in ripe perversion by the pillow.

So doubt was the order of the day.

"Maybe Stella is no great thing."

What could he doubt about Stella? She had crept into his home and stolen his invaluable painting when he had asked of her a favour. Was that not certain?

He laboured to find any certainties at all. There fawned upon Thomas that "uncanny" feeling, what one man had called familiar, and what others had called the ill of life. What he believed to be dead, what he believed to be gone and spent was still there. An irreparable and inexplicable anxiety.

"Oh Eleanor… Oh Stella… Oh Flora" he said again in delirium, not understanding anything at all, not understanding what Christ had to do with him in this moment, he, a gardener, in this bedroom in Surrey .

Repeating it again a second time, he felt he could understand some sense in what he had just said. Why had he pronounced these three names of three different women?

He struggled to tell the difference between Flora's, Eleanor's and Stella's face. It appeared to him that he had incarnated the face of his loneliness in three persons. How could it be that just now as he tried to think of all three of them individually, he could not? He struggled to find lucidity in image. He misplaced colours and details as an artist with tendinitis. They were all one. Was it truth? Or was it just his imagination?

Those three women he knew, of three generations, seemed to blur and fuse into a single face. A single toil. How did this face come to life? All he had to do was smelt three names together. "Oh Eleanor... Oh Stella... Oh Flora". And then his longing of woman morphed into a different form:
> *Porcelained an olive-oil white*
> *Incarnating the face of emptiness*
> *Algae gentle green eyed*
> *Yesterday wan and freckled*
> *With Manifold incomplete slabs*
> *as hips*
> *Put to waste*
> *Here is*
> *In crumbles*
> *A continuous warp of woman*

The fusion of the arts he so craved came in this fusion of faces. His Russian doll-heart cradled the wooden madder added to the toy.

He stood up. He had tired of rest already and rose to search the studio's drawing table. He needed to look at the letter FLORA had sent him. The letter to prove that the house in Tuscany was his. Rustling between the papers made a powder-blue, the old parchments he collected, between the chaos of laminated cards, he could not find the letter. Displeasure turned to unease, and in a bout he was making a mess of the desk, just to find the letter. He pulled out all the foliage of newspapers underneath his binders but still it was not there. Where was the letter? Had it been stolen along with the picture?

It probably had nothing to do with Stella. Who could want it? Only Eleanor and Bradley could. There fell upon Thomas the anxiety that perhaps it had not only been Stella to enter his home without him knowing. Or maybe it had not been Stella at all. Maybe Eleanor had been the one. Maybe he had made a great error.

Thomas did not stop to meditate the importance of these details. He passed over them with bathetic mood. In his head, those three women's faces were still welded in one, and so it could not matter who the culprit was.

Thomas descended downstairs. In all this he had forgotten to eat. When he passed by the kitchen, he went to inspect the fruit bowls but the pears and the apples had begun to rot. He dropped them back into the bowl and saw the pulps squashed by their fall. Towards the threshold between parlour and kitchen, utterly dazed; he had no idea what to do with his time now he felt averse to activity or thinking. Then the enzymes in his gut began to churn and he was gripped by hunger. One hand on his stomach and another on the wall to support himself, as he almost fell again to the sway of instinct. With his forehead resting on the glossy windowpane, he saw the damsons again at the end of his garden. The damson tree had ripened and had grown three metres above the ground, on its precipice he could see the softest fruits almost burst in joy if a zephyr touched them.

He unlocked the door and stumbled out into his garden; he let the door slip and the handle cracked the glass of the sliding door on the other side. The thump of this noise struck a similar crack in his own tearing eye, as he dried out the shards of plum in his vision of fruit-skin. Without caring at all for all the work he had done to preserve the grass, he stamped hard and forcefully to reach the tree. Behind the slender, cigar-like holes in his fence, he could see the neighbours playing in their garden on a trampoline, and he too felt buoyed towards restlessness. He lifted up his head to look at the damsons right above him, and his spine creaked and tingled and burnt with many sensations. His skeletal fingers coasted backwards and forwards to touch them, but they were much too high. He jumped as high he could but could not reach them.

To the side of the garden was the shed with the ladder and all his utensils. It was on the other western extreme of the garden, just a dozen strides from where he was now. The sultry heat began to have its way with him. Thomas unlaced his shoes to feel his bare feet caress the moist blades of grass. He trod on them and the blades swung back to reveal the effect of a shimmering arsenal. Now his feet were lurid with soil. Here was the shed. It was derelict and neglected; he had always wanted to renovate it but had never had stopped lying to himself that he hadn't the time. Still it had its appeal like this too. There was a spray of vine on the inside that girdled all around the small window. The vine covered the whole window save for a round space in the centre, large enough for a head to fit. He had dreamt to take a curious picture of someone in the shed, with their head in the space, so that they seemed verdurely swarmed by an ocean of green leaves. That was a splendid idea for one of his shows.

He opened the shed's door and felt a lurid smell. Mumbled a few curses. The fox had made a home in his shed again. He took the ladder from the clutter of saws, tables and old furniture and shook his head. How did fox enter the shed even if he locked the door? He tried to be tender. Why hate the fox? Perhaps he had someone to take a picture of by the window in the shed after all. One could place the fox's head, there behind the tempest of vines, and it would make a devastating image of foxy auburn with points of green leaf.

He dragged the ladder with him; opening it to then trap his fingers in the mechanism. A sigh of delight at the sting just above his knuckles. The stands of the ladder needed fixing before ascending. With his nude feet touching the cool metal, he began to go up the ladder and the fanciful flicker of a smile began to return to him. With every step he and the ladder began to tremble, but this time he did not feel fear. He felt a delectable fantasy in trembling, as he ascended up to the damsons. There passed to him one of his many bizarre ideas he had and had written in his picture book. Another of his ideas similar to the one about the pleasure in the number three and similar to the one that art needed to be liquid.

He was convinced that in trembling movements like the one of the ladder, there was something extraordinary. All movements sublimated, because the eyes, by instinct, were attracted to movement. Beauty was not, as Joyce thought it, improper for being kinetic. One just needed to think about gyms where people lifted weights, ballet rooms where dancers swayed, and beds were people trembled to know it was true.

As the ladder shook, he closed his eyes and enjoyed the rocking sensation. Then doubt was still in him. Why were shaking movements pleasurable? He thought that all movements seemed to desire knocking down a great flask from above that could smear people who moved with jets of happiness.

High up on the ladder he could see the children playing on the trampoline. His theory about movement knocking down bliss was proved again. The children's faces were inundated with joy. From this ladder he almost forgot about the damsons right above him altogether. He had a perfect sight of all the neighbour's windows. Outstanding to critique pretentiously what bad taste they had. A family was having lunch in the patio and for a moment he stared at them.

But who cared for theories about art! Who cared about the neighbours! Here were the damsons. They hung above him and were so numerous that they could crush him to a pulp. Now he was alone on the ladder and a breeze, that accomplice of solitude, came again. The damsons rocked backwards and forwards and glistened in the air, as ripe nipples dancing above him. He tried clasping one in his hand to squeeze it, but failed terribly and lost his balance. He grabbed hold of a branch and brought it down with him, falling to the floor with the red fruits that rained on him.

Laughed and smirked, like someone rolling in filth, howling with laughter. Squashing the damsons with his back, until his knee began to pop.

"Help! Help!" he called but no one answered him.

He changed mood abruptly and stopped rolling when he noticed he couldn't get up. He continued to call for help as he looked towards his house. The glare of the sliding doors blinded him; he looked at the back gate hopelessly. To attract attention he began clapping; clapping and crying out. The neighbour appeared on the other side of the fence.

"Is everything alright?"

"Oh!"

"Do you need a hand?"

"Yes."

"How shall I?"

"The back-gate is open. Can you please come and help me up?"

The neighbour nodded apprehensively. A few minutes later and the back gate he always left unlocked began moving. He saw the latch fall down and the door swung open.

"Are you alright? Are you alright?" the neighbour kept repeating.

"I'm fine."

"Good."

"Thank you for that."

"Thomas?"

"Yes?"

"Are you expecting someone?"

"Sorry?"

"Are you expecting someone?"

"When I passed by your porch just now there was a young woman waiting outside. I think you ought to let her in…"

Chapter 13.

When Thomas and Stella had re-entered the house, the ladder was still upright in the middle of the garden and the damson tree was partly destroyed. Thomas was drying his face that Stella had sprayed with water with a creamy towel. He scraped the fabric against his face and alternated between glimpses of cream and glimpses of Stella sitting by his dining table. Her elbows were perched upon the glass; her arms were long and morbidly delightful. He had never seen a sight more frightful than a woman with hairs on her arm. Stella had none. On her index finger was a gold plated ring.

    Stella had come here because Thomas had made a scene and put her integrity in question at Ted. So she had been fired. She needed to speak to him for two reasons. She needed him to formerly withdraw his complaint so that she might have a chance to get her job back. Secondly she needed to stand up to this person who seemed to want to destroy her life. Stella was never one to shy away from an argument. Stella was always one to take action. But it seemed as if now she had lost the control of her life to this man. In this respect, Thomas had been Monsieur to Stella, although without his subtlety and without his monocle.

    "May I offer you anything?"

    "Some pomegranate?" Thomas said as he held his back and limped from the kitchen towards her.

    "Look… This is isn't a leisurely visit."

    "Because of you! And I don't even know you! I've been fired."

Stella stopped by the mantelpiece to look at this object that had enchanted her. He saw her begin to admire the gramophone in whose horn he had placed Narcissus flowers. In this gramophone he had distilled the narcissus flower's fragrance and poured it inside so that one could smell it from the dining table. It always conciled his appetite. He had thought about somehow incorporating this piece at the Chelsea Show.

"These are my absolute favourite" she said as she closed her eyes and put her nose by the gramophone horn to inhale. There passed on her face an expression, one he wanted to capture as soon as he saw it. It was here he used his impeccable memory. Thomas could always remember what people said and now he applied this faculty to the facial expression in front of him. He saw the black eyeliner spread on her closed eyelids, it was far different to when they were open.

"They're my favourite too… if you start turning the gramophone's handle you'll see what happens."

Stella did as he said. She began turning the gramophone's handle to make the board spin and he saw her wave-crest ring revolve. The gramophone let out a sprite of perfume and made the sound of a potent trumpet blow; the narcissus flowers were catapulted out and rained on Stella's face. She was startled; her face damasked by these petals that had fallen on her; they covered her eyes, her cheeks and her hair entirely. Only her mouth was left bare.

"Did you make this?" she said.

"Yes. Do you like it? Let me show you something else."

"No, no, wait" she said as he was already half way across the room, leaning by a drawer.

"We have to speak."

"This is serious" and she went to sit back on the dining table and gestured for him to do the same. He felt a guest in his own home.

"Look, I don't know what you want from me, or maybe I do, but you do understand that you can't treat people like this."

"You do understand don't know you?"

"Look, allow me to explain myself."

"I have reason to believe" perhaps he was not so foolish, "That when I asked you to come here and water my plants, you broke in…"

"… And stole my painting."

Stella was flamboyant, inquisitive, often a burst of diversely filtered impressions, but not good at arguing. After an argument she always came up with the wittiest responses, but then it was far too late. The esprit de l'escalier was of course hers.

"It's not..."

"It's not like that."

"I haven't stolen anything from you."

"I never came here. I never came here to do the favour you asked me."

"Why would I be here otherwise? Do you think I'm so stupid?"

"No, no of course not" Stella being stupid was a bastard idea.

"But" he began still not fully convinced, "Do you have an alibi?"

"An alibi? Well actually I do?"

"And who?"

"My son."

"You have children?"

"Yes, only one."

"Right" he said as he took one of the fruits he had squashed before in the bowl between them.

Stella had children? He thought he knew everything about her. He remembered when he had been in the hospital he had compared himself to a gambler. When he had been gambling and guessing what she was like, when he had styled himself with the shirt and bowtie of a croupier in the roulette of possibilities.

"So?" she said after he had been staring blankly at the fruit bowl.

"So young and yet with children?" he replied whilst still not looking her in the face, still leaving his ruminations slowly.

"So old and yet unmarried?" she retorted. She had taken offence at this last remark of his, especially because he had stopped looking at her. Stella admired most those people who were warm and held her stare for long moments. Stella however was also enchanted by those persons who at times looked away, and became devastatingly serious, those persons who, in this respect, became manly and pensive.

Thomas put down the glass and turned. He saw a trace of the expression Stella had made when she had smelt his narcissus flowers, an expression of delight. He copied it again and stored it in his memory, his chest seemed to overflow with faces; and flesh and make up dyes began to spill down his tummy.

"Alright I believe you" he said as he was walking back towards her, still copying as best he could.

"Finally"

"So who do you think?" she said as she held her right hand far from herself, curled, as she would always do, to emphasise her ring. She had pianist's hands, later Thomas would discover she was a violin player.

"…It was?"

"If it's not you, then it has to be Eleanor."

"My godmother's daughter."

"So what does Eleanor want from you?"

"Her and I are fighting over my godmother's house."

"My godmother promised it to me but she can't stand it."

"She's taking me to court for it."

"The trial is in a month."

"You see it can't have been me" she said laughing.

"…"

"I'm so sorry Stella I've put you in this position."

"Look… tomorrow I will come down to Ted and withdraw my complaint."

"Those flowers" she said.

"Where did you get them? You can't get them here in the spring."

"They're artificial. The scent is an imitation too."

"It's just like the real thing."

"I know."

"…"

"Anyway, so you'll go? Speak to my manager?"

"Yes, I will. Tomorrow."

"Great."

"..."

"..."

"Oh, you're leaving? Already?"

"Aren't you staying for dinner?"

"Actually someone at home is expecting me."

"Your son?"

"Yes my son."

"But maybe another time?"

"Yes another time, we can arrange it tomorrow when I come by the store."

Her politeness always ruined her. She smiled, semi apologetically, and hoped he would forget to ask her again. Having exhausted much of the conversation possible between them, Stella stood up and folded her hands together. He took the hint, he pretended to not understand only for a moment, but then muttered a "I'll show you out" with a very dry tone of voice.

As he was leading Stella to the door, he reimagined the expression he had seen fading in her cheeks. Stella saw his shoulders slouch and his entire body seemed to curve to form elastic sways of mood. He looked at her; he seemed to notice that she hadn't removed her shoes when she had come in but didn't say anything. He opened the door. His belly occupied part of the space and she brushed by him.

"I haven't stopped thinking about what you said by the way. The point you made about the arts."

She heard him speak when he was behind her and she was staring out on to the road and the chantries behind it. His voice had sounded different altogether now his body was out of her line of sight.

"Sorry what?"

"What you were saying about the fusion of the arts having to be liquid. I haven't stopped thinking about it."

"Oh that! That's just something silly."

"No it's not... it's really not."

"I'd love to talk about more of those things with you. I've never known a person with whom you can really talk about things like that."

"Yes I suppose me neither."

"Maybe.."

"We can talk more tomorrow if you come by."

"You've actually given me an idea for my own work."

"Oh really what is it? What work?"

"Songs? Song writing?

"Yes, for song writing. I don't know if you know about cadence."

"What is it?"

"It's when a song can end on a masculine or a feminine ending. Anyway I thought it strange-"

"That songs can have a gender: masculine and feminine. People are like songs then and songs like people. It's a mixture like the one you were saying about Wagner."

"You put the idea in my head" and she raised her long hands and drilled her index finger into her temples to demonstrate.

"I'm so glad" he said as she began to distance herself from the door.

"I'll see you tomorrow then."

"Yes tomorrow."

Later that night he considered what it had been like to watch Stella leave his home from the spyhole. It had been a pink and velvety, phantasmatic glory.

Chapter 14.

"We open in five minutes" the waitress gestured to Thomas from inside the café. He nodded and continued to wander aimlessly outside, as impressions and new ideas arranged themselves on the rim of his temples as a princely diadem. The summer's cerise blush effeminised him too and one by one his impatience began to bawl at the waitress's stare. How much longer do I have to wait for a cup of coffee? - he thought. I have work to do.

For Thomas, this café on the high-street, with its pecan and maple muffins and prawn sandwiches, was the perfect studio where to work. He had come here early in the morning because it was the place where the best ideas came and where the worst ideas could be discarded, together with the complementary caramel sweets which he always dropped in the bin after paying. Whenever one of his shows was on, whenever creativity was lacking or work needed doing, he came to this café to sit. To observe and work. Then for months he would never return and he would only work from home. Then for months ideas for shows only came from the bedroom or the bathroom.

The CLOSED sign turned on its face, the cafe's door opened and he brought to a stop his march to kill time. He entered and bought a cup of coffee, then paid with coins and discarded the complementary sweet as soon as the waitress had given his back to him. Today he felt he hadn't the courage to openly refuse it. A booth by the window. Took three times the napkins necessary for he had forgotten his writing paper and needed a space where to draw.

He would spend an hour and a half here at the most. It was early morning and he had two errands to run, the first being finding a lawyer for the trial. There was a law-firm in Artillery road, just by the Anglican Church. Then of course he needed to go to Ted and repair the damage he had done. He wanted to help Stella get her job back. Then their relationship could change for the good. She was almost in the grasp of his friendship. She had even mentioned that he had inspired her. How inspired he felt to think that part of her life depended on him in this moment. Perhaps he truly was a Monsieur.

He looked up from his blank napkin canvases and took in the desultory sprawl of this studio. Yes, the café, for men such as him, was the place most comparable to a studio, that place where late men and women indulged in their art, with Monteverdi's laments of nymphs by tables. The napkins were the paper, ashtrays and straws ingredients for music, and the occasional pretty girls the self-same figure who sat or walk or leaned in an artist's imagining.

His last show at Chelsea was a few months away and he hadn't come up with any concrete ideas. He knew that in this show he wanted to treat the theme of the *all-embracing art form*. Recently he had reread a piece about Wagner and then Stella had said that the fusion of the arts art would be liquid. But these were only abstract ideas for the moment. In short, he had nothing. He drank his coffee and tried sketching some ideas. The coffee's steam sent up effluvial veneration to his three-personed chin.

On the napkin he began drawing a figure. First its body and then its head. The figure's hair he made out of musical crotchet notes – so that a lock of her hair was an undulation of music. Three of these figures on the napkins. He felt proud of himself until he looked up and realised they were all drawings of Stella.

Stirring the teaspoon in the cup, he tried thinking up something different. Impossible. How could music and painting and sculpture and theatre and writing fuse together?

When he finished his coffee the waitress came to clear his table. Perhaps the waitress knew. Maybe it was worth asking her. He slouched in his chair and looked around at the other tables as more people were coming in. Artist's studios had ornaments that were always the same, but here the ornaments changed every moment. Men and women entered and left and decorated the café with fair variety. A young boy with his mother were sitting on a table next to him. The boy began to make silly faces and Thomas waved at him. As he waved he saw the edge of his palm was stained with ink. On the last napkin he had left, he began to draw a small pedestal. Perhaps that was how he could start. Whatever idea he would up with, he would place on this pedestal. He drew the legs and then the face of table. It was a start.

He spent a few more moments looking at this empty pedestal he had drawn on the napkin. Then he decided he had had enough and stood up, adjusted his shirt and put the pen back in his right ear. As he left, he gifted the three napkins with Stella's drawings to the young boy.

He left ideas and abstraction altogether and began walking up to Artillery road to consult a lawyer. He had seen their advert on a poster paper. Thinking of divorce? – it had read. The law firm specialised in family law. They could help him put to rest any trouble about inheriting Flora's house, he was certain. Men and women were on their way to work as he came by the top of the high street. Some builders were doing road works and made him wait a few minutes before crossing the road. The builders' torsos had rosy moon-marks near their arms, fresh from sun-burn. A line came to mind:

Monsieur, coated in a white euphoria of gesso, walks down the avenue with prune coloured shoes dried to a coarse and fashionable glow.

"You can cross now" they ushered him on.

When he arrived in front of the law firm he saw the same poster paper. It had a woman on the front smiling. Thinking of Divorce? He read again. Why was this woman smiling? She seemed to advertise her impeccable teeth. Someone came out of the edifice and held the door open for him. In the office there were women in long suits, sumptuously engaged with the telephone. They all acknowledged him and he sat down and waited. A desk was soon freed up for him and he went to sit down and explain his case. He explained how his Godmother had left him a house in her will but how her daughter had destroyed the proof. The woman in front of him took down everything he said in schematic bullet points he admired. She told him that he didn't need to worry, they were here to help him and they had seen many cases similar. She advised him to find a witness that could prove that it had been "Eleanor" to break into his home.

When he left the law firm, the lawyer reinstated that he needed to find a witness. That should be his primary concern until they got in touch with him next. Who could be his witness? Perhaps the neighbours had seen the break-in. But his relationship with them was lacking altogether. Stella. Perhaps she could help him.

The builders had taken a break and he crossed over to the other side of the road unencumbered. Now that he had procured himself a lawyer, he could go to Ted to try and help Stella. He felt particularly motivated now he needed her help too. It took him a few minutes to reach Ted; he was out of breath and began walking slowly. Every time he had walked a few strides, he tapped his trouser pockets manically to ensure his wallet or keys had not slipped out. There was a guitar player by the pavement and he stopped for a moment to listen without giving him any money. His envy became highstrung as he observed the guitar player. Such a shame that he had never learnt how to play an instrument.

Now instead he made the men and women he bumped into on his path into his piano keys; he pressed his shoulders against them as he strutted in-between crowds and arranged scherzos in passers-by. There was a woman in an ivory white coat whom he played with the most force, she became his ivory key, and he became one great piano hammer that swung through and fulminated. He continued to bump shoulders and the street became alight with minors and majors; rudeness and violence became his musical expression and ladies in black or white his *doremi*. The Ted sign appeared in front of him.

He had arrived. A young boy was running down the street and hit him with his elbow. Thomas was knocked back, flushed and embarrassed, into his red crepuscular decrepitude.

Having spoken well and eloquently with the lawyer, he entered Ted with the confidence to believe that he could explain and put things right. The sales assistants that had seen him for the third time, gathered and began to whisper as he came in. They had given him a nickname. They often did this when a strange personality came in their midst. Just the other week they had called one of Stella's admirers a typical Italian name that had later become a sensation. They wanted to call him by this name too but he was far too old. Besides, they had tired of Pepe.

It took him several minutes to abandon the memory of having met Stella here. She had been standing there! He pointed and began filtering the projection. And he had been standing there! just a few metres to her right. Except they had moved a rack of clothes and it wasn't the same. He was tempted to rearrange the scene, just like it had been that salient time. Trying to restrain himself, he focused and remembered why he was here.

At first the cashier did not want to call the manager; she tried brushing aside his request. It was only when he insisted and slammed his fist down on the counter that she yielded and picked up the telephone. He was still speaking to her loudly and violently and he could not hear what she was saying. The manager arrived soon after and he too was dressed in a style that Thomas admired. He was also beginning to grow bald, just like Thomas, even if he was far younger.

The manager had dealt with many problematic customers like Thomas before. For a moment Thomas was still admiring his clothes and was polite in his manner, until he recoiled and made sure they got the message. Stella needed to get her job back. In the same way that the sane entertain the mad, the manager pretended to absorb profoundly everything he said, "Yes, you're absolutely right" and nodded and shook his head, "Yes I understand", whenever the conversation needed him to.

"Aren't you taking any of this down? I insist you take this down."

So the manager nodded, not meaning it at all, and took out a clipboard and a pen.

"Look it's easier if you do it in bullet points" Thomas said nosily, remembering how the lawyer had done it just half an hour ago.

This irritated the manager. He looked up from the clipboard and exchanged a glance with the other employee at the till, whose look just seemed to say: "I don't know".

Thomas stood over his shoulder to make sure he wrote everything correctly; he felt Thomas' miasmic inundation of breath. "Look, why don't you write?" he said to Thomas and handed him the pen. Thomas began to write systemically.

"Finished?" the manager smirked. Thomas nodded, looked up from the clipboard, took it back and then added one extra line.

"Now if that will be everything" the manager said as he walked towards Thomas and held him by the waist to usher him out. As his hand touched him, he felt the pain of yesterday's fall in his leg. He gave the manager his clipboard and without another word, began limping out. As soon as he had left, the manager took the paper from the clipboard and crumpled it up.

Out on the street again. He was christened and pastelled by the shades of the summer morning whose basin absorbed him again into a mile of cobblestone. Baby girls on push chairs with drooling mouths passed him by; he idealised them too and them of their spit new grandiloquisms he found hard to pronounce. The rest of the day was his. What could he do to occupy his time? Perhaps he could leer into and sway in between these shops lackadaisically, buy perhaps an ice cream and relieve himself of this sultry heat that was palling on him, or he could go home to work. Or he could go back to the coffee shop for more ideas. He passed in between these options capriciously and none of them satisfied him; finally he began walking down the high street as a last resort. The street was inclined and he rolled, as balls roll, without direction nor meaning. There were many teenagers in the centre that had already finished the semester; they skipped around the shops and Thomas lampooned their youth inside of him. His hairy chest turned a blue suede. Some of them who sat on letterboxes stared at Thomas as he went to sit down by the bench opposite the scholar's statue. This statue was one of the two here in Guildford; the other was at the end of the street and commemorated the arch bishop.

Thomas knew that the statue in front of him had been erected some ten years ago to celebrate the Holloway grammar school. It was a great and slim delicious boy of bronze that held four books in his arms and raised his hat in curtsey. He had a cloak that also spread to his side with a semi curve. Thomas dropped his thoughts about Stella altogether and looked at this scholar's books to consider knowledge and the great academy. Here in this miniature square he looked at the scholar and the dream of the *all embracing art form* returned to him. His last show! What was the formula for music, painting and writing to meet in one collage? Surely this scholar new and surely the formula was written in his books. He wanted to get up and push him aside, to take these books in his arms and see what was written inside. But he could not. The books' secrets were sealed in bronze.

"To hell with it" he said, got up; to leave the bench, the statue and everything with it. Who could know the answer to this question that ghosted his mind?

"Perhaps Monsieur knows" he said when he was a few meters clear.

Right as he said this, Monsieur, who had been watching all the while dripping in bronze paint, tightened his grip of the books and blinked.

Where was Stella? What was she doing? Would she forgive him now he had done as she had told him? Now he needed her help for the court case his dependence on her duplicated. He browsed through men's and women's faces on the high street but could not find her.

"To hell with it" he marched on again, "I'll find

her" and he laboured under the illusion that stumbling in between streets, he truly could meet her by chance. He passed by the bishop's statue and was still convinced he would. She had made no mention about where she lived and he had not guessed either. He guessed now. Epsom road! He turned and began walking beside the terrace houses. These impressions sabred into his minced nerves. "Where is Stella?" and the intolerable whim corroded him to the bone. If only he could know where Stella lived he could go deliver the good news in person and ask her this favour to be his witness for the trial. Epsom road was one that stretched far all the way to the next town, and he would have walked to the end of it if it meant communicating with her. Carcasses of dust bins passed him by; to Thomas' melodic snorts. Eleanor's home was somewhere near here. What if Stella and Eleanor were neighbours? And Stella's son? What if he looked like his father? As he came to the traffic light he stopped and began walking back; full of sweat and fears.

The hill in front of the G-live theatre took him up and made him pant as he walked back home and saw familiar faces everywhere sprinkled. Shortcuts became useless. He took one to bypass Castle Road but it proved of no use when he saw that a man he had been observing before arrived at the same time as him. This was the penultimate jab into his patience; the last came when the hill that led him home became so steep he had to rest to regain his breath. The street so steep and the temperature so warm, that he became passionately and dispassionately exhausted in this hot exercise. Slave to calefaction, lost to his withering bones, only the downhill slopes permitted him some slack in his performance with the bed and linen of the road.

There was a great house in the style of a villa that Thomas always stopped to look at, stooped to observe, whenever he took this path. It was just before the bend on Wilsmere Road and during Christmas it had the most enviable collection of lights and decorations. Despite his mood that shunned everything and absorbed nothing, he stopped by the arrow-pointed gates and rested his head on the metal. He stared at this house as was his custom, and placed it at the top of his list of the best properties in the neighbourhood. There were the fountains he admired most and the bushes that had been pruned to form delectable ogee curves.

His particular attention to detail was eclipsed by how big the building was. It was far larger than his home. It had six bedrooms; two of them unoccupied, he had observed. It belonged to a Swedish family. During Christmas they would put out the Scandinavian candles on the windowsill.

In the window there was one of the children; she opened the window that looked out towards the gate and Thomas was caught staring. The girl looked at him apathetically. He continued to stare at the house, and the blonde child inside it, and became envious. Flora's house in Tuscany. It became even more important to him; he had to win the trial.

Back at home. The telephone rings but he ignores it and goes upstairs to file the lawyer's transcript. The windows dirty again –grumbles and sighs. His room is unusually tidy and he is disappointed that he cannot waste time to clean it.

Rebelliously he throws the napkin with the

drawing of the pedestal somewhere towards the desk and it lands on the floor. He needed to start his work now that he had an idea; the pedestal on which he would place his creation for the Chelsea Show. But first he would make some marmalade. The damsons he had collected yesterday were still in his kitchen. He threw off all his clothes in case they would get stained whilst cooking and left only his undershirt. Then he left the room and knocked down on purpose the heap of books and pens, just so he would have something to do when he came back.

In the second drawer of the kitchen Thomas had a set of aprons. He put one on and tightened it around his body, simultaneously discerning the recipe for the marmalade. These were the simple tasks in which he found consolation. An old recipe book, two rusty pans to boil water.

"The difference between marmalade and jam is that marmalade contains lemon bits."

His love of the ornate often made him dazed. Cooking tranquilised; especially when he carried out many instructions one after the other. At first he began taking out the stones from the damsons, then he began cutting up the lemon peel. He dropped the fruits into the pan along with the sugar and began to stir; nextly lowered the cooker's temperature and continued to stir the fruits with a spoon for half an hour. An hour later and the marmalade was ready. Thomas poured it into a jar and spread some of it on bread crackers. The crackers on a plate and then forgot to close the fridge, permutating heat with frost in the room. On the staircase to the third floor, one could sit down and observe the street through the windows. Thomas decided he would sit there and eat his marmalade. Almost fell on the steps as he ascended and risked staining the carpet –no rather foibling the floor with character. Sat down, looked out onto the street and the hills behind it, and wondered if in Italy marmalades like this were welcomed.

The spoon fed him slowly. It gave to him the taste of plum and cold metal. Even if he was eating, he felt "blue with famine after love". Why hadn't Stella come to thank him for what he had done; he'd gone to speak to the manager as she said? Maybe it was her on the telephone earlier. He thought that it was another salesperson that had called; maybe he had been a fool not to pick up. Perhaps Stella will come in person, just like yesterday. When will she come? Will she ever find an interest in him? He cannot bear to be alone. This is the refulgent and endless solitude that he must hate.

Chapter 15.

Three days later Stella and her son appeared outside on Thomas' doorstep; dirigibled by gaiety. It was a Friday; Fridays had always been a lucky day ever since he had won at canasta. Before they arrived, Thomas had started sketching out the design for his next show; he had decided to place some bushes around the slab that was to be his pedestal. He had started well but then had begun to procrastinate again when he saw what other shows rival gardeners had been planning. So he had gone back to making his marmalade with new experimental ingredients. Cooking could make him delay and avoid his work. The kitchen became full of jars with slightly different tasting marmalades; for almost half a week he fed only on this type of jelly and became a fruity vegetable. The only exercise he did was to pass his spoon on the rim of each jar, as if playing a boiled set of tambourines.

The neighbours often exchanged food or other gifts like this one, and as the jars began to pile, he thought he could offer some to the young couple opposite his home, even if their relationship was lacking altogether. Children liked marmalades and this couple's child might like it too. He also basked youthfully in all the jars he had prepared and reconnected with the childish love of sugar and sensations. Oh wait, that was salt; slight mishap. He did not know that his marmalade would instead be tasted by Stella's son.

When the two of them arrived, Thomas was still wearing his apron; he had grown to like it and refused to take it off, even when he had gone to bed. The apron had given him this duplicitous luxury; it made him feel womanly and manly and all at once he became spouse and bride of the home. Just by tying a knot, the apron turned him into a culinary cross-dresser; a chef whose arms were grotesquely hairy but whose dress was feminine and soft, and he cooked for himself and ate for himself and pinched his own bum. Where the love of woman had always been an outward projection; this time it became an internal and magnetic whirlpool that drove him to seek femininity within himself.

Where the postman rang the doorbell, where the charity workers just stood outside his porch, this time Thomas was called with a thump! at his door. Three beats. The wooden spoon was still in his mouth, his cheeks were gorged with the stuff and he dropped everything to go answer the door. Opened; there was Stella holding hands with another man. Her son.

"Hi."

"I hope you don't mind me showing up like this."

"I tried calling and no one answered."

"I need to speak to you."

"This is Leonard by the way."

"Come in, come in" and he stepped aside to let them pass. This time he didn't even look at Stella. Thomas could only stare at this young boy who was passing beside him; who must have been no older than seven or eight years old.

"Are we disturbing you?"

"No, no, not at all" he said as he removed his stare from Leo and looked back at Stella.

"I was just cooking. Marmalade."

"Look, about your job" but he did not continue when he saw Stella inflate her eyes and shake her head as if to say, "not in front of him please".

She leaned down and kissed the boy on the cheek and said:
"Look Leo! Why don't you go out and play in the garden" and she nodded for them to go out into the parlour or kitchen where they could speak in private.
"Sorry, what were you saying?"
The fat boy in front drew out the greatest shame in him; ruined any pleasant taste an idiot's marmalade could conjure up. Stella spoke, waved her hands, even spurted some spit whilst talking, but behind the sliding doors there was a sight more distracting: a plump boy playing on the patio, staining the door with his breath and hands on the glass. Where he would always groan and complain at the sight of dirty windows, this time he said nothing as Leo continued to press his hands on the doors, without a care in the world of the consequences. He was so fat, obese really. The scene reminded him of a fascinating fat man he had seen in London carrying a quaint, suspicious briefcase, one that had made him imagine writing a book called: "Biography of a fat man". It was a working title.

Thomas leaned back on his divan shaped as an "L" and cabrioled his arms behind his head as if they were legs. He was in the middle row of the divan and Stella was on the extreme with her back to the garden. For a moment Leo disappeared behind Stella's shoulders and then reappeared at the edge. The boy's blue-breath hitting the glass perspired into the parlour, to whirl around Thomas.

Besides jealousy for Stella's affection for her son, which she had kissed with two quick pecks not too long ago, it was Leo's appearance to ruin him. He had inherited everything from his mother except his hair and stature. Whatever Leo had not taken from his mother, he had most probably taken from his father, that man; that man who, let us say it! had slept with Stella! He didn't even know her a month and this intense jealousy, foliaged-yellow, smothered him and became his seasonal august sorrow.

"Thomas are you listening to me or not?"

Thomas shook his head and wringed out of himself this terrible feeling.

"I'm sorry, I… what were you saying?"

"I was asking you what you said to my manager about what happened."

"They've decided to stick to their decision. They don't want to take me back. They haven't even given me a week's notice."

"But I went. I went down there to tell them. They even took down what I said and promised they would consider."

"But they haven't. The reason why I came down here is because I thought you'd forgotten, in which case…"

"But can't you appeal or something?"

"It's not… It's not like that in retail."

"I don't know if you realise, but this thing risks ruining my life and…"

"But surely" Thomas interrupted whilst still looking at the boy, "you and Leo's father…"

"That's the thing."

"There is no Leo's father."

"My son and I live alone at the moment."

"Oh" he couldn't be happier.

"And I need to get my job back. I depend on it. I'm not asking for your help but…"

Stella was much too proud to ask for help. She would even refuse asking for money from her own parents if it meant that they would later "bang it on her" as she often said. Now it was true that she wasn't asking for his help but she was trying to reach a compromise.

"I have the perfect idea" - Thomas got up and gave his back to her.

"I need your help too."

"Hear me out."

"I'm going to court to settle this matter about my godmother's house with Eleanor."

"Eleanor broke in here and burnt, took, I don't know what she did, but she has the proof that makes me lay claim to this house."

"I spoke with the lawyer and I need a witness."

"You can be my witness Stella. No, no don't frown at me like that just listen."

"This benefits you too. If she's proven guilty then you're cleared too."

"But I didn't see Eleanor come in here. I've never met her. Ever."

"Yes but you know it was her. This would be a white lie."

"All you have to do is to testify."

"You just have to prove you were with me when the burglary happened."

"And in the meantime" he continued.

"You can come and work for me."

Stella rolled her head back and laughed.

"Come and work for you? What do you mean come and work for you?"

"Be serious now."

"I am."

"You're great at giving me ideas. You have taste. I know you do. Until you apply for a new job, until you get it back or until the case is cleared, you can work for me."

"I need help."

"You obviously do need help" she wanted to say.

"With my work."

"Look how much can you possibly get at Ted?"

"Twenty pounds an hour?" Actually it was eight.

"We can arrange more than that. What do you say?"

Stella had become inattentive in looking out towards the garden. She remembered the times when she had been of Leo's age and her father in Rhodes, after her mother had left them, had made her help with all the chores of the home.

"I don't know… it's a possibility."

Thomas clicked his fingers as if having made a great point and began to walk around the room slowly. He was both convincing and awkward; was well aware himself. Even the apron failed to tie down any consistency.

Was Stella a liar? Would Stella adhere to this plan of his? If she had any complexes at all it was precisely this; to be called a liar, to be dishonest and to be as her family put it, "unclassy", in appearance and beauty products. This second complex had come soon after adolescence, when her and her sisters had been humiliated at a family gathering and had been labelled, as it was in the Greek, "scatological" children. She would never want to be dishonest nor unclassy, and so she embalmed herself with expensive lotions in the evening and half lies in the morning. But what was the point? – she sometimes thought? What was the point in keeping up appearances? For Stella people were chance creatures with a twain set of hands, that could make and destroy. Duplicitous people, duplicitous hands, could apply lotions. Yes, people were, in essence, two hands; that's why men and women were double sided, deca-fingered as deca-diverse, or so she believed.

This last idea was not entirely her own; she had coined it soon after reading Dostoyevsky, one of her favourite writers, whom she read at the beach when her father used to take her near Kallithea, on Sundays. One of her favourite lines on the definition of man, "a being that goes on two legs and is ungrateful" she had altered to this image of the hands. She looked at her own hands, remembered Dostoyevsky; reminisced the red terracotta mountain she would picture whenever she read his books, the denizen mountain of the beach she always imagined when reading, even if it had nothing to do with the book. It was her son's hands, and the fence in the garden, to make her think of the Russian writer. Thomas did not know about her theory, just as he did not know that all of Stella's creams and lotions would soon come to decorate his shelves too.

"I have to think about it."

"Maybe."

"So you will consider?"

"I would prefer if you went again to explain. We could go together?"

Right as she finished speaking, Leonard came back inside running and hurled himself on his mother's lap. Stella scooped him in his arms and began playing with his cheek, then she made a silly voice and mocked him with a nose to nose; that game that mothers play with their children.

But what about his theory? What about his theory that there was bliss in every moment? Stella's and Leo's noses shook and yet he was proved wrong; it was agony to look at them together.

Why was just looking at Stella and Leonard so unpleasant? It was strange to see his pain embodied by these two people. He imagined that this was the mind's way to cope with emptiness; to give a name and a face to an emptiness inside, that was what he was doing. It was impossible, he reasoned, to actually picture emptiness; that much was known to man, that infinity and nothingness were barred to his understanding. To picture nothingness? It was impossible! and so his longing to not be alone became these persons he could perceive; a way to flesh out a desire, quite literally.

He watched Stella with this boy in her arms. Leo, who looked like his father, had his father's hair, enjoyed all of Stella's warmth. He watched them brioche together their noses. Whatever passion and youth Stella and this boy's father had enjoyed at adolescence, whatever pleasures, they were enjoying again now in childhood. That man's image lived on this child and the secrets and the promises of all ages, child to adolescent, adolescent to man, could be known to him as a timeless prince who ghosts every époque. What was that man's name? Was he more successful than Thomas? He couldn't dare to hear it.

Stella smiled and he remembered the expression she had made of extreme delight when smelling the gramophone horn. What if she had made that face the night, the morning or the afternoon, in which she had slept with that man to conceive this child?

What could he do? Now he was old, decrepit, withering, Stella was unobtainable. He had to have her. He wanted to be this boy in her arms, yet far older, far greyer and yet just as desirous. But he knew it was impossible. Impossible to have her. Impossible to make love to her and become "one flesh", his wrinkled, hers full of youth and olive-like; one expired olive oil flesh; together they would make a juvenile senility.

To make love to Stella, that was just as impossible to picture as nothingness. And so he felt disappointed. Ah- but what can an empty man do if not find vanity supreme in his work? If he could not have Stella, then he had his work. The Gesakuntswerk. The *all-embracing art form*. His last work at Chelsea. That would be his cataclysmic vindication. His work, his retirement, became evermore important now that he was presented with everything he did not have.

"He's probably hungry."

"He can have some of my marmalade" Thomas spoke and excused himself to hide his shame. He went to the kitchen and then began spreading on some toast one of the types of marmalade he thought was best. Out of jealousy he would have given Leo the worst he had prepared, but then he thought that Stella might try some and he could not risk making a bad impression. He carried the plate over with tremulous hands; he never ate on the divan, but would have to make an exception.

The boy's mouth became full of marmalade-spackled crumbs after having eaten. Stella also tried some.

"Did you add some cinnamon? You could definitely add some cinnamon."

"No I didn't but good idea."

When Stella and Leo had left his home, he was still unsure how it had ended. He did not look at Stella leave by the spyhole this time. Instead he just repeated in his head, "cinnamon, cinnamon, cinnamon".

The following days Thomas applied cinnamon wherever his hand could. He sprinkled it first in his milk and then on grapes so that the taste began to tire him. Stella was right. The marmalade tasted far better with cinnamon. If only he had known that Stella used to make cinnamon tarts for Leo's father than he would have spat out the powder and his tongue with it.

The lawyer called and asked him to confirm a few details. The lawyer also wanted to discuss the value of the property in the inheritance and if they wanted to hire a personal investigator that could follow Eleanor to find out more about what happened. He accepted. He told her he could do it himself but she didn't seem amused and urged him to go down to the office to sign some papers. Another trip down to the centre. He sighed.

Besides these few days of inactivity, lately he felt as if he had done a lot of walking. Perhaps it was the light injury after having fallen from the ladder to emphasise the feeling in his legs. Besides cinnamon or Stella, walking was the other alternative to his loneliness. And the *all embracing art form*? That was also the occasional riddle in which to indulge. Now he could combine all three; he could walk to the centre thinking about the all embracing art form with the taste of cinnamon still in his mouth and Stella in his head. Before leaving the house he decided to put to use the spare laces that had come with his shoes. He spent almost half an hour criss-crossing the laces into his shoes and tangled to his feet all sincerity.

Walking. This and memory were the light-headed fool's poetry everyone was capable of. Was walking poetic? Admittedly so. The language of poetry had terms all to do with walking; the meter, the foot and the step of a stanza revealed every poet's desire to promenade. Between Shalford road and Pilgrim road he wrote a poem of two stanzas, with his new lucent shoelaces.

> *the darkling faults of 1.681*
> *montage and dott all over the avenue*
> *As I"m passing by the bank, euclid drives the point home to tell me*
>
> *I've seen you again*
> *ascending park stairs*
> *Or alleyways, with deviations by old Shoppes*

> *I have remade you now*
> *your personable intensity*
> *I*
> *have remade you*
> *but without the dimples dear*
> *Because your copies strut with their back to me*
> *and*
> *I cannot see like this*
> *When I walk, just before the bend, your filamentary tempo*
> *pierces*
> *lapels*
> *on new men's coats*
> *Undying beacon lampposts lights then bring me*
> *to*
> *strangers*
> *that bow down*
> *to imitate you in piazzas*

Crossing the road without stopping a moment became his enjambment, and the occasional shoulder he bumped into a rhyme that had not quite rolled off the tongue. Theatrics of course did not come without their consequences. As men despise poetry, so Thomas was despised and suffered the judgment of people who thought he was walking by beleaguered with bizarreness. He could have spared himself this trip to the town centre. He could have signed the papers the lawyer wanted next week, there was no great hurry, but chose not to do so to have an excuse to get out of the house and entertain one of his curiosities. Where did Stella's son go to school? He wanted to know. After passing by the law firm he decided he'd pass by the catholic school in the near vicinity to see if Stella was there to pick up her son.

When he arrived again at the law-firm, still the telephones, still the long suites. The lawyer, who he needed to stop calling "the lawyer", even if it pleased him to say it, told Thomas that they needed to schedule a mediation between both parties, him and Eleanor. Eleanor's lawyer had called her to say that Flora's will had emerged, in Italian. The language barrier had certainly been a problem. Nicole, Thomas' lawyer, would have dropped Thomas' case immediately if it wasn't for the fact that Flora's will, which left everything to Eleanor, had been written two years ago and could so be overruled by other evidence. The pompous tangle of names and clauses and laws was a mess. The letter Thomas had, the one where Flora had shown to have had a change of heart and had decided to leave the house in Tuscany to him, could change the case entirely. Speaking about the trial tired him and made him feel numb with complications; he left the office ever more annoyed by the practises and rules of justice. Yet there was a recompense at the end for him. That great villa would be his. And Stella with it. That was the next corner his persuasiveness would have to point her towards. Stella could come and live with him in Flora's house as soon as he won the case and retired. Without Leo of course. He could stay in England and go to a boarding school. Wasn't that prestigious in England? To go to a boarding school?

"Think of the honour" he would tell Stella.

These were the types of thoughts that proved Stella right: people were a tumult of two opposite hands. Thomas was a man at once forward and a man at once shy who didn't like to talk much, a man who basked in the thick and ornate lace of embroidery, and a man who just wanted stuff to be simple. Contradiction. That was the atonement for having been born with just one life to live. Where he had initially been quiet and unable to speak to Stella, now he took it upon himself to intrude into her life amicably and ambitiously. Having formed the bond of jealousy, he took the liberties of thinking about Stella all the time and treated her as if she had always been a timeless friend that was soon to be much more.

He decided he'd go outside the Catholic school on North street to see if Leo was there and if Stella had come to pick him up. If they would see him he could explain that he'd come to pick up his grandson; he could bribe one of the children passing by and escape unencumbered without being too embarrassed. Most of all he wanted to see Leonard more than Stella. Thomas believed that if pain became familiar, it could be less alien and impersonal. Whenever a painful memory returned to him, he did not reject it, instead he often explored it, passed between its changing shape until it became hurtful no longer and he was married to the memory. That was what he could do now. He could see Leo again, inspect him better and vaccinate this jealousy congealed in the blood. Yes. Was that not the principal idea behind vaccines? To inject the same poison that would later become cure?

The electric possibility, the idea to also kidnap Leo, to vivisect him out of this perfect life, certainly passed through him. For the moments were jealousy still lingered, he became a dangerous man.

He admitted to this as he leaned on a car on the street and waited for the children to come outside for "home time". Where catholic buildings or churches in other places of the continent were ornate and decorous; this one was appallingly simple. The church in England was meagre. Bricks collaged together to deliver the façade of a school impoverished by sin or whatever judgement from above. He would have been wrong however to think that there was no richness to enjoy here. Instead, the wealth of the catholic church had taken on a new uniform Thomas would prefer to any arch or marble, it was this lottery; this frittering away of the desire for the baroque to young girls. Young girls. The dazzlement of the ornate, the evangelical worship of the beautiful, was given to these fourteen and fifteen year old girls that were coming outside the school. This place was both a primary and secondary school.

In short these young girls aroused Thomas and gave to him a lingual erection. He saw them exit through the great door with uniforms in dark navy blue; with similarly dark hair. They most probably were all of Irish descent; English people had no business with Catholicism and just thought it something stupidly old fashioned from another century. He remembered Greece was orthodox. Stella probably didn't send her son to school here. Yet now it was much too late to make sense of this detail with feeling in prey, and these girls that added to the cradling orbit of passion and jealousy.

More of the teenagers came out, some with tight sweatpants that emphasised their glutinous buttocks, and others with skirts that reminded one of the elegance of legs. Thomas watched and the young girls began to take out cigarettes, indifferent to what anyone might think. As they loitered outside, the cigarettes they held in their hands puffed out in clouds their vaporous youth.

Thomas thought again about kidnapping Leo and yes! he felt he could do it. The younger classes were coming out. He moved forward to get closer to this boy, made contact with the girls raining their smoke upon him, and felt ready, to commit the crime of passion. Leo, or Leo's copy, was facing the other way and Thomas could not make out his face clearly as he tilted towards, on him. He could only see that short hair that was so unlike Stella's; that hair which smacked of his great dread. That man. What if Stella had pulled at that man's hair the nights they slept together? That was the unnerving possibility just at the fringe of his toils. He was half a meter away from the boy and his hands were ready to pull him by the hairs and his brains with it, so that any memory of Stella concealed there could be destroyed and made his.

"Excuse me" he said in the politest of tones that brought him back to mercy. The boy ran off in the distance. His mother had arrived. She took her hands in his and walked away whilst scrutinising Thomas. There was a bevy of children everywhere around him that amplified in great numbers how cruel and evil he was becoming. He felt terrible. He had actually considered! He had actually considered hurting this boy that looked like Leo; that was the effect that seeing Stella and her son had given him. A sound seemed to play in his ear, a *peal* of thunder; he had two options, to accept its toll and return to normality, or to coat himself with the electric *peel* of a sound, so his own skin could become just as villainous and sudden and blue as lightening. He did the first. He zipped up his jacket, to hide his sin and began walking away from the school whilst bumping into children.

He accidentally stepped on a boy's heels and had to bend down to apologise; that made him feel even more guilty and indignant. As he crossed the road, with the cars passing by, a desire of penance passed through him; to ask for a type of forgiveness, that was what he wanted. He lingered on the road and was frightened; became paranoid that if a car would hit him he would go out of the world at the worst of times, in the most unheroic conditions of the soul.

Towards the high-street, walking back, he tried being kind at random; he let a woman pass before him and also took a magazine that young people outside of supermarkets gave out for a tip. He hated the serialised editions; he had also never taken one before, but did so to exonerate himself from feeling any more guilt. It didn't work. Just before the clock-tower, he turned the corner and passed by Guildford Castle. He entered this park where the castle stood and began walking around the walls that sealed off the place from the town, to make it his panoptical prison.

He spent the rest of the day in this park, for two reasons. Perhaps Stella would bring her son here to play after school finished and then he might bump into them and be offered a chance to make up for the ideas that passed through him, even if they did not know it. This would be his expiatory punishment.

A few hours. Stella hadn't come. When night began to fall, he went to hide in the bushes so that the guard that closed the park didn't see him. Instead of returning back to his bedroom, he slept by the grass and the piercing, abrasive thorns became the warmest blanket one could hope for. A verse he had once written in his picture-book:

In sleep and repose serenity find, solemn grace of dormant eyes.

Chapter 16.

The morning he returned home Stella was waiting outside his door. After barely having slept for more than a couple of hours in the park, he decided to take a taxi and spare himself any more exercise. True, he would abstain from poetry, from walking in fabulous meters and steps and anapaestic distances without stress. In this sense he was foregoing art but didn't care at all. In the taxi he watched the fare charge rise exorbitantly. With every winding turn of the road he was centrifuged in the car as if he were a salad lacquered in sauces.

Twenty pounds; that was much he had to pay for just a five minute car-ride. He almost hesitated in giving the pound notes to the driver, but then Stella was in his head and he remembered the dangers of being frugal. Women didn't like men who were tight with money. So against his greater will he decided to be generous and paid without complaining. When he got out he scratched the taxi's driver's car with his keys. What would Stella have thought if she saw him?

He truly needed to be careful with any more maleficent outpourings because Stella was there in his driveway, with her hand pressing on the doorbell. He had never seen her before from this angle and he took the bearing just as a sailor might have done; a hundred and sixty degrees and seven meters.

Pushed on; the gravel in his driveway betrayed his step and as he neared the porch she turned and realised he was here.

"I'm going to have to take you up on what you said."

Much too tired, he nodded and let her in and almost fell asleep by the stairs. Stella had decided to come and work for him. But "only for a day", to "give it a shot" she had said. He made some coffee, and also offered it to her, because he couldn't concentrate at all. He found it hard to believe that she had accepted his offer. She needed money. That much was clear. Stella told him that at Ted there was almost no chance of her being hired again because she was already on her second disciplinary. The first two had come after arguments with her manager where she had entered into a dangerous and petty rivalry. Stella's job description stated that she was classified as the visual manager of the store; and it was her task to arrange the windows and the clothes inside. But this manager, whom everyone in the store could clearly see was more than just a little on the feminine side, often overruled Stella's choices for the store's visual and made her life difficult. She would arrange socks in this manner and he would change them; she would add a contemporary touch to the window and he would dislike it. After a while this had led to vehement arguments between Stella and the manager, where she would always lose.

It certainly did not help that Stella had a playful and teasing character that got on the manager's nerves. Sometimes, just out of the spontaneity inherent in Stella, she would say, "Oh but you never told me", "Oh but you never said" and he would never understand that she was joking and didn't mean it. At one point he'd called her a liar; the worst of offences Stella could imagine. That and being called unclassy she could not tolerate. When she had stood up to him, he had said, "So you're calling me a liar?" and so there was always this confusion about who was the liar, who was the saint and who was the woman of the two. The manager had been dreaming of firing Stella and Thomas' "fracas" as the newspapers often called it, permitted him the perfect opportunity to do so. Stella had also tired of working there. She had gone there out of desperation, after her acting career had brought her nothing but a few third rate roles in a theatre in Woking, the nearby town.

She had for long wanted to leave Ted but because of circumstance, the incorrigible Monsieur, had not managed to do so. And yet in a way Monsieur had listened; Monsieur who was always just in the next street parallel, in the bathroom's cubicle beside, had bent his ear to her requests and had mustered up his generosity. The truth of the matter was that Stella had no wish to return to Ted; that was a life that had brought her great unhappiness and misery and above all, shame. Having graduated with just one point below full marks in her theatre degree, she considered herself far above these people that worked in retail. Stella's contempt was not unfounded; she was never a snob without reason. These people that surrounded her in the work place struck her as mediocre because they were happy to live with monotony.

It had actually been easier than one could have imagined to convince her to come and work for Thomas. She had been thinking about quitting, but then there was Leonard and she could not take risks. She had thought about applying for jobs elsewhere but after work could find no other time other than for Leo, music and poetry; the principal pass-times and obligations. So circumstance had forced her to accept the changes which in truth she desired all along. The sexism in the office, the constant jokes made about her in the fitting rooms, could surely not be as bad as Thomas' sexism or light racism. Even if she would work for Thomas, she wanted to make one detail clear, that she would not help with work that was too manual or that had to do with cleaning.

"Look, I didn't go to cleaning university."

These were the thoughts that often passed through Stella whenever her manager ordered her to clean the ceilings or mop the shop floor, because "dust too was part of the visual". She had no idea what it would be like to work for Thomas. Could it be much worse than having to stand on high heels for ten hours to blister her feet with a pallet of wounds?

One of her personal beliefs was that in life "it would be nice to be like a wave, without knowing the direction ahead".

Thomas sipped the coffee and made wry noise as he sucked the contents from the cup.

"I'm so glad you came round."

"You'll see this won't be too bad."

Twenty pounds an hour… Twenty pounds an hour.

Chapter 17.

Their partnership began. They began to work together to help Thomas with his last show. The first nuance that needed taking care of was the fox. The fox had continued to dig holes between the grass and the fence and had ridiculed him many months, even when he had planted a stem of "fox gloves"; the plant in the shape of horn-like pillows feathered in white, with spots of dark violet by the rim. Putting its paw in the petal, the red-headed feline had snarled. The flower-gloves didn't fit.

"First thing we have to do" Thomas said, "is to take care of that animal". The two of them left the kitchen and went into the utility room that in turn led to the boots room.

"There are three keys here, kitchen, garage and boots room" Thomas slowly revealed the secrets of his home. Stella saw that he had tied to the door all three keys to the wall with different coloured ribbons and naming tags with laminated card. This attention to detail at first she found quite frightening and feminine but was then persuaded to celebrate it. The gardener had simply acquired, as if through osmosis, the femininity in the bed of every Flora. She was one to play close attention to detail. When she had still been at school one of her relationships had almost ended when the boyfriend in question had refused to let her pluck out his eyebrows. She always looked at eyebrows.

She looked at Thomas' eyebrows as he was unlocking the door and thought that not too far from now, she would have to pluck them out. Otherwise they would not get along. The boots room had shoes in one corner and different boxes of fruits in the other. She waited for him to hand her a set of boots that would fit her and slowly began to envy and admire his home. As soon as she put on the boots, she was delighted to let her feet slide in the soft rubber that cushioned her blisters, so unlike the long heels that were mandatory at Ted.

Thomas showed her the places of the garden where the fox had dug holes and urinated. They needed to seal up the holes once and for all so that the fox could not enter, then to sow new seeds and repair the grass. When hearing the instructions, and how numerous and manual they were, she repeated "I didn't go to cleaning university for this" although this time she changed it to "gardening university" and expected twice the share of ingenuity. Thomas promised this would be the only manual task before they got to work together to plan out with pen and paper how he could go about this last show. Even if Stella complained, and if even she doubted his promise, she soon found herself solace-bound. She was disembodied by this outward projection –her admiration for these plants. They both took two spades and began digging and it was relieving to sweat and exercise, especially for Stella who hated sports but was always energetic. Watching Stella work was the third voluptuousness of his garden; the other two were staring out into the neighbour's balcony next door and the blue thickness of a branch of woodbine whose occasional curl seemed to want to pull him into its flattering snare.

When they had finished, Thomas brought out some tea. Even if Thomas hated tea, he felt that that was the moral and correct thing to do at the moment. They enjoyed this drink out on the patio and Stella enjoyed the asphyxiating pump of adrenaline. Being away from that store where there were no windows, just constant artificial lighting, easily convinced Stella that this was no bad day after all.

"No chance of it coming back now" she said to Thomas and smiled out towards the garden. And she, unlike the fox, the next day would come back to continue working with Thomas.

The only worry in her mind was that after her first day, Thomas had not paid her. He excused himself saying that he had not had time to go out and take cash, and that he had not even expected her to come. She conceded the point. He was right.

The following day the two of them found themselves in the patio, at the table again drinking tea, as if they had transitioned seamlessly from one bowing out of the day to the other. Thomas had convinced her to help out with one more manual work, that was the last errand and they would start, he promised. They needed to move a plant out of a broken vase, paint the vase to make it seem as if the damage were part of the design, and then move the plant back.

After having finished this translation of the broken to the beautiful, Stella slumped in her chair and kicked off her boots. She extended her legs, catapulted her feet high as if to see-saw and then said:

"Ough, damn it!"

Thomas, who was coming back from the kitchen after having brought with him a chocolate, he had learnt that Stella always took chocolate after lunch, laughed and said: "What's the matter?"

"A piece of wood just got stuck in my leg."

What happened next was at once embarrassing and provocatively opportune. Stella was forced to remove her clothes. A better opportunity to see Stella undressed could not have presented itself. Stella was not a person who liked to openly admit to pain, if not only emotional pain. But here she didn't want to seem so weak. Without looking Thomas in the face she started to walk slowly, almost limping, towards the kitchen and muttered, "Some tweezers, get some tweezers".

Thomas did as he said. To be emasculated, to be told what to do when it should be him trying to help her, did not at all displease Thomas; instead he enjoyed the military satisfaction of Stella's orders. He went upstairs to the bathroom to get the tweezers and worried more about what she might think of him if he somehow did not help her, than her injury.

"The bathroom?"

"Down there on the left."

Thomas waited by his breakfast table whilst Stella was in the bathroom trying to pluck out the piece of wood stuck under her skin. Of course this had happened to Thomas more than once before. The chairs and the tables in the patio were run-down and had thorns of wood dying to enter men and women's bodies. But Thomas had never removed them and his body was full of many of these insidious pieces of wood that had carved out in him their own ornamentation. There was a thorn in his palm and then one right behind his shoulder; this last had tangled with his nerves and was forming a fat cist. Occasionally his skin would swell and he would feel the light prickles beat under the tissue.

The thorn in Stella's leg threatened one possibility: it might discourage her from coming here again and make her say, "I told you so", "This is because you made me help with manual work"; it might make her somehow connect his home to pain and injury through trauma. Thomas always lusted after these psychological absurdities in other people's brains that might make him fall out of their favour. Then there was his pathetic obsession; he worried that Stella's body might be less attractive with this thorn that stained her olive skin. Or it could be as a tattoo. In which case he would not complain.

After fifteen minutes that Stella had not come out of the bathroom, Thomas had been watching the kitchen's clock, he went to check on her. He pressed his ear against the door of the bathroom and heard an intermittent, "Ough, Ough, Ough".

"Is everything alright in there?"
"Can you help?"
"Can I come in?"
"Yes."

He opened the door and found Stella with her back to the mirror, turning her head on her shoulder and without any trousers on. Her jacquard underwear was not the only irresistible textile to draw out on a loom rapid and intoxicating blotches of arousal. He pretended to not look. He looked only at the wound like a superior and noble doctor.

"I can't quite get at it" she said right as she was pinching her leg with the tweezers.

"Can you try?"

She handed him the tweezers. He nodded and bit his lip as he went down on his knees. His masculinity was on the line, or so he thought; he didn't want to seem like a fool who didn't know how to do anything. Surgical concentration. That was what he would require now. He needed to see precisely where this thorn was and extract it out with one final and infallible movement. And yet it was almost impossible to do so. On his knees, a few centimetres away from the flaccid flesh on Stella's leg, he saw her painted toenails and then looked up to see her from below, then turned to see another reflection of her in the mirror. On his knees, he could see her from all angles. It was this all-encompassing sight to shipwreck any sobriety he could have wished to have in this moment. This all encompassing sight of Stella, holistic and round, just as round as Stella's bottom in front of him, reminded him in his thought process of the all-embracing art form and slowly he began to connect this esoteric dream to his visions of people and solitude. To reconcile paint to music and ink, with marble too, was that not the same as trying to defeat solitude; the ultimate reconciliation? Yes, perhaps he began to realise, that to want to mix the arts was just the same as wanting to mix with people, to defeat solitude; at last it was this cataclysmic communion he wanted.

Whatever theory was there in his mind, now practice was calling. Stella was waiting for him. He needed to hurry up. He took the tweezers and began snapping them together as Stella began to squeal. He told her to be patient; that he knew what he was doing. He did not. As he thrusted with the tweezers, he could not help but think about buttocks. Plump bottoms like apples, saggy bottoms like rotten pears, or flat bottoms like cutting boards of the kitchen. Others instead inflated like balloons camouflaged with clothes on.

He managed to get the thorn of out her leg. It was actually easier than expected. He'd understood how to do it but then lingered a few moments, so she could keep her trousers off just a little longer. He stood up, had the thorn in his hand and showed it to her.

"There."

She sighed. She took the thorn in her own hands and looked at it closely.

"Thank you" she began laughing.

"That was really annoying."

"What are the chances of that happening."

Actually they were quite high. It had happened to Thomas many times before but he didn't say anything in case she would blame him for having been careless for not telling her. He didn't want to ruin this triumph of theirs. He stood there idiotically as Stella put back her trousers on and then began playfully: "Now it's my turn".

Stella wanted to pluck out Thomas' eyebrows. At first Thomas thought that she was joking and went to clear the table outside in the garden. After a while Stella forced him to sit down, that they couldn't resume their work otherwise, that his eyebrows "really needed trimming". He stood there with eyes closed as Stella plucked them out and accepted more for this chance of intimacy with Stella, than for his trust in her taste. When she had finished, Stella said, "there" and was just as satisfied as when Thomas had taken out the thorn. When Thomas looked in the mirror he admitted that she was right. He looked much better. That would not be the first time Stella plucked out Thomas' eyebrows and that would also not be the first injury that Stella would suffer in his home.

Stella left to go pick up her son at school; at which point they parted ways thinking about each other in this new humour the day had given them.

Chapter 18.

Thomas and Stella continued to work together in this way for the rest of the week. Stella arrived at around nine o'clock each morning and Thomas would wait for her for two hours, after having risen early. In these days where she had left Ted, she had started applying for a variety of new jobs. These ranged from other positions in retail to secretary and administration roles. She had always wanted to begin this process of seeking something new. One of the positions she applied to was in the administration office of the faculty where she had studied at Surrey University. This was the place where she had spent the best years of her life, despite having fallen pregnant after her first year. Surrey University was where she had met her first love, Leo's father, and also where her second love, who was younger than her, had studied.

  This interdisciplinary university, with its range of faculties from engineering to theatre and hospitality, made all the important persons of her life, mingle in one memory and academy. Those times at university she had described as "four years overflowing with happiness". This was another of Stella's "aquatic" phrases, together with the one about her being a "wave", which she boasted with a casual nonchalance and smile. Those times had been liquefied by memory to become far better than they actually were. When Thomas later heard about them, he judged them to be quite overrated, considering what else Stella told him that contradicted her initial appraisal. He knew that he was guilty of having done this too; of thinking the past better than it was. He knew that memory was just another vanity; all things made of glass were. How was glass made? Ah, with sand? That was why his lashes would fill with grain-gold sand when in reminiscence.

There was an entire entourage for Thomas to be jealous about in Stella's past. There were these two lovers and then her son. Of course Stella did not tell Thomas about all the particulars of her life all at once.

They were not intimate yet even if Thomas had already seen Stella's bottom. Exactly a week after the thorn incident, Stella helped Thomas make an important break through in his work. That morning she had come with a small gift for Thomas; she felt guilty that she had made over thirty applications for new jobs, whilst still making plenty of money from Thomas, much more than Ted. Whenever she went to other people's homes, she would never come empty handed. She couldn't think of a person more rude than someone who arrived at a dinner or a lunch, without having brought anything. This quality she had inherited from her father, the man who, despite all his shortcomings, was always generous with his friends, especially when his leather shop had become the most profitable in all of Rhodes. Despite her father's abrupt and sometimes cruel manner, despite the fact that after her mother had left he had brought many women home, generosity was one of the few qualities she looked up to her in her father. These gifts were Stella's distinguishable mark, even if they betrayed her actions; surely if she had the sensibility to buy coaster cups and other gifts for the home, she had the sensibility to realise that her lies hurt other people?

That morning she had brought Thomas "Romeo y Julietta" Havana cigars. Spanish was another language Stella purported to speak. If Flora would have met Stella she would have liked her immediately.

"I brought you these" she had said that morning.

"Romeo y Julietta cigars". She had pronounced the words with a smile that slendered her. The "y" in the name of the cigars expertedly. Spanish had been a course she had taken as an extra curricular at university. As soon as she had given him the box with the cigars, part of her regretted doing so. She feared that he might misinterpret the gift and think about them as a Romeo and Juliet. Her politeness always ruined her.

No ideas of this sort passed through Thomas. The casing of the cigars fascinated Thomas with its feast of the ornate, the heavy gold and brown and the constellation of coins like pennies on a forehead.

"Right, let's get started then."

With most of the manual work put to the side, now had come the time to actually begin their work. What he had been dwelling over for such a long time, would start. What he had put in the periphery, now would finally come back in the centre. Stella did not know that she would enjoy working on the brainstorming of this project far more than she could have expected and far more than any window arranging at Ted. They would work in Thomas' studio on the first floor.

She had not seen the first floor yet. As she came up, he told her to remove her shoes, which she did reluctantly. She saw some of the paintings of the house that he had made and was quite impressed by one of them. Besides generosity, she also looked up to her father's talent in painting. She had brought over a few of his paintings from Greece and had even put some in the office at Ted to try and sell them.

"You do some too?"

"Yes."

"Can you draw well?" he asked.

This was one of the questions that one should never ask Stella. It was one of her complexes; not being able to draw. The fear of not being able to draw was what had initially pushed her towards painting. She had tried drawing the simple outline of a woman but then had gotten very frustrated and so she had thrown blotches of paint on top, just to prove that she was talented after all. "It's all about how you do it". Since then, she had given up drawing altogether and whenever someone asked her if she could draw, it reminded her of the shameful moment; her terrible drawing. The drawing, subsequently sanctified by paint, had then become the front cover to an anthology of poetry which she called, "Hunting Ideals". Yes, besides drawing badly and singing well, Stella also wrote poetry; this was her principal interest that had started just a few months before meeting Thomas. Her poetry had started after another mistake, just like the drawing. She'd started after the man with whom she had cheated on Leonard's father, her primary school friend, had encouraged her.

Thomas was yet to know about these events. He did feel however the need to somehow enter into that space crumbling into lunacies of dust, the past, and so he used his memory to preserve her now in every detail, to make up for all the moments they had not passed together. Whatever she had felt for other men, whatever other men had felt for her, he could eclipse with the accuracy of his memories.

In the studio Stella received the opportunity to admire Thomas' taste. At first she had been impressed with the wealth and variety of his taste but now found it a tone too classical. He was not to be blamed too much for this, that was to be his expected with his age and she was actually happy to implement her "twist". "I always add my little twist" she would say to newly acquired relations. One time, when speaking to her second love, she had been debating the question of faithfulness and had concluded that even faithfulness, though she considered it, needed her "little twist". Her lover had then sent her to hell.

Thomas' worked needed her twist even if it was not lacking already in perversion. She would have started with the decoration of the studio, which she found too emphatic, but said nothing for fear of sounding rude. They sat down by the desk; Thomas had kindly brought a spare chair.

"So what ideas do you have so far?"

"I was thinking of having a pedestal or some sort of space where to place the work."

"Like a window in a shop."

"Right."

"Then of course we said that it needs to include water or liquids."

"Why did we say that again?"

"Because any fusion is liquid."

"Oh yes, that's right."

Thomas proceeded to show Stella his picture book with all the shows he had made so far in his career. At first Stella was impressed by the richness and vibrancy of the types of gardens he had helped to make. The obsessive refinery however, the worship of delicate gusto, began to slowly tire her and flowers and gardens became second to her theatre; the place where action superseded taste. Thomas and Stella would soon come to inspire each other. She would slowly acquire a penchant for the extravagant and Thomas would learn about the thrill of melodrama in Stella's behaviour.

For the moment she did not think that he had any good ideas for this last show. The idea to have a shop-like window reminded her of the workplace which was all too familiar and besides, it went against the idea of gardens being in open spaces. She suggested that they should have something simple to leave space for the principal idea in the work; the *gesamtkunstwerk*. She explained to Thomas that in her opinion, if he covered the entire exposition with the richest and noblest flowers, they would detract from the original point, which was beyond plants and flora.

"If you could just have a base like this" she began saying as she sketched out some lines on a paper in front of him, "Five meters by six".

"We get a much bigger space allotted usually."

"And then somewhere in this space you can place what you had in mind to represent all of the arts."

"I had a pedestal in mind, look" and he showed her the napkins with the drawings.

She saw that he was better at drawing than her.
"I don't really like that."

"How about an old travel chest?"

"Right at the end of the garden."

She began drawing it out enthusiastically as Thomas leaned over her shoulder.

"And then you can put materials of every type of art inside the chest, like tubes of paint, instruments and a slab of marble to symbolise painting, music and sculpture."

"You can make each item out of flowers, like a pen made of flowers for example.

"Okay. How do you think we can justify this choice of the travel-chest though? At one point during the show each gardener has to justify his work."

"Well - " she began.

"I suppose you can say that entering into a garden is much like taking a trip. In this case it leads to a type of wonderland, where at the end, the traveller finds Wagner's dream: all the arts fused together."

"In your garden the jury will walk down the path, to see what is at the end."

"And on the bed of grass where this travel chest will lay, you can put flowers of your choice. You can attach flowers to the lid of the chest. That's how it works at these shows, isn't it?"

"We should probably make the garden longer then and less wide, so the jury will actually have to walk to the travel-chest."

"Yes, the important thing is to convey this concept of travel or journey, how stepping into a garden means stepping into another universe of green."

Thomas listened to her ideas and lazed in her easy way of explaining things. He hadn't thought about a travel chest but the idea excited him and was far more practical than anything he could have come up with at the moment. He nodded and then gave his consent before explaining that this year the Chelsea show was taking place in autumn, in September, and that he wanted to add this seasonal effect.

"Like I said you can think about the colour scheme of the grass and make it autumnal".

At last Thomas had his idea. He clapped his hands and began walking around the room, forgetting to thank Stella for her contribution. At lunch-time they smoked the cigars Stella had brought and Thomas ensured all the chairs outside had cushions to prevent any more incidents with thorns. Thomas was clumsy as he held the cigar in his hands and tried imitating the debonair Stella to his side whose mouth vaporised with a rouge flame the atmosphere between them. The papery crumple of these cigars, together with the succulent pears they were destroying with their mouths, began to break the intimacy between them. Stella asked Thomas how the trial about Flora's inheritance was going and he told her that tomorrow the lawyer had organised a mediation with Eleanor. Then he also asked about Leo, not because he cared. She told him that her son was excited because next week they were going on a school tip but she didn't know what to make of it.

He nodded and pretended to be interested as the swerves of smoke showed to him the coarse edges of jealousy. The corpulence and breadth of this cigar smoke glossed over the rest of this garden, the green behind it and Stella's pale cheek, to make a body of sensations altogether mauve. This activity that asked of them to use their mouths, to smoke together, to talk to each other, unified them just as a kiss might have done.

They began to talk about relationships and Stella asked Thomas if he had been married before. He shook his head and then asked her the same question, which she elaborately expanded upon. Stella often made this mistake of revealing everything about herself to people who never did the same. She would often talk about herself and her friends would use her as an analytical platform on which to vent their own frustrations. Then she would regret having spoken at all but would make the same mistake after not resisting to speak about herself again. In this case however Thomas did not dissect every detail Stella told him; he was more of an immortaliser than an analyst. He listened and simply used the opportunity to continue to preserve Stella in her every minutiae and get to know her better. She found this silence encouraging. It became easy to tell him about how she had been with Leo's father for almost five years after having met him at university but how there had been a series of crises which had moved her to leave him for this young boy, whom she had also stopped seeing.

Thomas said nothing and focused more on capturing the cadences tripping on her mouth; her accent which so often stressed double consonants, especially when she said the word "bottle", which made her sound oriental.

"Shall we open another bottle?" she said when the wine they were having for lunch had finished. Thomas nodded, and remembered to take a chocolate from the pantry for Stella.

At the usual time, Stella left at a quarter past three to go pick up her son from school. When she left they gave each other a hug and Thomas thanked Stella for her excellent idea of the day and paid her. She wished him a "nice and relaxing weekend" and left with her dimples in full show. As she was leaving, Thomas trotted upstairs to the first floor to watch her cross the road; an equine fleet in the reflected glass. His temper took another abrupt turn as he contemplated how he was alone again. Like many before him, Thomas began to suffer from the habit in men to compare women to other images or objects.

He looked at Stella leaving and everything seemed irreparably transformed into a bottomless pit whose continuity had no end point; strands of her hair seemed to transform to rugs; polished and pale skin to old holy-water basins in turn. He was bent over and the touch of his kiss was stone. His grope was a pearl squeezed to a pulp. Can things not be as they are? Can Stella not be as she is? No he says, simile is a paranoia; and plummets.

Chapter 19.

The weekend in which Stella and Thomas were apart would be the solidifying glue to the memories he had captured so far. On Saturday afternoon he had the mediation with Eleanor, whom he had gone back to obsessing about, now that this new life with Stella just seemed an optimistic and unrealistic imagining. But then Monday would come, he would see Stella again, and he would cradle in this rebirth. He had no intentions to negotiate anything with Eleanor, but this was the practice necessary the lawyer had said. The first problem had been to find a place where to convene. His home was out of the question and he didn't want to meet in a public place either. He was curious to see Eleanor's home and he hoped the mediation could take place there. He pushed for it be so. On the telephone he was uncooperative and refused to come to an agreement until Eleanor proposed that they could sit down as civilised people in her conservatory. Why did he want to see Eleanor's home? For the same reason that he had wanted to see Leo outside the school, to come to terms with his pain, his "Algos" as Stella had taught him, the word associated to the suffix '-algia', denoting a painful condition; arthralgia, dorsalgia, (the worst) nostalgia.

Since Stella had started working with him, he had revised some Greek words that were in common with the English language to impress her. He had charmed her for instance when he had slipped in the word "panacea" into his discussion, when she had telling him about how she had once had to find a solution to choosing between Leo's father and another man. In revising his vocabulary he had learnt the word "atelophoebia"; this was the awkward fear where a person was afraid of not being able to overcome his problems. A fear of fears. A quite apprehensive paranoia. There was perhaps no better way to describe Thomas' behaviour that led him to indulge into the details of his sorrows, to not reject them, than to use the word "atelophoebic". He feared if that he did not charge into these problems they might crush him. And so the thought of Eleanor, a sympathy of his past, with her husband - how often did they make love? - made him want to see their home, to explore their marriage, so perhaps he could stop thinking about them. As he left the house to go to the mediation, he was "adamant", from the Greek for "diamond", that this was the way to solve his problems.

Every stroller of the street has his suffering. Most of the time it is boredom to push him out of the home, or a monstrous idleness. Waiting to cross towards the bend of Shalford Park that led to town, whilst thinking of Stella and Eleanor in bed with other men, became Thomas' valentine crucifixion.

After he had made it to the other side of the road, he desired something different. This path, which seemed to be the continuous bridge or loading point between him and some next event, began to be sickly sweet. He would have liked to change something, perhaps to walk it backwards, and as he passed by "The Wayside Pub" he haphazardly criss-crossed across the path because he had not done that before. He looked at his watch to see if he was late and this measure of time that came in shivers gave him a nod. Walk faster.

The following streets he passed; swollen plump crowds flitting past shops. Lit in tumescence. Right before the scholar's statue there were some tourists, some pensioners with a tour guide, and Thomas stumbled into them. Soon after he had passed by the bishop's statue, and a new Chinese shop, whose kitchen steam baptised him with a flavour of prawn, he arrived at Eleanor's home. Eleanor lived near Epsom road. He remembered that he did still know where Stella lived. It might be a good idea to ask her the next time he saw her. In the driveway he recognised Eleanor's car, the same that had been parked his driveway when her and Bradley had come to visit him. When he knocked on the door, he noticed the rust on the knocker and the green mould that had began to settle. With a decrepit house like this, it was no surprise that they didn't want to forego the villa in Tuscany.

Eleanor's home was similar to a sordid set of china; a conservatory blended into coquetry. There was a narrow corridor, which Thomas passed through, that made one slide into a space as if having fallen to the bottom of a great and white teacup. The contradictory effect created by the curtains, simultaneously dark and light, also gave the room an almost tangerine aura.

"Lovely to see you both" he stumbled in their living room.

There were the photographs. He had mainly come to see these. They were arranged on a bookshelf that encased the television and a few other ornaments. There were the pictures of their marriage in silver frames. He had learnt that Stella didn't like silver. These black and white photographs arranged in Thomas their own torturing dichotomy. There was a picture of Eleanor and Bradley on a vista, with a promontory in the background and the two of their macabre smiles. Then there were the pictures of the children, their graduating ceremonies, and the occasional birthday special. Thomas sat down and considered how everything, this entire room, was just as painful as he had imagined. Perhaps standing up to these fears, the anxiety could ease, slowly. On Eleanor's cabinet there was the most incumbent piece of all; a picture of his Godmother holding a baby in her hand. The strawberry hair, the peach orange skin and Saturn peach bouffant; a flesh fruit salad. The past's suckling of fat which made her seem slim, far younger than he remembered. She held her daughter in her hands and had a long dress down to the ankles.

This photograph of Flora made him remember that his painting had been stolen. And if it had been Eleanor to break into his home, which it certainly had been, then the picture was here in this house. Surely Eleanor wasn't so careless to have it in sight now that he was here? His lawyer had urged him not to make mention of the picture, nor to "go off on another outburst" when they were in Eleanor's home. Thomas had to greatly restrain himself from crying out and searching the house to repossess what he thought was his. Instead he just sipped the water Eleanor had brought, that was all she had offered them, water! his godmother would be appalled.

Thomas did not intend to come to any real agreement in this mediation. He did not want to divide half the house in the inheritance, nor to forego whatever else was in question. The part he looked forward to most was wasting Eleanor's and Bradley's time. Bradley had taken it upon himself to take care of Eleanor's defence. He was a lawyer, that was part of the irony he supposed, and it would be up to him to defend his wife. Bradley was just a few years younger than Thomas and yet not a single one of his hairs had begun to grey; his youth was still in full flight in a corvine black. There were only the occasional blades of white hair, but these seemed more part of Thomas' imagination, rather than any palatable reality. In truth these moments before him were quite unpalatable; there were the photographs, the anticlimactic waterfall of water being poured in front of him in jugs, and the rest of the furniture of this house. The furniture here had been chosen by Eleanor and Bradley together; another feature to be jealous about. His sorrow became ornamentally specific; it was a Cuban woven armchair or a sunrise floor mirror.

    It appeared to Thomas whilst laying back in his chair that this case was similar to an argument between couples; Eleanor and Bradley were one, and his lawyer was also a woman. He let her speak. He dangled himself only in his nonchalant silence; the same that Stella had liked when she had been opening up to him. In remembering what Stella had said to him, he felt a light din of guilt; his lawyer and him couldn't be a couple, that would be breaking the imaginary vows he had formed with Stella. He continued to let Nicole, the lawyer, speak on his behalf and only occasionally nodded or added a remark which was altogether quite unhelpful. He wanted to leave as soon as possible. At first Bradley proposed a type of buy off; that they could not go to court at all, that they understood Thomas' concern and could come to an agreement for a sum of money, a "compromise", as he had put it. Did they think he was stupid? He rejected.

Bradley was less rude than his wife. She, rather, crossed her legs arrogantly and looked in another direction of the room, at times interjected with her opinion that was always the self-same; Thomas should have nothing and she should have everything. After all, it "was only right for it to be this way", it was "the greater good, what she would have wanted". An hour later and Thomas and his lawyer were shown the door without having reached any new agreement in the mediation. It could have been just as well, just as self-same to not have gone there at all, had Thomas not accidentally told Eleanor about Stella.

When he was escorted outside, Nicole had already left moments before as she was in a hurry, the telephone rang. Bradley went to answer and it was *Monsieur* on the line. Whilst Bradley was occupied with the crackling voice of circumstance on the other side of the telephone, Eleanor and Thomas were left alone on the porch.

"You should pull out of this whilst you can."

"And why is that?" he heard himself say.

"Because it isn't right for you to get my mother's house."

"Even if" it was here he made the mistake, "someone saw you breaking in?"

"And who would that be?"

When Eleanor slammed the door, and Thomas was already unto the other side of the road, Monsieur put down the line and almost choked on some raisons he was enjoying.

Thomas proceeded into the rest of the day having mediated only between himself and thoughts of Stella. And it had only been one day that they had been apart.

When he passed by the Oxfam charity centre, he brought his walk to a stop and entered. As soon he came in, Thomas, the collector of other people's memories, emphatically surveyed the racks of postcards. He often came in these charity shops to find the quaint item in which to nuzzle into his reproach of the present. He noticed there was a new boy at the cash register, "how nice to get a new volunteer" he thought as he came close to the counter, but then didn't greet the boy back when he reconsidered that altruists were merely confused egoists; alike to broken compasses that inverted north and south. There was a similar altruism and confusion whirling in him. Old belongings, his own sense of belonging; wanting to be Stella's. "I want to be yours", "I want to be yours" he repeated in his head.

The only things he could make his in this moment were these postcards and birthday cards on the rack in front of him. He had already bought two items here before, a birthday card with a great and glittered "9" inside and a "map of the midlands" where the driver had written on the drawings of the motorway. Those items, still impregnated by ink, became like props to the story of a past. It was curious to collect the matching memorabilia; a postcard and then the same reply the other sender had sent back, so he could see both sides of the story. He collected these postcards as if they were persons, no, not just persons, but personages with their essences and habits; idiosyncrasies stapled on the back of cards like paper maché.

The vitriol heaped on these items might not only drop from the pen of good people; these postcards and maps or posters of the charity shop might have once belonged to cheaters, liars or saints. Though he captured, treasured, collected the energies innate in this memorabilia, as if trapping flies in jars, he wanted to give, to give himself, to Stella. So he bought for her some vintage photo frames and one postcard made of tin he hoped she would like. He paid and left this charity shop to which he had donated his tempestuous energy.

There came the Sunday. The second day of Thomas' and Stella's separation. He decided to sleep in, to make time pass faster, and at around noon began to hoover the kitchen floor whose parquet was full of breadcrumbs. Besides these errands which occupied him for an hour, Thomas also cleaned the windows still stained by Leo's hands. He had to clean the windows twice because the stain kept returning right after he had wiped it with the cloth, and the outlines of his fingerprints returned to leave their mark. Afterwards he listened to the radio; another pass-time that kept him occupied whenever he was sumptuous & solitary. A vintage Roberts model transistor radio that made him tune into the radio stations of surrey, not mainly for the music, but for the voice of a woman whose volubility was, to him, voluptuous. It was the continuity of her programme that he liked; the presenter never seemed to run out of subject matters and very often interviewed listeners who had phoned in to speak with her. A Sunday he had even called, but then had put down soon after he realised he was live with all of surrey or the whole country.

The best feature about this radio was that it was portable; he could carry it outside and lounge in his deck chairs or even take it with him to the bathroom. Taking the radio with him into the bathroom, with that woman's voice imprisoned inside, had required a few years. They had first needed to break that barrier of intimacy of course, before he could make water beside her.

After a while that he had lazed on the bed, he realised that had been silently entertaining the radio far too long. He had its buttons spin and swivel. What might Stella think? He squashed down its antenna and played with the buttons a last time to turn it off. This faithfulness moved him to take another walk. He would stay faithful to Stella, but didn't want to lead a sedentary lifestyle. He supposed that some of the best things in his life went unnoticed; going out on the street now, without needing hat, gloves or scarf, forgetting that it was summer, certainly suggested so. He wanted to go visit a place he had been away from for a while. He had been thinking about it in all the trips to the centre he had made in these days. On Shalford Road was a park with a great field; to the edge was a cluster of trees densely pressed together if not only for a small space; a speck of open ground. He had been observing the open space secretively in all these times he had passed by Shalford road. It was a space of forest carved open, like an artery that led one to a greater fantastic vein. Just now as he crossed, it was late afternoon, he scrutinised the space from afar, it was perhaps two hundred meters away, and saw it pulsate.

He arrived at the other side of the park and saw the entrance to the forest at a much closer distance. There was a pool of mud he crossed that splashed on his shoes and shoelaces, and the branches that snapped on his heels, to scald him for his clumsiness. What followed next was a long and slender corridor-shaped path that led to the River Way; a path that was so mansion-like that it might have possessed its own balustrades. Perhaps it even had a butler; nature's gentleman. Thomas walked and was surrounded on either sides by wild grass that had grown to the height of his midriff.

It was not this wild grass to attract him, neither was it the occasional young person that came to jog here, it was a specific type of flower that surrounded him. This path that led to the River Wey had astrantia type plants. Fountains of stars were inseminated into these marshy flatlands, and he, wearing moons for want of fantasy, decided to stop and inspect them. He saw that it was a vulgar type of Astrantia major; he rested his eyes on the cushioned releve that shone with its cosmic and minute white; a trembling and tremendous smallness. Astra came from the Greek for star, that was another of the words he had revised, and it was here that his connections to that plant and Stella began. He plucked out a shoot and placed it in his shirt; it tickled him between the buttons and his hairy, virile chest.

He could hear a railway track thump not to far away from him as he came to the end of the path and stood by the River Wey. To his left was a bridge that crossed over to the other side of the bank, just ten metres apart from where he was now. "Historic Guildford"; the sign often displayed when one drove into the town. The council often liked to boast this historic quality with whatever few relics or important buildings they had. To his left, on the way to the bridge, were some signs with pictures and descriptions that explained the territory's history. He did not care at all for these; it was action he craved, in truth it was Stella he craved most of all, even if she was already here pinned between flesh and silk. He just wanted Monday to come. He opened the small gate that led to the bridge, walked upon it looking at both sides of the river, and then took a right.

If he continued on this path, on this other side of the bank, he would find himself in the town. He continued to sit instead on a throne made of pebbles just a short distance away from the lake. It was in front of a shallow stream that then led into the river. He sat, waited longer, and then became bored to the point that he kicked his shoes off, just as Stella might have done, and put his feet in the stream. The frowning stream was just up to his ankles and he splashed and pressed his feet on the pebbles until Monday soon came again with its own ripple.

Chapter 20.

At last Stella arrived on Monday. She came half an hour later than usual and Thomas became quite apprehensive, having had to wait an entire two days to see her again; the rank, rancid wait cleansed only by the trip of the evening before. She apologised and explained that she had had to accompany her son to the bus station because him and his class were taking a day trip out to Stonehenge and would return tomorrow. Even if the semester in most colleges had finished, Stella continued to send her son to summer school. It was a way to put Leo's time to good use without having to hire a child-minder. She also cared to a great extent about Leo's education. Stella was often one to lead by example, was easily persuaded and dissuaded by the soever next sensation.

Her father, despite the fact that he didn't care at all to read any of Stella's poetry, despite the fact that he had not even attended her own graduation ceremony, had deeply cared for her and her sister's education. When she had been in high school her father had driven her to afterschool tuition every day, had made her learn the violin and piano, despite his desire of wanting his children to be part of a political party when they grew up. Stella took great enjoyment in ascribing to her son shards of her own vanity, in the way he dressed and what subjects he would be good at. She did not want Leo to be skilled in the subjects she found boring, like the sciences for instance. At the same time she did not want for him to lean too much on the romantic side of literature, "because he also needed to be popular with girls… many girls".

With these types of ideas was she ready to be a mother? Whatever the answer, any baby she saw was enchanted whenever she clapped her hands in their cheeks and arranged in them a scintillating worship.

Stella had actually been looking forward to returning to work with Thomas. She had found him to be much more of an extrovert than she imagined, or at least was surprised to see that he was not shy all the time. Stella did not know that in her absence Thomas had indulged in his mental machinations - yet even he seemed to have forgotten them now she was here. When she came through the door and hung her bag on a column that formed part of the stairs, Thomas noticed she wasn't wearing her ring; the one he had admired every day they had spent together.

"You left your ring" he said as she was ruffling through her bag.

"Yes, I was in such a rush today."

Thomas enjoyed this minute change in her appearance; he would have to appreciate these changes, for both of them were running out clothes in their wardrobe which they hadn't already seen on each other before. Stella was easily impressed by these sudden changes in style in people's appearance, just as she was easily bored by people that wore certain clothes too often. When Thomas was at home and by himself, he almost always wore worn out clothes. He did not care at all to be fashionable in his own home. But that had to change. Now Stella was coming everyday, Monday to Friday, he could not risk being caught at his worst. So he changed shirt everyday, sometimes twice a day, even when they were out in the garden.

"Those trousers are melting on you."

"You should go to Ted and buy a new pair" she said whilst laughing, as if she were still working in that shop. This had not been the first time Stella had made fun of Thomas. The week before she had joked that Thomas looked ridiculous when he had changed shoes to go outside in the garden. He had been wearing a fleece and had put on elegant leopard striped shoes to go outside on the patio, and she had found it ever so funny. He had looked like a tramp who had invested his entire patrimony on shoes. Thomas enjoyed being made fun of by Stella. He could have been considered a type of masochist in his behaviour; he did enjoy pain sometimes. Thomas let himself openly be roasted by Stella, for the flame of her critique was languid, lugubrious and lovely.

He did not have a schedule in mind for the work Stella and him were to do this week but he did have the modicum of an idea. Listening to the radio the day before, he had heard about a few bonding exercises that employers do with their workers, or that men try with women. The presenter of the radio station had said that men and women bonded when they were doing an activity together. That was "the key to any healthy workplace or home." He regretted not having known this the first time he had walked into Ted and met Stella. He wanted to redo the scene, to rewrite all of it, under this new simple persuasion he was acquiring. If he could meet Stella from the beginning again, he would have come up with a way for them to do an activity together. Improvisation. Surely as an actress she would have been fond of spontaneity. He could have walked into the store, asked for the pocket squares perhaps, and then asked her to show him how to fold them and make patterns. They could have folded the pocket squares together and he would have followed her lead; she would have been attracted by the opportunity to be in charge, and for him to copy what she did.

To make up for his terrible first-impression, he decided that they could do something similar. He made up an excuse that in the travel chest of his show at Chelsea, amongst the other items in the chest, he wanted to place post stamps. They would contribute to the theme of the all-embracing art form.

"We can put in some post stamps. I've been thinking about it all weekend" he lied.

"That's actually a good idea."

Thomas had a room full of past stamps. Besides the items from the charity shops, he collected these in order to have another pass time. He had not however, taken the same care in tidying this room as he did with the studio for instance, or with the utility room, where he had labelled all of the keys with tags and ribbons. He was always contradictory. Much like Stella as a matter of fact. "I think you would really like my father's paintings" Stella said as they were coming up the stairs. "He has a similar style to you", although she obviously thought her father's was better. They entered the room with the postcards and there was a heap in the corner of the room, so numerous that they seemed to slide between each other as a pyramid of sand. "Oh my" Stella began. "Now we have to pick the best ones" he said. This was the task he had thought of for them to bond, and later he had thought of another. "There's so many" she continued as she went to sit down. "Do you have a small book we can put them in perhaps?" He nodded and then began to smile, they were already solving problems together.

They spent an hour in this room, sitting on the floor, amongst the innumerable number of post stamps piled around them. At first they had not agreed about which post stamps should make it into the travel chest. They had divided the heap into two piles and each would extract the ones they thought were best. "How about this one? No?", "How about that one?", "Neither".

She rejected all of his suggestions and then said, "You have such terrible taste.. though better than most people" and he could have ended the day there, so much did he adore her twisted compliments. Whenever Stella became comfortable around people she almost acquired a different face entirely. She always put up her hair, especially when she wanted to concentrate, and her nostrils became slightly inflated to make her seem an extrovert. In comparison Thomas was a problematic, overthinking, Tartarus school of an enigma, with proto-existential deviations. But now he also enjoyed this scene as she did, and he hoped that she would make fun of him again. He had abandoned the idea that he could have any say in choosing the past cards.

Instead he just laid down and put one elbow on the floor unto which he could lean his head. They weren't doing this together as he had intended but they were bonding, that seemed apparent. He looked at the types she had chosen and they seemed to be all familiar, except for a couple, because "you also need to have some random ones once in a while, otherwise it just gets boring".

It seemed as if this statement was not just applicable to this situation, in her opinion. When Thomas' elbow became heavy from leaning he stood upright. She had finally finished. She asked him if she could keep a few of them for herself because she wanted to place them in a frame and have them in her living room. Of course he consented. Before they got up, Thomas became playful, almost as playful as Stella might have been, and took a heap of post cards and threw it on her. These postcards falling on her became the global mark of her seduction; behind her ear was Amsterdam and under the silk of her sleeve was Paris. If he would have kissed her, he would have kissed a city, as if to press his lips on towers and alleyways organic with grime and cosmopolitancy; in their smooch would be a shabby-chic.

Both of them were hungry and had lunch earlier than usual. So far Thomas had been preparing pasta everyday; the recipes his godmother had taught him. Stella had tired of them, much like she had tired of the beige trousers he wore at all times.

"Maybe I can cook something" she said as Thomas began setting the table and she was poised over the kitchen counter, considering what to make.

"But I don't think you have the ingredients."

One of Stella's greatest regrets was that since she had gone to live in a shared flat with strangers and her son, she had stopped cooking. The house where she lived did not feel her own. Her previous partner had taken almost all of the kitchen utensils and she had lost her habit to prepare her favourite recipes, if not only for Leonard. Stella had lost ten kilos in consequence, even if she often remarked how she "would like to die whilst eating", amongst lard and lavender.

"You can cook here anything you want" he said as he came to the sink.

The thought appealed to Stella. She was slowly beginning to trust Thomas, and if she could cook in this house as if it were her own, then she would be very, very happy.

Just as he spoke and passed behind her, he touched her lightly behind the back. He did not do this perversely; he did it just at the right times, to establish a certain type of intimacy. That was another common trick he had heard about on the radio. He did this, he sometimes happened to brush his fingers by hers, to bump his shoulder into her shoulder, to erase the times that had been pencil-sketched on her body in whorls before he had known her. He knew about her desire to cook properly. He had picked up on her allusions during conversation, "In my old house in Reading, I used to make" she would often repeat. Thomas, the collector, had been preserving instances like those well. Storing those instances came with unpalatable consequences, pain mostly, but this would be way for him to get closer to Stella. As they looked in silence at the kitchen counter, one could have that thought that both of them were marinating their prey.

"We need to go out later and buy that travel chest. I need your help in choosing it."

"Maybe we can get the ingredients whilst we're out and you can cook for dinner."

"But I have to go pick up Leo."
"Oh right, he's away with his class."
"I guess that works then."

It had worked well this technique. He could finally have dinner with her. Stella did not reproach his insistence in this circumstance; the thought of cooking in Thomas' home had been with her the entire week. For the moment Stella suggested that they have some bread with butter and some mortadella she had seen in the fridge. Soon after they had finished, they left the plates and the table just as they were. Thomas was eager to do this next task he had planned with Stella; to go out and buy the travel chest for the show. She would be his stylist for twenty pounds an hour. They drove together to Guildford. "How do you push it back?" Stella was saying as she got in the car and found her long legs press obtusely against the carpet. Thomas had never had this problem before. He took his hands off the steering wheel and bent down to help adjust the seat with the lever below.

They drove through Echo Pit Road, then past Chantry View Road, and the splice of her fascinating way of being, her bouts of happiness, was repeated with every bend. He found it distracting when Stella began to reapply her lipstick, to echo, after all, the same phantasmatic collusion of lips and wax and mannerisms; the same she had elicited before the lunch hour. The men who had kissed Stella before knew that this was one of her idiosyncrasies after eating. When Stella had painted her lips, she could not be kissed any more. This habit formed the litigious, always at war, always at trial, love and hate relationship men had for her lipstick.

It was not so much her own lipstick being ruined that she cared about, but more the fact that her lover's face would become stained when smooching. Then it would be too obvious that she had kissed them. It was not that Stella was afraid of public displays of affection; she just did not want other people to know how and where she placed her lips. "Do you have some paper?", "No but maybe check on the side there" Thomas replied when Stella needed a tissue with which to clean her mouth and reapply certain traces of the lipstick.

"This will have to do" Stella said as she took one of the business cards she had found in the glove box compartment and began to drain into it her lip's exuberant colour. Thomas had needed that business card, it had his mechanic's number written on it, but he could not care at all to complain; he could keep this card with the stamp of her lips. If only she had put her hands in his whilst he moved the stick shift then the manoeuvre might be complete, the break inarrestable, and their contact a type of abrasion. They parked in Castle Road Car Park and as they drove through and the bar lifted to let them enter, Stella thought that she should pay, considering that he was paying her for doing something that was actually quite enjoyable. They stepped outside onto the street and the castle that Thomas had seen before when he was alone, that castle which had almost swivelled like a dancer, with locks, necklaces and V lines, did not appear the same to him. It was just a castle. His woman was by his side. And they were partners, partners at least for this last show he had to prepare.

Most people did not know about this castle in Guildford, or even if they did, they did not give it as much importance as it was worthy of. If there were ever a place where Thomas wanted to kiss Stella, or to just become the paper with which she cleaned her lips from lipstick, it would be there in this park of Guildford castle. That would be his idyllic scheme. He had to put to rest these possibilities however, however improbable, because now there was work to be done. Stella and Thomas needed to find this travel chest that would form part of Thomas' show. They passed by the charity shops first and Thomas learnt that Stella was also a type of collector who came into these charity ships in search of a secret or a special item. Just like with the postcards, he knew that he would have no voice in choosing the chest. Stella would take over and he would have to accept it. But that was what he wanted. This woman in front of him, so happy, so joyous, so radiant and trembling, if he were fragile, she was vibrant still, so simple and everything, often had the tendency to interrupt other people and talk about herself. That was what she did now, this shopping, which should have been for Thomas' work, quickly transformed into Stella's own shopping spree. No, spree is perhaps too harsh a word; there was only one principal item of worth to Stella in this charity shop and it was a velvet cloak.

When they had browsed around for this travel chest and had found nothing but a few second-rate boxes, Stella stopped by a rack of the charity shop to inspect a great long cloak of velvet. "This is perfect" she had said, and Thomas had come over, not knowing how this related to the ideas they had discussed so far. Indeed it did not relate to their work together at all. Stella had for long been obsessed with velvet. Ever since she had started singing Lady Day's songs from the album "Velvet Mood" at the bar Amora Amora, she had been obsessed with the fabric type. That word, velvet, which seemed to be everywhere repeated, became one of her many trademark symbols. Her new anthology of poetry, Stella was always working on new things she thought would be successful; she had called "Blue velvet vision", because, as she put it, "in life you should put on these glasses and see life through this opaque".

The rest of their time out in the town-centre also became about her. They left the charity shop after having bought Stella's cloak and moved through the high-street to scan through some more prestigious and expensive shops. Of these was "Anthropologies". Thomas had decided that his budget for this travel chest would be unlimited, money was not the problem, it was more a problem of taste; Stella's excellent attention to detail, her vision for the new, needed to aid him here. So far she had not been helpful, although Thomas had not minded, her remarks about her new poetry anthology intrigued him, and he treasured them just as well as if they had found what he was looking for. They were in this store, Anthropologies, just by the section for the "house & home", and he encountered the same problem. Stella was an egoist. She passed by these objects spread out on tables inhaling identities, exhaling personalities; moving between this exhilarating turn into pottery, shelves, and other items of the house, that seemed to confuse Stella with an animation of two pasts, her previous life in Reading, and her life in this current moment in Guildford. Thomas knew what she thought. He had noticed this behaviour in Stella in the short time they had worked together. Stella was indulging in her memories; in this inebriation of time. Just as he had heard her lament about not cooking anymore after having left her own house in Reading, he knew that she regretted not being able to buy these ornaments.

"These would be nice" Stella was saying as she fingered some plates and then went to look at a toile wall panel, one that was "perfect for her future home". "Future home" were words Thomas would hear often in his time spent with Stella. She often alluded to this futuristic, mutable idea of the future house she would one day be able to afford, the one that she could decorate as she pleased. As she spoke Stella was melancholy, solely melancholy, if not for these expensive ornaments that kindled variegated sensations in her.

Where Thomas had been clever to spot an emotive weakness in Stella by asking her to cook dinner, this time he could do nothing but feel the same sadness she felt. As they were browsing this immense shop of three floors, moving between department and department, he imitated her in her swings of mood.

When they stopped by one shelf, and Stella was perusing a porcelain chameleon, Thomas also became similarly impressionable and adaptable to what was before him; yes he became a veiled chameleon that shed his colour on his wrinkled coarse skin, to every changing drop and blotch of feeling passing through Stella –in dissipating intermittence. And it was when Stella remembered the coffee she used to make for Leo's father, in the coffee machine she once had, that Thomas turned a stainless metallic grey, and was incinerated by hot water bubbling inside him; was tattooed by dark cocoa beans.

Soon after all these transformations, jealousies and melancholies, Thomas and Stella found the travel chest they were looking for. Whatever thrill Thomas had hoped to find in describing this chest in his mind, in weighing it up in his arms, was eclipsed by Stella's meddling of the past. Stella had spotted it; she had made a few important suggestions but then had returned back to her solitude. He had nodded and then they had gone to pay, in silence, as if they were a couple that had been arguing. The thought of them as couple was perhaps the only means to atone for this uncomfortableness that Thomas had felt during the outing. They left the shop and Thomas carried the chest in his arms. To console her he said, "Let's go buy those ingredients so you can prepare something" and Stella had nodded.

Like a hypocrite, for he was often in this same mood, he just wanted to tell her, "Be! Happy!", but if he would have done that, which one of Stella's lovers had done before, not Leonard's father, the other one, she would have said, "Okay, let me pretend then", and she would have smiled, would have lubricated the stretch of her lips with her tears, to make a face sombre and terrifying. All these things he would have done, would not have done, to kiss her, to tell her to be happy, to just violently clasp her towards him, they were just wild scenarios. Just as the M in "M & S", the supermarket where they bought mince meat, became the "M" and the "S" in her being morose.

They bought the mince meat and parsley because Stella wanted to prepare one of her specials,

"Youvarlakia", a type of soup with meatballs made of lamb and rice. They passed by the fruits and vegetables of "Marks and Spencer" and Stella, riddled by the m, morose, seemed happier until she said:

"I used to hate working here."

"You used to work here?"

"Yes, right before Ted."

"The worst part is they give you these naming tags as if you were at the zoo."

And that person he hated, Leo's father, was also mentioned, in a duet of hatred, but he tried to repress him and soon after they had paid for all the ingredients, or rather he had paid, they were out on the street again. He was carrying the travel chest and she was carrying the plastic bags.

Did these subtle unhappinesses begin to make him love her less? If anything it was here he began to love her *most*, in all this wealth of the things they could not do, had to stray away from, as if the entire of Surrey needed exorcising. The music in the car thumped loudly on their way back home, in benedictine choruses; after new-wave and pop. Stella was changing through the radio stations and hoped that she would find the station where they played one of her favourite singers. Thomas hoped that if she was so easily impressionable, a song might lift her spirits. "There's a singer I like, sometimes they play his songs on Radio 2" she proceeded to explain whilst pushing the buttons of the stereo. Stella told him about the Italian singer she liked. He forgot his name as soon as she said it, and she explained how she had been to one of his concerts and had written about it in her anthology.

"I have to get round to reading those sometime" he said as he was watching the road. Ever since jealousy had kindled its spark in him, Thomas thought about the following: where had he been in the precise moment when Stella had made love with another man? Where had he been, what had he been doing, when Stella had first met another person whom she had found interesting? It was this transfusion of reality, these knots that dangled down from above and arranged them as puppets who trudged into the house with strings attached to their back, so that they seemed a ventriloquism out of synch and time.

They began to prepare Stella's youvarlakia. In the kitchen Stella became authoritative; she soon forgot her unhappiness and ordered him around the kitchen with a flurry of commands. She made him cut up an onion and one by one explained each instruction of the recipe and frowned at Thomas when she found him eating the ingredients. To be scalded, just like to be made fun of, made Thomas chuckle. When the coriander had been pinched, the pepper ground and the eggs smashed, Thomas and Stella found themselves at the dining table.

"Nice to not have to go pick up Leo today" Stella admitted as she sipped some of the soup and Thomas agreed, happy that she was relieved Leonard wasn't here just as much as him. The food gave Thomas an opportunity to veil his silence and not make him seem rude or awkward. He ate the soup and looked up at her as she was speaking, telling him about another anecdote, a centesimal confession, and he could appear to be a good listener whilst eating, tranquil, at the same time. For dessert he proposed they have some mandarins, or some kiwis, and Stella refused both for she never ate fruit. She would have left soon after eating had it not been for the fact that Thomas asked to see Stella's poetry anthology. Her own father had not asked her. Leo's father had often been supportive and had read her pieces, but in truth she knew he had only done it for her and was not very interested nor skilled with matters of art. Stella often mentioned her poetry but only showed it to people who knew she knew would like it.

She was yet to release her work to the public. The market for poetry was meagre, she had said. In this instance however she hoped that Thomas could give her advice. When they were on the high-street earlier, and she had bought that cloak, he had said something that had inspired her. She didn't think he had more taste than her, but sometimes he had a way with words that surprised her. Especially when he read and she could not see him; that was his miraculous enigma.

Stella stood up from the table and went to get the bag where she kept her notebook with her poems. Thomas was tidying the table and was making noise by bashing the plates together. She waited for him to finish without helping; she did not want to think of herself as a maid, even if it might seem rude. Thomas came over and spread out his palm, to motion them over to the divan, where they both sat and put their feet up. Then she opened the notebook, which she explained was also the notebook she used for work and sometimes wrote in when her colleagues weren't looking. It was a ring-binded notebook with an elastic latch. Her poems always began by listing random nouns, "Steam Cookers" for example, and always included dramatic turns of phrases by using the word "the", like "the sterility… the awakening… the crying". The most fantastic quality however in Stella's poetry was her use of Greek words in English; the language of those glorious and naked days.

Those translucent rhythms and tonalities seeped airily through, into the parlour. Of these was the word, "threnody" that she had written, a type of cry or lament. The word was the precursor to other words such "melody or rhapsody" and whenever Stella began to read, her voice acquired this rhapsodic flair, a light and compact sound, that in truth did not do much justice to her most grave poems.

"And I will be waiting on the oak platform."

This was the line that Thomas had liked most. He crossed his legs and reconsidered it as Stella was to his side, with her head dipping into the white pool page of the notebook.

Instead of complimenting her like her friends would do, "I liked the part where", "That bit was really good", he waited for her to finish and then said:

"Can I read it?"

She nodded, quite surprised, and as he stood up to come get the notebook, she curled upon the L-shaped divan so that she was staring out into the garden and could not see him. He proceeded to read and just like when Stella had admired Thomas' work the first time she had come here, she was subdued by two powers, his voice and her work. These two attached themselves to enter into her ear.

Right when he had finished, she said: "One more time", to cabriole again into what she had made. He suggested about making a pun on one of the words in the poem and she made a mental note of it. When he had been reading she had thought again about the belted mountain in Rhodes, by the beach, the sight she would always think about when reading prose that she liked. Afterwards they indulged in entertainment less noble. They watched television. Thomas feared that she might leave at any moment. She laid in repose, not taking her eyes off the television, even when Thomas stood up. There was really no one else in her life. There would have been, had she not brought all of her relationships to breaking point.

Stella was exhausted. Ten minutes after he had returned from the bathroom, he found that she had fallen asleep with her hand under her head. "Stella! Stella!" but she did not move. He began to go about his routine of the evening; checking all the windows were closed. Later he went upstairs and took a blanket. Oh, wait, I forgot to floss. He returned and spread the blanket over Stella who was still asleep, with her hand under her chin, as if she had died of an ineffable toothache.

It was right as he spread the blue plaid over her, as if arranging her tomb, for the death of this day and the rebirth of the next, that he remembered those Jacobean tombs where barons used to lie, petrified by solace.

"It's alright, you can sleep here."

She nodded and went back to sleep.

Of the saliva that was slowly slipping from her mouth, he made a new champagne.

Chapter 21.

The afternoon after Stella stayed over at Thomas' house, she fell from the ladder whilst picking plums and sprained both her ankles. The morning she awoke Thomas had already been up for half an hour and was drinking his coffee in the kitchen whilst standing up. Sometimes he had breakfast the entire week without sitting down. "I can't believe" Stella said when she woke up, "that I just fell asleep like that". This was another of Stella's expressions, "I can't believe", together with "you won't believe". Every time she said these two she forgot to add the "it" in "I can't believe it", as if "it" were so small a word it did matter if "it" were left behind. It was not that Stella was not proficient in English. She was a mother-tongue. These were just her minute idiosyncrasies, as minute as the word "it", which she always left for dead.

She got up from the divan and threw off the blanket and looked out towards the kitchen where Thomas was standing, trying to not sit down as if he were in a hurry. "What happened?" "I didn't even take off my make up" and Thomas looked at her face which was smudged and began laughing. Stella knew that she had been guilty of falling asleep many times before. In her past relationships with men, she had always fallen asleep when they were on the bed, at precisely the wrong moments. It would then be an undertaking for her partner to convince her wake up, brush her teeth and remove her make up. If they didn't then she would become insufferable, if they woke her up she would also become insufferable. Those two lovers she had often mentioned, Leo's father and the other one Thomas had not yet dared to ask about, had come up with two different names for the sleepy Stella. One of them had called her "Asteraki" because in Greek "Astra" meant star and "aki" was the ending given to make names sweeter and baby like. And the other had called her "mousy" "It's the same concept as Asteraki except with a mouse" Stella had said.

Thomas had not yet come up with his own name. He simply began washing his cup and said "You really don't need to worry at all". Stella excused herself to the bathroom and came out of the bathroom repeating again, "I can't believe" , "I can't believe". Stella felt angry with herself that she had fallen asleep like a fool; she felt lurid and regretted not having all her lotions and personal belongings.

"Like a fool" another three words in Stella's arsenal.

"You can't just go out there looking like a fool" she said to Leo when he refused to get dressed.

They spent some minutes by the kitchen counter and she found Thomas so much more relaxed, so much more colloquial even, than when she had first him. After clearing up, they began their work again. The travel chest they had bought yesterday had been a connoisseur's capture. They went into the studio and made a mental mind-map of how and where they could place it, what items they could put inside. She suggested that they should not put too many things inside lest it become cluttered, but Thomas argued that Wagner's songs, the man who had coined the concept of the *all-embracing art form*, had been full of clutter and cacophony. They were torn between these choices until Thomas proposed an avant-garde idea. The travel chest could be empty.

"No. That's a bad idea."

It would also have been a "bad idea" that day for Stella to go up on that ladder. In becoming friends these few last days, they had grown to use their time together to eclipse the solitude present in both of their lives. Thomas had said that the damson tree needed picking and he wanted to make some more marmalade, so at around noon they went out with the ladder into the garden. "I want to try" Stella had said, and he had been chuckling to himself as he was loosening the ladder. They were by the shed. Thomas looked again at its window and its spray of vine that covered the entire frame except for a space the size of an oblong. "I've always wanted to take a picture of someone's head in that space there" he said whilst removing the ladder from the other tools. "Maybe we can" she said smiling; anxiously taking the ladder in her hands to go and pick the damsons.

At first he had forgotten that this ladder was faulty. He had bought it just a few years ago and yet it was already beginning to rust, but worst of all it had a complicated mechanism. Stella, eager, as was her wont, had taken it into her hands and was marching towards the tree she would dismember to make marmalade. "You wish it were that simple" he said when she was trying to set up the ladder. "This one's a pain to assemble every time". At once he feared that if he were not able to open this ladder in front of her, she would think him a "fool" and he "would be standing there just like a fool". For a moment he considered failing to set up the ladder on purpose, just to make her angry, for there was a type of languid joy, even in her anger.

Soon after he had considered this, he found that he could not assemble the ladder, even if he wanted to. It was made all wrong. It had latches on the bottom but needed pushing at the top. It was made in a type of sliding mechanism. It almost certainly required two people to open. "Give me a hand with this" he said as she was watching him and beginning to frown a little. This was his work, not hers. Stella bent down and pulled up the latches, almost cutting herself, and Thomas also pulled up the latches on his side, and pushed upwards with his other arm, so that they became a statuary figure in strange positions. The ladder finally opened. Their faces had come very close together by this ladder; the metallic mediator of their relationship. Afterwards Stella said "finally" and began to mount the ladder by the damsons that were farthest above. As soon as she put her foot on the third step the ladder, it began to tremble. Thomas put his foot on the base to not make the entire structure collapse. In the first two steps that Stella had ascended, he had touched her again, lightly, not perversely. Just at the right time. She had her back to him, her hair was in a bun; she had become comfortable around him and had a shirt with spaghetti straps that left her shoulders bear.

As she was going up the ladder, he was behind her and had put both his hands on her waist to help lift her up. Right as she ascended and his hands were all over her, all over her but just in the right amount, part of Stella's shirt lifted up behind her back. Behind her back, assembled a slender streak, a horizon of skin. His hairy fingers were on the either extreme of this line of skin, and this trembling ladder, together with the addition of these two, his old fingers, her young back, seemed to make his hands swirl into other times and other futurisms complete with dynamism. Stella did not mind what he was doing. He was out of her line of sight, he had said something and his voice had made everything better and besides, she just wanted to pick these plums.

Thomas had called these plums "damsons", something she found interesting and strange. He had also called the oranges they had had the other day, "minneola". Stella found these names for everyday food pretentious and unnecessary. Her poems however would often express her taste for the different word, for the sublime, "It's in the word: sub. Below, hidden, obscure" she would often repeat. So whilst she shunned these frivolous names, she also used them in her work. Perhaps she just wanted to be the only one doing it. Anyhow, she would pick them, whatever they were, damsons or plums. She was high up on the ladder and could not see Thomas, but could see the neighbour's house, their patio and living room, their extended conservatory and the new terrace they were planning. Later Stella would ask Thomas "How much do you think a house would cost here? Half a million pounds?", and he had just nodded, pretending that he did not know that it was more than three times that.

Just as Leo had been the abrasive sandpaper to his jealousy, so these houses, so these beach-like covered walls of yellow, became the sandpaper to Stella's jealousy. It was not that Stella despised Thomas for living in this neighbourhood that was quite luxurious and aristocratic, although she would have done, had she known that his Godmother had given him a small loan to help buy the house. Stella despised privilege, but not because she was a moralist, not because she cared at all for the respect of society. In truth her "future house" would become the sanctuary to the circles of money, privilege and taste she claimed to despise. Although to do it she would "do it all by herself", because "I always prefer doing things myself and not depending on other people". And yet she had depended on Leo's father. Based on what she had told Thomas, that man had been successful, not a sugar daddy, no, not something so crude, but someone who was successful.

Nevertheless the wealth she wanted now was sprinkled in the air everywhere besides her; it was these damsons that would be hers. "What do I do with them?" she was saying to Thomas below her when she had filled one fist full of them. He had been looking at her all this time she was on the ladder. "Drop them down" he had said, and she had made them fall and he had seen them drop as succulent meteors. One of them hit him right on his forehead and he mumbled a few curses, regretting them instantly when he remembered that Stella did not like it when people swore, although she often swore herself. It was this profusion of pain by the side of his head, the damson that had hit him, that made him remember one of his theories. In every movement there is bliss; beauty is never static he had thought in his half-baked aesthetic theory.

Stella moved above him, her arms reached out in all directions to pick the fruits, but he could not see her entirely. With the desire to see Stella better, with the desire of movement on the flipside of his mind, not really thinking at all, he took his foot off the base of the ladder to distance himself for a better view. He could see her better, and there was even the movement and trembling he wanted, the ladder began to shake and she fell, holding on to a branch with scintillas, torched by the abrasion of her grip slipping from the damsons.

And seeing what an idiot he had been, he moved back towards the ladder to pretend he had not left his post, but by now the entire structure had fallen and Stella with it. Two sprained ankles. That was the bliss movement had bestowed to Stella. Besides seeing her face when in pain, which he could later copy in his memory, what followed next was quite unpleasant. Stella was on the floor, she did not emit a loud cry, she just stood there with her eyes closed, biting her lips, trying not to disclose her excruciating pain. She began to rub her hands over her ankles but it was of no use. There were streams of tears falling on her cheeks, but they were silent tears, for she was not crying, it was just her body's response.

She had written a poem about tears not too long ago, "sapphire tears" she had written, an expression that Thomas was unsure about. Didn't that just sound cliché? Sapphire tears? But now he was in so position to criticise. It had been his fault that she had fallen, even if Stella did not know it yet, she had had her back to him. He went over to her and tried helping her up, and it was then she began to cry out in pain, when she put pressure on her ankles. So he decided to do what was chivalrous, whilst Stella, determined not to let anyone see that she was suffering, kept rubbing her ankles. He picked her up in his arms. She was heavy. Stella's figure was slim, but she had strong legs that reinforced her stature and added to the bulk of her beauty.

Weeks later, when Stella's ankles would heal, Thomas and Stella would play a game of leg against leg whilst laying on the floor, the same game that she would play with Leonard when they connected their legs and made a bicycle-like kick together. In this game Thomas would see how strong Stella's legs were. At present it was his strength and vigour, and also his manhood, just like with the ladder, that was tested as he held Stella. He walked back towards the house trying to not trip, and for a moment hesitated when he arrived. How could he open the door with Stella in his arms? "If you could just reach to open the door" he said whilst spinning round to make Stella level with the door handle. She opened it and he almost dropped her head in his arms. He continued towards the parlour and finally laid her down on the divan, where she had slept the night before, except this time it really did seem like he was laying her in her tomb.

She had not said anything in all this time, so he anxiously shook her, "Is everything alright?". "Obviously not" she snapped. "I can't feel my ankles". But she did not proceed to complain, nor to talk about herself, which she almost always did. She had someone else on her mind.

"What time is it? I have to go pick up Leo."

"You can't like this..."

"I'm going to have to go."

He came back in with a first aid kit and worried more about how inept he was at applying bandages and other medicine of the sort, than the pain Stella was experiencing. He offered her some painkillers that she immediately refused, for Stella disliked medicine and shared a similar opinion to the one she had about privileges. He regretted having taken aspirin just a week ago when had felt a light headache. In retrospect she had frowned when he had excused himself; she must have thought him flimsy –and weak. "It's late!" Stella said, "you have to go pick up Leo!", she continued to shout, not knowing that this man who had made her lose her job, had also sprained her ankles.

Chapter 22.

He entered the car to go pick up Leo and the presence of Stella was still not dislocated, broken out of the nerve of his own jealousy. But at least he would benefit from Stella's injury. She would stay in his home longer than expected. She was slowly beginning to settle there, just as she was slowly beginning to settle and amalgamate on the bed of his brain.

In thinking himself close to Stella, he found himself saying, "we". "Why did we have to have this child?" he was thinking, as if him and Stella had become one.

He came close to collision when he drove to retrieve Leonard. The last time he had driven Stella had been by his side and now the car felt empty. He already missed seeing her in the periphery of his vision. If his eye was shaped spherically like the world, then Stella, by his side, with her olive white skin and streaks of sandstorm yellow hair, was the colouring atmosphere between globe and space in the periphery.

"Obtrusive thoughts". He had heard about them on the radio, on the fatidic programme he always listened to. "Obtrusive thoughts" were when random negative thoughts perforated the mind of a person. Sometimes they were comical; they were always absurd. Obtrusive thoughts came to almost every driver, the radio station had said. The station had said that without explanation, a driver cruising in his car, begins to think, "what if I drive into that car?" , "What if I run into this old lady?". "How many points is a baby in a pram worth?".

"A driver looks over his shoulder and realises that so many people's lives are in his hands". These obtrusive thoughts were not lacking in Thomas. He had listened attentively when they were discussing them on the radio and felt relieved that he was not the only one to suffer from them. "It's normal" the presenter had said, "as a driver to have these crazy thoughts" and then she had continued to talk, in her affable manner.

The obtrusive thought to crash his car, or to hurl himself from a precipice, occurred to Thomas when he began to think that Leo would be his passenger. Leonard would be killed, he would survive, and Stella would be his. He could collide into a car just on Leo's side, to his left, and feel the impact: Leonard's bones breaking. All the love Stella had given him would slowly begin to emanate out of his corpse. He would catch it in whiffs and suspire, and then, perhaps then, he could claim to have been loved by Stella.

A short while after he had slowed down, he let the engine tremble so that the clogs romped to the tempo of his own hatred.

At the traffic light, he was kind enough to let a man and a dog pass before him. He grumbled as he paid for parking but then remembered again that women did not like frugal men. By virtue of generosity, he even put fifty pence more than necessary in the parking ticket machine, and it swallowed his hand still benighted by the traces of murder and complot. He walked to the bus station, just behind the friary centre, where he knew Leo and his class would arrive. Stella had urged him to not to be late because he was a sensitive boy and hated it whenever she arrived last. So he slowly cantered and tried taking as much time as he could.

When he arrived he saw the double-decker buss parked in front of the "Friary Shopping Centre". Friary? It had once been a church, but the place had nothing to do with friars or monks currently; it was a shopping mall, just as American as the next. The friary centre, ever so distorted, ever so congenial to marketing, had credos that had become credos of money and church bells that toiled to the sound of expensive perfume. They needed to rename it. Religious persons might find it offensive, Thomas thought, although he did not care. He was not the type of person, at least under the letter of the law, to care.

Other parents had come to collect their children that had spent the day and night in Stonehenge. There was a teacher, a woman of thirty, that was dismissing them off her list as soon as the parents approached her and she recognised them. Thomas went up to her, he began to mumble, "I'm here to pick up Leo, and she had replied, "hmm I don't remember you" as she looked over her list. Thomas tried to explain what had happened but the teacher, all too aware of strange men like Thomas, would not let Leo go unless she spoke with his mother. So they had to telephone Stella. Thomas telephoned to his own home, that was where Stella was, but she obviously could not get up to pick up the telephone, seeing she had sprained both her ankles. He thought that he had come here in vain, that they would not let Leo come away with him, until Monsieur, camouflaged as a school teacher, came by with a yellow raincoat and clipboard. "No, no, I know this man, I've seen him before" and he winked to Thomas as he took the schoolteacher by the shoulder. It seemed that Monsieur was on his side. Even if he had shaved his sideburns, this time.

Thomas and Leonard walked to the car. "Your mother's had an injury" he began gravely, trying to hurt Leo, "although she's going to be alright" he said afterwards, for he was starting to worry himself. Leo was in the periphery of his vision as they were walking and Thomas noticed how much he looked like his mother and nothing like his father from this perspective. If Leo could linger there by the side of his eye, continuing to look like Stella, perhaps they could become friends and his hatred would begin to wane. As they crossed the road, Thomas took Leo's hand in his hand, and looked at him, vis-à-vis. He remembered just the day before when he had been out with Stella and she had been disconsolate. Her son was different. He seemed neutral and otherwise happy, as if he were one to always remain positive and rarely admitted being sad. He was just like his father, Thomas knew it.

The obtrusive thoughts came even before he started driving. He considered to let Leo cross the road, to leave his hand, and to usher him onto a car speed that would take him away as if on a tomb with four tires. Yet he was not so cruel to let Leo be run over by a car, and as he squeezed his hand in his, Thomas realised that this was the closest he had come to holding Stella's hand.

Just as if he were holding Stella's hand, he began to worry that perhaps his palms were too sweaty and he might find them disgusting and somehow his mother would find out, and he would be embarrassed. Instead he untangled his hand and put his arm over his shoulder as they came to the other side of the road. In seeing the resemblances between this boy and the woman he so desired, his hatred began to crumble. What would it be like to hold Stella's hand? Her fingers were far longer than Leo's and yet they seemed just as soft; they would probably wrap around his hand and ribbon the flipside of his palm.

When Leo entered the car the seat was pushed back, so that Thomas could not see him in his line of sight. Out of the wish to not feel alone in the car, he said to him, "Look push here", and moved the seat forwards so they were level. Thomas did not have a seat booster but Leonard was of age and height to not need one. He had inherited Stella's height and not his father's; that man was short and Thomas cherished the fact that he was probably taller than him.

Thomas began to be annoyed by Leonard's serenity. He began to speed and then slowed down just a couple of meters before another car, to frighten him, so his body jerked forward. Leo's neck could whiplash, and the fluids of love and affection that Stella had injected there, with her kisses, might dissipate to fill up Thomas' nostrils. They did not.

"That was fun" he replied and began laughing, clapping his hands, those hands like Stella's that joined together like two cymbals of a drum, a callous clap! to mock him. Maybe he had been much too kind to tie Leonard's seatbelt. He continued to turn his head sideward to look at the boy and then at the road, and nothing seemed to upset him. But Thomas soon relented from hating Leo any more when the boy began playing with the stick shift.

Changing the gears, he had just passed the house he had stopped to admire the other day. Leo put his hand on Thomas' as he moved the stick shift. As soon as Leonard's minute hand had seized his wrist that was controlling the gears, and Leo began to laugh, for a second just like Stella, one of Thomas' wishes from the other day came true. When Stella and Thomas had been driving to the town to buy the travel chest for his show, Thomas had wished that right after she had finished spreading her lipstick, Stella would take her hands in his and they could drive dangerously, palm in palm, as brusque lovers do. This desire which he had expressed came late and in another form; he was enjoying it now and it was Leonard's hand like Stella's mantling over his. A stupid, irresistible smile came over him, he turned the bend, down Echo Pit road, and found the echo of that desire come again, that wish whispered in his mind had been repeated the day after; satisfied him almost word for word.

He took his stare off of the road and looked at Leo who said "I'm sorry", and then puckered his face and shed a gleam of laughter in his eyes. That gleam, that laughter in the gaze, that puckering of the lips, was the same one he had seen in Stella when he had caught her going through his box of chocolates. She had laughed and had said "Do you want one?" and he had proceeded to study the exact impression she had made. Out of instinct Thomas took two of his fingers and pinched Leo's cheeks playfully just as if they were Stella's filled with chocolate. "That's alright he said" and found himself draping away a smile that was creeping luminously through. They arrived back at Thomas' home. Thomas noticed that Leo did not slam the car-door like Stella. His admiration for him began to grow. "Is she here?" he said to Thomas as he was opening the door. "Yes she is here". He saw Leo running down the corridor into the parlour, check both his shoulders, to then find his mother laying down on the divan.

Before Thomas had made it halfway down the corridor, Leo had gone to dive into his mother's arms; they were rubbing their noses again. There was so much more livelihood that was beginning to throttle around the walls of his home, no matter whatever pleasures and fantasies he had hoped to find in his gardening. If there had been space for another nose in that game Thomas would have liked to join. "Someone called" Stella said as she held her son in her hands and put her fingers on the back of his head. "Yes it was me. They almost didn't want to let me take Leo. But then I was lucky enough that" he interrupted himself when saw her ankles resting there in front of him. "Are you better?" he continued whilst sitting beside her, with the perfect excuse to flesh out any more intimacy he wanted. "No not at all. Although I don't think it's as bad as you may think. These things always seem to happen to me, ever since I was born. You won't believe" and she proceeded to go off on another tangent whenever she said, "You won't believe".

Stella explained that besides these two sprained ankles, her life had began with an injury. She had been born as a "lucky child", with a "cowl" as it was medically called, a piece of membrane that covers a new-born's head and face. She had been born with one of the rarest types; a tissue type that adhered to the face and head by attachment points and was looped behind the ears, making the removal process more complex. The doctors, having never seen a birth like this before, it was one in a million in probability, removed the suspect phenomenon in a hurry for fear she could not breathe. They had pulled the cowl off the new-born Stella so violently that the tissue, in brushing so quickly over her face, pulled on her eyes and made her become cross-eyed. For the first month of her life Stella had lived with her irises out of place. They had healed soon after, but she had been lucky, a "lucky child" indeed. Leonard was by her side whilst Stella was speaking and he had taken the blanket and wrapped it around his head. The picture of Stella's own cowl when she had been born became more vivid and tangible to his imagination. Just as if Leo were the projection of Stella's story, he was prickled by the glow of the translucent bubble that had enveloped her in this slithering and fantastic fashion, that had been the sac to her unveiling –perhaps the protection to his own fragility as a man.

"And then, one time, you won't believe."

"Stella!" he interrupted her.

"We have to get you to the hospital, you can tell me about this in the car."

Chapter 23.

Besides the theory that thoughts were in a person's ear, besides the theory that the fusion of the arts needed to be liquid, Thomas was beginning to come up with another of his unique ideas. It was the following. Thomas was beginning to believe that in tangling his emotions to Stella's, he would begin to acquire part of her memories. It was only now, when he was in the car, that he felt the idea begin to grip him. If only he could telephone the radio and tell them about it, that would be just as good a topic to discuss as the obtrusive thoughts.

As they were driving, it appeared to him that Stella and him had been in this position, that they had driven to the hospital together once before. "Déjà vu", that was some of the other magic everyone was capable of, apart from walking of course. This déjà vu, this distortion of memory, poured itself into the seams of his brain so that his scalp began to overflow with cerebrospinal fluids, and he had to wipe away the mushy sweat by his cheeks. Déjà vu! The word was just as liquid as language could make it, "Déj", which made the tongue spume just by saying it, and "vu", the light zip, the corkscrew coming off, just as if the word, "Déjà vu", were a tavel rose'. Now he did not care to think about the word Déjà vu as much as he cared to think about this phenomenon he was experiencing. He had driven Stella to the hospital once before, yes, he was certain.

"Is your throat alright?". Re-living the time Stella had gotten a mackerel bone stuck down her throat. Leonard's father had driven her down to the surgery to get it removed. "My throat? It's my ankles that feel broken" Stella said.

"Those two people you always mention. What are their names?"
"Who?"
"Oh you mean Paul."
"And Daniel."

He would have continued to ask her more questions but soon after he took a right turn and they arrived at the hospital. A parking officer ominously haunted the vicinity. Not a good idea to park in the disabled bay. He helped her out of the car and she was leaning on his shoulder; there was a scent of perfume that stumbled into his nostrils, and he carried both inside, Stella and smell. Leo was trailing behind him, characteristically optimistic, even if he had just heard his father's name, "Paul", mentioned in the car. They waited two hours for Stella to see the doctor.

"Don't put your hands there, it's extremely dirty" he was saying to Leo, thinking that if he was going to hold hands with him again he did not want to get sick. Leo wasn't listening so he said it again. He did not want to get sick.

After he had read a few out-dated magazines back to front and was educated just as well as a stylist about the fashions of three years ago, he began playing a game with Leo. "Chopsticks", the game where each player has to transfer scores from his hands by tapping the other player's fingers.

This game, "chopsticks", became the rival to the game that Stella played with her son, "nose to nose". Leo had never played it before and Thomas found pleasure in explaining the rules of the game to him. Leo's enthusiasm for his number game shadowed Stella's enthusiasm for the postcards. Stella had responded well to that activity, but not as much as Leo now. He considered that perhaps Leo liked this game even more than his mother's "nose to nose" and Thomas, always in competition with other people it seemed, hoped to rival Stella in Leo's affections. He was beginning to hope that Leo found him more fun than his own mother. They were having a good time, stealing scores off their fingers, until Stella came out with two casts around her ankles. "Three weeks" she sighed. That was how much she would not be able to walk for.

Back in the car, numbers still capered in his mind. There were "three weeks", those "two" men, "Paul and Daniel", and then, unexpectedly, "2" again, that also came creeping to him, when Stella said "It's quite hot in here" and removed her gown to expose her 2 shoulders. These shoulders added themselves, one and one, subtracted torment in him, and multiplied all the possible things he could think about; squaring his cerebralness^2. So lost in these calculations that Stella had to repeat herself.

"Can you please take me home?"

"What do you mean? I thought you were staying at mine, you can't walk, I can give you a hand."

"No, no. Don't be silly. I'm alright."

She began to consider how much he had helped her already. Would he later "bang it on her" as she often said? Would he bring up how much he was helping her, how he had given her a job?

"No you're not, it's alright, don't worry. I can take care of you" he said whilst rubbing her knee, as if he were saying it to himself. "No, no, really" she repeated again, "all I want to do is go home and write a poem about this". "Do you know what? I'd really like to write something right now" and she reached into her bag to search for her notebook. Stella liked to talk about her work conspicuously, in order to boast. She consumed poems just as if they were cigarettes, just as if they were, her embellishing addiction. It was only when she could not find the notebook in her bag, and Leo was leaning in-between the seats, saying "Can we play another game?" that she reconsidered.

"Where is it? I need my notebook. Right now!"

She began fondling through her things violently with an expression that disturbed Thomas. "You've probably left it in my house" he tried calming her. "Well we're going to have to pass there then" she said. "So look, you can stay at mine after all". "Leo is hungry, aren't you Leo?" he said whilst frowning to him violently, to make him say yes, "and you aren't in any condition to move yet". She looked at him as if she were doing him a favour, in truth she was, and remarked "Alright then. But first I need to get a couple of things from my place". He nodded.

"Thank you" she had said after a while.

"No, thank you for having helped me with my work."

"And", he added, "thank you that you will be my witness for the trial."

"Without you everything would fall through."

"Oh yes" she had said whilst looking out on to the street, as if she had just become aware of her importance in his life.

Chapter 24.

That home that had for long been empty, if not only for the imaginings of an old man, rich with debauch, soon became the cornerstone of hospitality. Thomas scooped up Stella in his arms after having parked in the driveway and ushered her into what he would make his sterling hotel; a last-minute option with defective plumbing, but impeccable service. He had driven in with a flamboyant swerve and almost hit the plants just as the postman might have done. Out of the car, into his arms, as if he had come from a wedding, although perhaps a tragic marriage, with someone else's son that had already been born.

The innkeeper resorted to making omelette for the two of them and soon found himself regretting his invitation. He rued the beds he would have to make, the towels he would have to clean and the plates he would have to wash. This was the price for company, he surmised. Down the corridor, there were no longer squeaks and tremors in the dark as complements to his solitude. There were those two people he cared about, one of them with sprained ankles and legs the length of limousines.

Up the stairs, Stella needed help, how exhausting -more than he had felt for a long time. "You and Leonard can sleep in the room next to the studio". It was to the left as soon as one came up from the stairs and to the right of the studio. He put Stella down in the room and then went to get the linen. Five minutes. "I'm coming just a moment!" Ten minutes. He tarried in coming back because he spent a quarter of an hour, with his eyes bloodshot, looking at the linen to see if it had holes. One couldn't risk making a bad impression. "Perfect" he said as he saw the sheet was intact. He returned to Stella and Leo that had been waiting. They were just as tired as he. Stella was leaning on the wall whilst he was making the bed. He beat the sides of the bed to remove the wrinkles and then saw that the linen was uneven. Sigh, oh; Leo was helping him. The boy had gone over the other side of the bed to help him straighten the sheet. The spontaneous act of kindness slowly began to tangle Thomas' emotions to Leonard's. What memories could Thomas absorb from him? Perhaps the piñatas he had seen burst in Mexico, when him, Stella, and Leo's father, had gone travelling when they were still together.

Goodnight, did you lock the door, I did.

Stella had begun to notice the relationship between Thomas and her son. She hugged Thomas when he brought the notebook where she wrote her poems. He had been reading a verse when going up the stairs that he thought was addressed to him. "Machinations of sky in a room when you are by me". Quite unsure if he liked it or not. Pleasant however that down the corridor there was company. Even if it did not change anything in truth, even if the side of his bed was empty, the idea calmed him. His tranquillity soon turned to pride, and he remembered the lie he had told Eleanor, "Her name is Stella and she's soon coming to live with me". Well, it had become true. If she were to ever appear at his doorstep again, perhaps Stella might answer and he could boast about the woman he had found. He wished Eleanor would come tomorrow. Stella could answer the door, and then he could appear just before they began speaking, to prevent Eleanor asking too many questions. If that would happen then Leonard would need to be hidden somewhere upstairs. Otherwise it would be quite embarrassing.

Before turning off the light he considered that Stella's notebook was probably a type of diary. He could learn much about her if he could begin to read it in secret. How was her poetry? It verged on the abstract, but it did have potential. He liked the idiosyncratic use of Greek words. The bizarre thing was, he philosophised, that almost any poem could be enjoyable if just a single line was read out loud.

"Monophonic sounds of woman snap and arpeggio in company of ten."

What did it mean? To make up for the missing rhyme in the poem, the lamp's button made a sonorous click when Thomas turned it off. Behind his eyelids falling down as curtains, he looked for other enigmas, backstage and asleep.

Chapter 25.

Thomas put to use his habit of rising early in the morning. If he was going to win over Stella, then perhaps he could do it by bringing her breakfast in bed and lauding her work. "I really liked the snap and arpeggio" he might say.

Stella had a savoury breakfast and not a sweet one as he did. That had been one of her only defects, in his opinion. He spread some butter on some bread crackers and then sliced the mortadella to align it well on the plate. The "painter's thumb technique", to ensure all the food was aligned. Presentation was everything. He squeezed some orange juice and hoped to finally convince Stella to eat some fruit. Wearing his fuxia-lined apron again, he was effeminised; he wanted to hug himself as if he were man and woman and had a sweet-tooth for caresses. When he had finished squeezing the oranges and had seen that it was just seven-o'clock, he remembered how freshly squeezed fruit lost its vitamins if it was not consumed immediately. Stella would perhaps wake up more than an hour from now, surely all the vitamins would be gone by then. The pitcher where he had poured the orange juice seemed to have an hourglass inside, slowly slipping away into the pulp; an hourglass shaped in fact, shaped just as sensually as Stella's curvaceous body. Oh even he knew his mind made associations much too easy!

It was the thought of the orange's vitamins being lost in vain, together with the fact that he realised that he had not made breakfast for Leo, that made him worry. He had forgotten to make breakfast for Leo. Perhaps he was becoming much too cruel. What had Leonard done to him? He had helped make the bed yesterday. So would he just let him starve? Perhaps if Thomas came into the room with breakfast just for Stella, she might like the privilege, or she might hate it because she disliked privileges, or she might find it rude towards her son, or she might not like the breakfast at all. What he could do? He would just have to trust that it would be alright. No. That was a risk. He made breakfast for both.

He set out everything he had prepared on a tray on the kitchen counter and found himself bored in waiting for them to wake up. There was no one with whom to play "chopsticks", unlike yesterday at the hospital.

With every invaluable second that passed, more vitamins were lost in the orange's count down. He decided to go wake up them himself. To spoil the surprise. He arrived outside their room and the door was closed. His hands were occupied so he had to knock by thumping his forehead against the door. He was dazed and almost dropped the plates. No reply. He banged his head again. No reply. He needed to wake them, there was no question about it. In prey to another of his idiosyncrasies, he balanced the tray on his head and opened the door. He found them laying besides one another. Stella had wrapped her arm around her son and was sleeping with her face pointing towards the ceiling. He deposited the tray on the small table to the side of the room before announcing himself.

"Good morning!"

Stella turned on her side and mumbled something. Leonard opened his eyes.

"Leo… Leo needs to go to school" she whispered in the byway between sleep and wakefulness. Stella continued to sleep, ravelling herself in hibernation. Undoubtedly she had to recuperate all the hours she had lost when she lived in Reading and woke up at five in the morning to take the train. She had run out of holidays when she was working at Ted and was, altogether, exhausted. She had managed to say something however, "Leo needs to go to school", and then had gone back to snoring. Stella often spoke in her sleep, or rather responded in her sleep when spoken to. The two men she mentioned, Daniel and Paul, had both had great fun in talking to her in her sleep. Daniel had asked her questions in the middle of the night to find out her secrets and Paul had done the same to tease her. The sleeping Stella they had spoken to they called "Asteraki" and "Mousy". Asteraki was abrupt and comical. She answered within a second and revealed what she truly thought. One time Paul and her had been laying in bed and Paul had decided to tease her by trying to give her an identity crisis. "What's your name?" he had said. "Mousy". "Do you write poetry?". "No I write trash" she replied abruptly and Paul had rolled over laughing.

Thomas was yet to find out this quality in Stella. He just looked at Leonard who was already climbing out of the bed to eat the breakfast he had brought in. "She always does that when she's tired" the boy said. It occurred to him that up until that point, he had been all wrong in his approach to winning over Stella. Leo probably knew more about her than anyone else. If Leo and him were to become friends, then he could discover more of Stella's secrets.

For now it was the secrets of parenthood that were barred to him. Leonard needed to go to school. Thomas did not know about a mother's or a father's routine of the morning; neither the teeth that needed to be brushed, the hair that needed to be combed and the shirts that needed to be tucked in. He was beginning to regret having invited them into his home. It was only when Thomas was helping Leo get dressed, that he was glad to have them here. He had just pulled off Leonard's shirt, and when he had made him spin around, Leo turned his head to look over his shoulder. Thomas captured this turn of the head, the profile, the nose continuing down to the shoulder in the curvaceous slope. His profile was similar to Stella's. In this boy were the reticent parts of what he coveted most.

On the way to school Thomas began to ask Leonard as many questions as he could about Stella. "No, it's really hard to get her anything she likes" Leonard said when Thomas asked him what he could gift Stella. "What you have to do is let her tell you what she wants, then surprise her". The boy knew what he was doing. He would be helpful. Perhaps it was Paul's voice, his father, who knew Stella well, that was speaking to him behind those sordidly unclean teeth. "Sorry" Thomas said as Leo was getting out of the car. "For what?" he smiled and closed the car door without slamming it; a typical vility of the bad-mannered.

Before Thomas returned home he wanted to buy something for Stella to surprise her. To linger in the town, just a while longer. There was no point in returning home yet, there was work waiting for him there. How would Stella help him now that she had been injured? She could no longer help in the garden. She would have to give him critical advice, there from the bed. He hoped his work would not suffer without her. Doing it alone, that wouldn't be possible. Leonard's benign advice about the gift returned to him.

Just before Stella and him had passed by "Anthropologies" to buy the travel chest, Stella had wanted to enter a cosmetics store. "I just don't feel confident", she had been referring to how her lipstick smudged whenever she spoke and wanted to buy one that lasted longer. "No it's too expensive" she had put the lipstick back.

He would buy this lipstick for her right this moment. Perhaps she might think twice before kissing someone else then. He did not feel out of place amongst the cosmetics; neither did he blush when he fondled the lipstick types that were arranged in chromatic numbers. He had sauntered in quite confidently. It was only when he had told the woman at the counter that the lipstick was for his wife, and she had begun asking questions, that he began to feel uncomfortable. "If you can tell me her name, we can write her in our books for the discount". He'd given her the name. "It appears that she's already on our books". He hoped that they did not know her already and knew how much younger she was than him, in case they would start speaking ill about him. He snatched the bag with the lipstick from the woman and left before she could ask him any more questions. What did they all want from him?

After he had lied and had begun to perform self-made stories liable to errors, he found Eleanor and Bradley snarling around the town. They had come into his mind last night, although he had not seen them since the mediation with the lawyer. They ascended the high-street and were helping each other walk arm in arm. Many times before had he seen them in outings like these. Bradley, the American man, always stood on the right side of the pavement to adhere to good gallantry. Perhaps he could engineer a scene where he could run into them and Stella would be by his side. Bradley would envy him for this young girl. True, her ankles were sprained, so they couldn't do it today, but they would heal soon, in three weeks the doctor had said.

Eleanor was on the other side of the pavement; he was just under the clock tower. Earrings dangled down from her lobe. The rollick of their tension, just above the shoulders. He observed Eleanor and then Bradley, who stopped by the pavement and put his open hand under her chin and then under her earrings, to complement them. What were they saying? They were out of ear-shot. He could only imagine what Bradley was saying to her; as his mouth moved in silence, he became Thomas' puppet.

"They're the same ones" he was probably saying whilst still playing by her ear, "That I got you when we first got married". "Oh, do you remember them?".

The earrings, from the other side of the street, dangled in Thomas a horrid feeling. Hadn't she worn them once before? They were fish-eye earrings; sterling silver jewellery made out of natural fish eyeball that had been processed into a clear opaque. He watched as Bradley played with the hook that the fish-eye was attached to. Even if Eleanor had her back to him, he knew that she was blushing. He thought that he had stopped being jealous about Eleanor; he thought that he was only jealous about Stella. Jealousy; it took on any name and face it could.

As he continued to stare at Eleanor's bejewelled ears on the other side of the street, a crowd of people passed between them. These convivial aquatint men and women drooly formed a stream between both sides of the pavement. The hook attached to the fish-eye reeled him in, pierced through men and women, and caught him. The earrings became as fishermen of jealousies.

Was the lipstick he had bought Stella as good as these earrings Bradley had once gifted Eleanor? No, certainly it was not. If he ever were to have Stella, would their relationship ever be as good as theirs? He answered himself again. No. It could not be, he surmised. It would not be same; it would not be the same because Thomas and Stella were of such different ages, they could not grow old together. That was what Eleanor and Bradley were doing now, arm in arm, they were helping each other walk in their old age. Stella and himself could never do the same, even if he would succeed in making her his. To make her his! What good was it to possess, if one had already had a lifetime to own? He had feared running into Eleanor and Bradley the moment they had shown up on his doorstop to ask about Flora's will. Seeing them had upset him; they were this intrusion in his otherwise crystalline confabulation. All the happiness he was beginning to acquire in his new life with Stella, slowly began to evanesce.

He began to follow Bradley and his wife and returned to his problematic way of being. The couple began walking up the steps that left the main street and parted towards the outskirts of the centre. Thomas lagged far behind, with his lips puckered; the hook of Eleanor's earrings still in his mouth. He covered the end of Tunsgate square and then emerged dripping out unto Castle road. He scanned both sides of the road but he seemed to have lost them. The only familiar face he could recognise was Guildford castle. Again? It seemed always the same, this orbit around the same places, the same ideas.

He passed through the gates of Guildford castle and became jealous about Eleanor and Stella, all at once. Then he remembered the other feeling that he had experienced in these two days just past. Stella's memories concealed inside him. As he came out towards the middle of the park, he saw the bench where Stella and Daniel had first kissed. Stella and Daniel had come here every day, in the summer of two years ago, whenever Stella finished work. How did he know that? Now it was as if it had been him to place his lips on Stella's, as if had been him to pull a strand of Stella's hair behind her ear before placing his hand up her shirt. Did experiencing these memories give him any joy? It did not. Instead of enjoying the luxury of these moments with Stella, that he would otherwise have no access to, he just felt himself an imitation. He soon left the park. The aftertaste of Stella's saliva was still in his mouth. He parroted another of her verses, as if it were his own.

"Comb my lips with cynicism. Rap your ribbon in my ear."

Chapter 26.

When he returned home he found Stella laying in bed, momentarily transfigured by a lackadaisical leg on leg, drooping blouse. Through the door, leaving his shoes laced by the stairs, he shouted to alert her that he had come back. Up the stairs he put his hand on his mouth, remembering having just kissed Stella in the park, again the lubricous mouth against mouth. From the stair-head he saw her applying lip-balm and then she began smiling at him as he was walking towards her. "Thank you for the breakfast sweetie". She had never called him by this name before. It was almost as pleasant as when she had placed her hand on his neck in the park earlier. Should he tell her about this feeling he was experiencing, how his emotions were becoming so tangled to hers? Perhaps she might find that strange, or the memories might stop altogether.

"How are *you* feeling?" he said as he came to sit by the bed beside her. On the night table beside her she had placed the notebook, fresh with new writing. "Great actually" Stella said. "I slept in all morning and then started working on my poems. This could be a blessing in disguise" she was laughing. Fain to see her spirits lifted. His mood was so dependent on hers. When they had been out in the town, and she had been sad, he had found it hard to not feel afflicted too; in the reflection of the shop windows he had seen two sullen Laurencin figures on display. "I guess this is going to force me" she continued, "to just sit down and write". "But of course I'll help you with your work" and she stroked Thomas. Her touch did not feel new, she had stroked him once before when by the riverside. Or was that just another of her memories he was acquiring?

"Are you sure you don't want me to bring you some painkillers?". He often seemed to be speaking to himself when he addressed Stella. "Definitely not". Stella would never take medicine. "I'm used to it. Didn't I tell you that when I was born", "You had a cowl and they" he interrupted her. "No! that was another time. Did I tell you how I almost lost my tongue?". He interrupted her because he wanted to show her that he had been paying attention to her stories. To get her back for something she had told him. Stella had mentioned that he told her the same stories, repeatedly. If only one could catch her out at his own game.

Stella proceeded to tell him what luck she had had in not losing her tongue. Her mother had been holding her in her arms when coming out of the bathroom and had tripped on the wires of a hair dryer. She had dropped Stella on the floor and the impact had made Stella clench her teeth so vigorously, that her tongue had been sliced apart and was left hanging by a millimetre. The doctors had said that her tongue would either fall off or that it would grow back. It had grown back. Whenever Stella told these two stories, about the cowl and the tongue, he saw her at her happiest. One couldn't tell why. Perhaps it was because they were marks of the personality she so craved.

Stella's tongue severed in two. When they had been in the park, he had not felt this wound she had suffered long ago; in the memory her tongue had fastened itself around his. Stella was a good kisser despite the fact that her tongue had almost snapped. Daniel had complemented her on the bench and she had said, "It's not about technique. It's not about how the other person makes you feel". "You were lucky, that your tongue didn't fall off". "Oh yes" she said laughing. It would have been entirely different if Stella had been mute. Would she ever have come to England? Would he even have found her inspiring if he could not speak to her? As if to put to use the fortune of having kept her tongue, Stella began speaking copiously again and went on another characteristic, long-winded tangent. He listened to her and began to absorb more of her arcane past until she mentioned how the same had almost happened to Leonard, when Paul had tripped down the stairs.

That afternoon for Thomas consisted of walking between his studio and Stella's bedroom, to show her what new sketches he had made for the colour scheme of his show. She would say, "I like that", or "You can't put too much otherwise you lose the effect", and he would return to his studio and start again. It had helped him to have a second opinion in his work. They also spoke about what Stella was writing and they began to influence each other. Thomas wanted to make Stella's work more ornate, and Stella wanted to make Thomas' work more theatrical. If they had anything in common it was this; their work. They both wanted to redeem themselves of the mediocrity they felt in their lives by making something that others could cherish and admire –to ensorcell others! Stella was intent on trying to exorcise this mediocrity in her life. She had felt it everyday she went to work and felt her talents going to waste.

As he was walking to and fro between Stella's bedroom and the studio, he noticed that in each room he was seeking the self-same pleasure. In the studio he would seek a reconciliation to art, and in the bedroom he would seek a reconciliation to Stella. To mix the arts he surmised, was just the same as reconciling oneself back to another person. For now he did want to stop too long to meditate on these details.

Lunch: he prepared another of Stella's recipes. She delegated the cooking from the bedroom and told him how to prepare another type of soup. It had not been the same to cook in the kitchen without her, although there was still the pressure of having to do well. He tasted what he made three times, to see if it was lacking in salt. They had lunch together in the bedroom even if Thomas never ate upstairs.

Stella leaning on the wall, trying to reach the bathroom when he brought in the food. "What didn't you call me?" he said as was trying to help her. "It's okay. I can do it myself". Sometimes she became very proud. He waited for Stella to go to the bathroom so they could start eating. The bathroom was just beside the bedroom and he listened to what Stella was doing. It was this manic attitude to detail, this microscopic analysis of Stella, to make the feeling of having seen part of Stella's past continue. He really wanted to telephone the radio and tell them what he felt, "Yes the strange thing is" he would say, "that it's as if I were losing my memories and acquiring hers". Impossible to remember what he had been doing the day before he met Stella. Eleanor had come in the morning but then what happened?

On the bed turned dinner-table Thomas essayed to chew his food and Stella had another mood swing. She became insufferable and over-reacted when Thomas told her that she should not place her glass on the bedside table without a coaster cup. "Alright, alright, easy" she had said abruptly. He said nothing and went back to eating. The Déjà vus thus robbed Thomas of any joy in experiencing new moments with Stella. She had just finished eating and had put her plate on the floor; she wasn't laughing anymore like she had done that morning. Just folded her arms. The sheets over her ankles covered the casts so that she seemed perfectly healthy, except in mood. It seemed to Thomas that he was taking care of her not because she had sprained her ankles, but because she was depressed. He could not explain why his mood morphed to mirror Stella's. Gloom gave him its mocking sash to wear. Emasculation also added the silk-stockings that didn't fit. Stella looked down towards her feet, just like when they were walking on the street a few days ago. He wanted to shake her out of her unhappiness again, to tell her, "Be! Happy!".

He stood up from the bed and went to open the window. His back to her –and stared out towards the garden, slowly bringing the emollience of memory. Undoubtedly the script he knew back to front; repetition ghosted him. He had been in this situation before. Had he not? When he turned around he wanted to rip the sheets that covered her legs, to see her casts were gone; her ankles weren't sprained.

"I'm sorry" said Stella when she noticed how upset he seemed.

"I'm sorry I sometimes get like this. I know it affects you."

"It's just when I was writing today I was thinking about."

"Daniel. And Paul" he interrupted her. That was the first time he had said their names with his own voice. It had produced the same effect in him as when he had pronounced "Oh Eleanor, Oh Stella, Oh Flora", alone in his room.

Now he could extinguish the mystery flaming behind Stella's life, he could ask her to tell him more about those times. Atelophoebic, with a fear of fears, after all.

All he needed to do was ask. He remembered when he had been hanging by her lips once before, except the memory was his. It was when she was singing in the bar, at Amora Amora, when everyone had been wearing tortoise-shell sunglasses indoors.

"Yes, alright. Then why don't you tell me about it?"

Chapter 27.

Before Thomas had met Stella he had not cared much about storytelling. Storytelling had had just as much charm to him as the drunk perfumed in gin. He had preferred instead to laze in the textures and sensations of life and had made his work his primary and sole ambition. The picture book he had, which had taken him a lifetime to complete, had tapestried together fragments of colour, fibres of his soul, and most importantly snippets of women, all by the name of "Flora". Yes, he was a gardener, he was a practical man, but it was the delicacies and fragilities of pleasure that had moved him most. And yet he had lived a life quite exempt from pleasure, if not only egoistical pleasure, whose sharp vibrancies remained inside of him as lambent hermits. He had been unmarried but he had had his house of flowers. He had taken up many hobbies; bird-watching, pottery and even kite-flying, but the mysteries of other people, besides Eleanor, had never intrigued him to the point of suspiring. For him even women were not people to be admired, hated or loved, but two parallels lines, two legs, that had merged into one line to venerate.

  Stella on the other hand, who had come to England to study theatre, was amazed by the talents and mediocrities of people; their failures and their triumphs. Without these her pursuit of art could not be possible, she believed. For Stella people gave purpose to art, even if true art needed no purpose, she found works of art without people to be ghastly. She just needed to think of the places where she had spent most of her time in these years, to realise that without people, the show fell apart.

What good was a stage without people? Would good were clothes if no one wore them? The spirit of art needed a body in which to live, and people, in prey to whatever passions and impressions, would be the ones to be become puppet and puppeteer, to turn the table unto mediocrity itself.

It was these two different opinions that would now conflate as Stella told Thomas about her life. Daniel and Paul; she had mentioned them already several times but had never proceeded to elaborate on the details. What had happened with those two men? In point of fact they were the reason why she lived alone with Leonard in a shared house; they were the reason why she was sometimes afflicted by bouts of depression and swings of mood. What did Thomas care? What did Thomas care to hear about her past life? Besides curiosity, he wanted to make sense of why he was identifying himself with those men. If he had begun to love Stella like those men, were they not similar to him?

Most of all he wanted to confront what he feared; his jealousy. He would never want to be a coward. He also wanted to know more about those men to compare himself to them. Now that he did not know what they were like, he had no means to criticise their personalities and failures. He did not know about any failure of theirs to make him feel good about himself. If he could know more about them, he could give personability to his hatred and lie to himself that he was better than them.

"Paul and I met seven years ago at university" Stella began.

"He was my flat mate, he lived just down the corridor. I didn't like him at first because I thought he was quite short."

There it was. The first point to hold against Paul! He was short. He, Thomas, was probably far taller. If him and Stella were to walk on the street and he would catch her thinking about him, he could have the confidence to know that perhaps she found him more attractive, at least in height. He wanted to know exactly by how much he was shorter than him. By how many inches was he shorter? Thomas wanted his inferiority to be exact. "But then actually he really grew on me". That was less like what he wanted to hear.

"I've actually been to a psychologist to talk about this. Did I tell you that" -he shook his head. "Well some time ago I had to go see a psychologist. And what I said to him was that Paul, he was like a nail that insinuated itself in my heart". He didn't like the expression but it was what she had said. How loathsome. What could he criticise in Paul based on what Stella had just told him? At least he was not a nail. By what he had read in the notebook he was a "machination of sky in a room".

Stella continued to tell Thomas how these two men had changed her life. At which point would Daniel come in?

"I made a lot of mistakes…"

Thomas had laid down on one side whilst Stella was speaking. One of his ears pressed down on the pillow and Stella's words poured themselves undiluted and with full intensity into his left ear. "I've always been a free spirit" –his left ear took in and funnelled down all her words into his brain. It was the word "spirit" as her story was poured down his ear, to make him think of spirits and brandies, just as if cognacs and calvados distilled from fresh apples whirlpooled down his ear canal. Why brandies? Thomas was a teetotal and the brandies evoked a duplicitous effect that made him feel at once languid and flattered and sick with the sting of alcohol. He continued to pause on this last word he had heard her say, "spirit", and the apple notes combined with traditional wood and flavours in his ear, in one cantata.

"And because I am a free spirit I always said to Paul that at one point I would want to date other people. And he was okay with that because he said that even if I did, he knew that I would always want him".

Thomas began to frown, he found this part of the story strange. What did she mean that Daniel consented to her dating other people? "I hope you're not going to judge me based on what I tell you. You're not going to judge me are you?" he shook his head, he was only here to judge Daniel and Paul, for the moment. "Well in the seven years I was with Paul I did meet other people".

"One time" she began.

"So you cheated?" he was stuttering.

"I don't really consider that cheating… because I didn't have any bad intentions". He tried imagining what Paul's reaction had been at the time she had told him this, just as if it were his own. How had he reacted?

"He forgave me, even though I don't really think there was anything to forgive."

"And then after university we moved in together. But I always thought about leaving him at some point, although I did love him, I really did". He didn't believe it. He wanted to interrupt her, her stories were beginning to tire him.

"And so you left him?"

"Yes. That was the beginning of me taking the step", "step" was another of Stella's words that she emphasised. She said "step" slurring her s, always, and pinching her fingers together. Whenever she said this word, "step", she also emphasised her accent. "To leave Paul" she continued.

So far he had gathered together a collection of things, a paraphernalia of contempt to hold against Paul.

"So you never really loved this person did you?" he began.

"No, I did. I really did. Even if all of that happened, that never took away my love for him."

"I'm sorry but that doesn't make much sense to me" he said as Stella was just shaking her shoulders, unable to explain.

"How did you meet this other person? Daniel?"

"At Ted and as soon as I saw him I liked him. I remember it perfectly actually. I was kneeling down by the fitting rooms picking up some hangers. You've seen the store here in Guildford, you know the place."

He did know it.

"So you met, like we met?"

He could not even lay claim to having met Stella in a personable or inimitable way. He was just a pastiche of that man.

"Yes! Our first kiss…"

"Was in Guildford park" he interrupted.
"Yes. How do you know that?"
"Just a hunch."
"So what" his voice was hoarse, "happened in the end?"

He wanted her to get to the point. She continued to tell him about those times, at times illuminating herself with joy, at times rescinding back into her depression. He listened and began to paper himself with other men's limbs.

Chapter 28.

After Stella had enlightened Thomas about the sombre modes of her past, had told him about those two shadows that were cast by figures as mannequins, Daniel and Paul, he returned to his studio for a while. Everything Stella had told him, he had immortalised inside of him; Paul's reaction to the third time Stella had cheated, and the way Stella had looked back at Daniel when she was kneeling on the floor and first saw him. It had been similar to how he had hoped. Stella had even said at the end of it, "thank you for listening. I really feel like I can tell you everything". It had hurt him to hear her story but he knew it was necessary. What type of man was Paul for letting himself be cheated on? And what type of person was Daniel to try and start something with a woman that still lived with someone else and had a child? What those men had done, or had not done, was far worse than how Stella had treated them. He had agreed not to judge her after all. But Thomas was doing more than just keeping a promise.

In the late afternoon, when Stella had felt better, he began to do some more work for his show. It was just a couple of months away; it might even coincide with the trial for his godmother's inheritance. He had been considering what to put in the travel chest. His ideas were in abundance. The travel chest he had bought at "Anthropologies" with Stella was perhaps too small. After browsing through some catalogues, he telephoned to order a larger one. When it was time for Thomas to go pick up Leo from the summer school he knocked on Stella's door to tell her. "I ordered a new chest for the show. The other one was far too small". "You ordered it without telling me?" she said disappointed.

"Well how big is it?"

"This one is immense. Even I could fit inside."

When Thomas left his home to retrieve Leo, he decided to walk. Taking the car had tired him. It was only four o'clock but much it seemed that Monsieur, an improvised arsonist, had set all of Surrey's watches on fire. Much later than four o'clock; the permeating afternoon burst and seemed suffused by treacle'd pigments. Semi-circling past Shalford park, he was maimed by the turquoise trickles riveting unto him.

As he walked he admitted to himself that he was omitting part of the story Stella had told him. He had shut out everything after she had said, "I couldn't forget Paul and so". He had not wanted to hear why she had done that, nor what the implications had been. He could not believe that she was someone capable of betrayal. Yet now as he walked, as he shouldered past the great quarry just before the "Weyside café", the rest of her story would return to him. He would begin to write dialogues again with his mind.

"One of the reasons why I ended it with Daniel is because he was totally broke, but worst of all lazy."

"And imagine, my nickname for Paul used to be Lord Sugar."

"Money was always a problem with him. He was younger than me. I told you that right?"

"Anyway, well, my life this year has been being torn between these two people, between being broke and feeling mediocre."

"Yes, but why?"

The rest of his journey to pick up Leonard was not as evocative. He was however still in denial about everything Stella had told him, how she had left someone for money, how money in fact, seemed to be the principal enigma in her life. He remembered the joke she had made when they first met.

"Money is the real total work of art."

When he picked up Leo, Thomas was similarly miserable and took his hand in his. "Did you have fun?" "Yes" Leo replied.

"They made us do a treasure hunt" –but he was not paying attention at all. Continued to walk, with Leo's palm in his; he looked into the boy's raucous face. Leonard smiled in a way so unlike Stella that it smacked of someone else.

What type of man was Paul? Was he as pleasant as this boy? Paul was successful apparently, but he had also let himself be treated in a certain way. What type of coward was he? Thomas would never want to be like Paul. Even if Paul had kissed Stella, had gone on holidays with her, had spent birthdays together with her, he would not want to be like him. To be a coward! The mere thought, it shocked him. Was he a coward? Had he not been particularly brave in his life; had he let people trample over him? He could say, almost with certainty, that he had not and would not, let anyone treat him like an imbecile. So he began to scheme against any cowardice there might be in his life; he crossed the street without even looking over his shoulder and then thought about Eleanor and Bradley and the trial. He would have to win that trial, he could not, and would not, let Eleanor take away what he considered his.

All these anxieties soon subsided when Thomas returned and found Stella, just as she had been all day, laying in the bed. The notebook on the bedside table; another of Stella's second-rate lines came into his head.

"Beautiful people are either superficial or unhappy, but never both."

Chapter 29.

Infelicity soon came to be replaced by Felicity, that other feeling with the name of a prostitute that smote his home and diffused an atmosphere vital and vitiating. Just the day after Stella had told him all those horrid stories, he had already forgotten them. He forgot about Stella's cruelty and was absolved by way of indulgence not into his fool's paradise, but his genius' paradise. Tricking the mind, which whimsically commanded how he felt, unhappy, sad, joyous, blue, maroon or soporific, was a genius' endeavour.

There would only be laughter between them and no more traces of other people's memories. Or so he hoped. The day after Stella had told him about her life, the window cleaners came and she was just as frightened as he had been all those days ago, when she saw the cleaning soap and the squeegees wrap around the house. When the cleaners came to clean her side of the window, she shouted Thomas! Thomas! And then realised she was being hysterical. "It's alright" Thomas said. "It's just the cleaners" and they began laughing together as they looked at the man by the window whose smile was toothless. She had a sense of humour; she must have been a good person after all.

In the days that came Stella's poetry anthology, "Blue Velvet Vision" came close to be completed. "I really want", said Stella, "for it to come with photographs". "We can arrange that" Thomas said enthusiastically, for his work was also coming into fruition. There was just a month left and he would soon finish and then he could dedicate himself to helping her with her work. What would happen to their friendship once his show would be finished in September? And would she leave his home as soon as her ankles had healed? He wanted her to stay, no, he wanted for both of them to go to Flora's house when the trial was over; he was certain he would win, and Leonard would come too, there was space for him after all. Oh, he could begin to remember that rustic house well, how Flora had always thrown herself on the sofas after returning from a day out, as if she were perennially exhausted, and then lit a cigarette and shook beside her tangle of wan strawberry hair. Did Stella smoke? She would have to if they were to go there, and Leo, he could grow up in a manner similar to how he had.

"Where can we go to take the photos?" Stella said as he came back into the room to ask her for advice, for which space he should ask to be allotted for the Chelsea show, whether he would want his work to be one of the first that appeared to the judges, or one of the last, so they could savour the aftertaste. "I've always wanted" replied Thomas, "to take a picture by the shed".

"Have you noticed how in the shed the vines cover all of the window except a small space?"

"Oh yes."

"It looks like a head in the hole photo board."

"When you're better we can take a photo there."

"Yes. In a couple of weeks."

When she would heal, he might become useless to her. Perhaps it was worth breaking her ankles again to delay her recovery; then she could stay in his care for another month.

When he went upstairs to the attic to see what other items he could put in his travel chest for the show, the thought of injuring Stella was still with him. How cruel of him! but it was necessary he persuaded, if he wanted to spend more time with her. He was not being cruel; these were the necessary precautions, no, the "steps", as Stella called them, to be happy and to avoid being alone. What steps could he take now? - he thought as he was opening the old boxes.

He needed to paralyse her; to find a way for her to remain in his care. In the attic he was alike to the perfumer whose cabinet filled with new vials falls down and shatters everywhere, and he, to stop the liquids from evaporating, goes to throw himself on top of them.

As he ruffled through the boxes in the attic, he considered that Leo could be his principal way to win over Stella. He was certain that Stella had come here in the first place after she had seen Leo and him play "chopsticks". He would have to be indispensable to Leonard, no matter that he looked like Paul, he would spoil him to the point of brim. Just moments after he had schemed this plan, he came across one of the old dolls he had in his attic. It was made of wood and had pins pierced threw it, as if it were a voodoo doll. Stella was calling him from downstairs, "Just a second!" he shouted as he turned the doll on its sides. This was another of the collectables he had acquired over the years; he had put it on display in the studio, but then had found it quiet disquieting. If only he could use this voodoo doll to break Stella's ankles a second time, then he might have another month at his disposal. He was mystified by his ideas and after continuing to turn the doll around, on its right side, then its left side, he felt guilty and put the doll back in the box. Was he a strange man?

It was not so strange after all, he considered, for men and women to conjure up bodies, in places where they were not. A voodoo doll was just one of the many examples of the projections where the body figured, in a shape outside of itself. He remembered passing by trees whose branches erected out their arms; the vagabonds who sat in parks and made of their bench a bride. The world, filled with people who built bodies outside of themselves, was similar to a ubiquitous studio where men designed women in their pages, girls in scribbles.

"How are your ankles doing?" he said when he returned downstairs and had put the voodoo doll back in the box upstairs.

"Feeling better actually."

Superstition continued in Thomas for the remainder of these days, except he soon abandoned all evil and simply focused on his happiness. Thomas had always been superstitious of numbers and on each day he continued to spend with Stella, he noted down the date of the most important times they enjoyed. He had grown to envy, or if not envy, to admire, Stella's notebook riddled with poems. Now he could do the same; he could compile a diary with the most important dates of the month and play the numbers in the lottery. It was July, the 7th month of the year, when Stella had come to stay with him. 7 would be the first number that he would try to gamble on in the lotto.

On the 5th of July, he had always liked this number, he caught Stella humming his name in the doorway. He had just told her that he was going outside to take out the rubbish, but then soon returned when he saw that he had forgotten his keys in the studio. He passed by Stella's bedroom and heard her singing. Singing had been the first art he had seen Stella perform, the poems had come after. Stella herself had never really considered herself to be a singer, but more of a poetess. Her tendency to not call herself a singer however, despite her talent, was just a means to boast how good she was at everything. Stella did not consider singing to be as unique as writing, and so this saying of hers, "I'm no singer", was one of the "steps", as she always called them, to being extravagant. Despite the fact that the door was closed, despite the fact that he could not see her at all, he felt her being extravagant now as she sang, alone in her room. Not because she was singing Lady Day, mimicking that person whose personality seemed yarned in tailor stores, but because she was charming him by saying his name, "Tommy can you hear me? Can you feel me near you? Tommy, can you see me? Can I help to cheer you?".

She sang "Tommy can you hear me" by "The Who", the iconic rock band of the sixties. How did she know this song? It was not of her time. He had just been sixteen when "The Who" had released this song. He put his hand on the door handle whose shape was just as comely as Stella's neck that carried the tunes from her voice box like a duke box. He slid his hand by the door handle, banistering the soundly shape, a dusty track; to usher out the music from her throat whilst she sang. His grip was not clutch; it was caress. He caressed out the notes from the handle and her neck; sometimes pinched the nape —when she was off tune.

For him to hear his name sang down the corridor like this was to go back to the first time he had heard this song, when him and Flora and Eleanor had gone driving and Flora had taken them down to the bar, thrown them both in a booth and played this song on the duke box. Yes, behind that door, Stella might be Flora, or Flora might be Stella, it did not matter. It was that verse of Stella's poetry coming true, the one he had fallen asleep to a few nights ago, "Monophonic sounds of woman snap and arpeggio in company of ten" – one woman's image snapping in pieces to make more people.

He pressed down on the door handle; he entered the room unannounced and said "I love that song!". Stella cried out because he had come in when she was changing. To his notebook to write down the lucky number. 5th of July.

He remembered that day, the 5th of July, as the day Stella had sung for him. Later when he asked her about it she had admitted "Yes you did make me think of it actually. Do you know *The Who* have a whole album named Tommy?".

On the 9th of July he witnessed a lucky moment with Leonard. It was right after he had gone to pick up the boy from school and had wanted to pass by a betting shop. He had entered the betting shop palm in palm with Leonard, he always took his vile hand now, even if it was populated by innumerable germs. When Thomas had just paid for the "scratch and win" card, he gave it to Leo to hold for a moment as he took out a coin from his wallet. "Can I do it?" Leo said before he was just beginning to pass the coin over the card. "Fine". He gave Leo the coin and he began scratching.

Soon after, Thomas won a hundred pounds. He scooped up Leo in his arms and began spinning around with him, saying "We've won", as if they had won the trial for Flora's inheritance. At the end of that day he had written down 9 in his journal with the heading: "Won a hundred pounds with Leo".

Many other dates he took down all had to do with Leonard. On the 15th of July, he had always thought this to be an unlucky number and would never have played it at the lotto, he witnessed another fortunate-infected moment with the boy. It was afternoon, Thomas needed to park but could not find a space, if not on double yellow lines. "Just park there" Leo had said. "I can't, I'll get a parking ticket". "No you won't". "Let's make a bet" Leo said, "that you won't". "Alright then". When they returned, Thomas had not received a parking ticket. "I told you" Leo was laughing. They "high-fived" each other and then began celebrating like idiots with "jazz hands" by shaking their hands around them like instruments.

These numbers and memories, they came to be more about Leonard than they did about Stella. Especially when Thomas had asked Leo what they had done at summer school. Thomas had always believed that life was much like a narrative with its own style; now with Leonard he bowed down to the boyish beauty of a mellowed children's prose.

"They made us write about our career paths."
"And what did you say you want to be?"
"A gardener."

"You get to live in a big house and talk about art with my mum."

He wanted to collect these lucky dates, the 5th, the 9th and the 15th, dates that had mostly been with Leo, and put them in a hat to extract the winning numbers he would play for the lottery. Perhaps he could put them in one of Stella's hats, the one she had shaped like a bell. He would shake the hat but Leo would extract the numbers.

"That's such a good idea" said Stella when he told her.

"That would be a way to write a poem too. To put words in a hat and extract them at random. I've got to try that".

His fear as a poet would be to run out of ideas. Yes, art was liquid, they had said that many times, but wasn't the water of the body (where poetry came) expendable? In a seventy kilo man, there were thirty litres of water and how many expressions could come to be from his ten litres of blood plasma, ten litres of interstitial fluid? Not many, he surmised.

He did not care to think much about Stella and her poems made from hats and bells. Rather the surprising Leo blessed with his good-luck. If he could bring him to the trial, he would certainly win the case against Eleanor, even if that was second to the mental peace these two people had so far bestowed him.

Chapter 30.

The trial against Eleanor began. Thomas took down the date in case it would be lucky or unlucky. The 19th of July; just two days before Stella would have the casts removed from her ankles. He had not realised his plans to make her injury more severe so she would remain longer in his care. Would she soon leave him?

The morning he was due to go to court Stella had kissed him on the neck, she had said, "Good luck". She had still been in the byway between sleep and wakefulness when he came in her room, and he remembered what Leo had told him, "She always does that when she's tired". This time she had pulled the sheets to the side of the bed. When she turned on her back, Thomas saw a mole on her left shoulder. He bent down to kiss it, she would never find out in her sleep, but as soon as he was about to place his lips on the spot, she lifted her elbow and hit him by accident.

He had noticed that same mole on her son's back when he was helping Leo get dressed. Tomorrow morning, the day before Stella's casts would come off, and they would not need him anymore, he would pull Stella close to him and press his lips on her back, to taste melanin and carcinogen, to taste a small brown sack that had absorbed sunlight and would explode in resplendent rays to his kiss. Stella's back would then feel warm and she would begin to giggle, it was innocent he convinced himself, it was only a kiss after all.

For breakfast Leo had expressed an unwavering preference for peanut butter. Thomas had bought a small ocean of peanut butter jars to put in his pantry. He spread the peanut butter on bread crackers every morning, just as the boy preferred, not only on the face of the cracker, but on the edges too. The day Thomas was leaving for the court, Leo had strangely said, "Isn't there something else?" and Thomas had taken the car just to buy some new biscuits he had never eaten before.

It was this desire to be liked by this boy, it was the desire for him to eclipse his father, in bravery and success, that made Thomas subservient to any one of Leo's whims. The quality that had made men worship Stella and depend on her, lived on in this boy with Stella's nose, with Stella's hands and Stella's smirks. Where Stella had used this power to obtain what she wanted, had used power like the girls he had seen at the secondary school with cigarettes in their hands, Leo used it so Thomas would buy him whatever food he wanted. "Actually if I'm not going to be a gardener then I might as well become a chef. Then you can eat all the time" Leo had said onetime when they were driving back. At the age of nine Leonard was the connoisseur of Guildford's delicacies and finesses of cuisine. He had shown Thomas the caramelised pretzels behind the friary alleyway and the falafels near Castle road. He could ask artistic advice from Stella and culinary advice from Leo, even if cooking was another art, with stirring spoons like paint-brushes.

The day Thomas was driving to the trial, the boy had said: "Tommy can we go and get those milkshakes again before school starts?". Leo had eaten so much peanut butter in the last month that his nose had become like a peanut shell.

Thomas blushed in remembering when Stella had sang "The Who", "Tommy can you hear me?" and he knew that Leo had said it on purpose to cajole him into giving him what he wanted. He stroked Leo's hair until he realised how cunning the boy was being and took his hand back. Though his care for Leo had become so great that he did not consider murdering him anymore, homicide was perhaps unkind, Thomas did feel pride streaming through his veins. He thought again of cowardice, of being humiliated, just like the men Stella had told him about. Was Leo, the expert of cuisine, who knew where to find caramelised pretzels in Guildford, beginning to understand how he was lily-livered? He could not let anybody, Leo least of all, think he was a coward. He was unlike Paul, he was certain of it, far taller; more cultured. As Thomas continued to drive, to show Leo that he was not a coward, he did not stop by a pedestrian crossing and almost put down a young girl. "That will teach them", he solipsised, "to stop thinking they can bully us into slowing down". Then Leonard could begin to admire his strictness.

"Anyway thank you for the biscuits, the double chocolate chip was extra delicious."

"You can't say extra in a sentence like that" he enforced his mastery and fatherhood but was smiling inside of him. Before arriving at the school, Thomas considered how he needed Leo's help, or his luck rather, for the trial. The lawyer had said how "It wasn't looking good". Eleanor's lawyer had relayed the transcript of Flora's will that clearly stated that her daughter would receive everything. But that will was out-dated, Flora had had a change of heart in the letter she had sent to him.

But he could not prove it. "We might want to consider not taking them to court at all. We could reach an agreement instead" the lawyer had suggested. Thomas had insisted they sued. The lawyer however had warned him that the case might even be dismissed immediately. "We risk turning up there like idiots". He insisted all the same.

As they were passing by the bench after Debenhams, Thomas began asking for a favour.

"Leo I need your help with something."

"Tell me."

"I'm going to court now for a trial."

"Yes, for your godmother's inheritance. Thomas, did your godmother used to make?

"Try and concentrate" he interrupted him. The boy could often go off on tangents like his mother.

"I need your good luck. In about forty minutes I'm going to be in the court room. Try and think of me there in forty minutes. Send positive thoughts okay?" he said this whilst demonstrating by bringing up a finger near his scalp.

"Okay. You want me to bring you luck? I can do that" he was laughing and was enchanted by how superstitious he was.

"Try and picture where I'll be. It's a big brick building with a roof like a pyramid. Actually it's quite ugly. But try and picture it."

"Okay."

"How long will the trial last?"

"Depends..."

"Could be one session. It could be a long time. Anyway it's not as fast as on television."

"Don't forget what I told you alright?"

"Sending positive energies…" Leo was saying as he put his hands by his temples to demonstrate. When they had arrived outside Leo's school, and the boy had given his back to him, Thomas traced the nape of his neck down to his back. He thought again about that mole near Stella's shoulder that concealed inside other energies; that solar bomb.

Thomas' return to solitude after Leo had quitted the car was instantaneous. He had grown accustomed to alternating between these two spectrums of the youth he longer had; the nine-year-old Leo and the twenty-eight year-old Stella. Yes, the spectre, or spectrum of this youth, phantomised his fear of solitude. Whenever Stella and Leo were gone, the effect of silence and solitude was heightened; and it was ghastly. Thomas wanted to tangle himself in the bevy of cars, between broken glass and metal, just to seek company.

Crown court. It was the most hideous place he had ever seen. When he went to the car park he considered not paying, just like the time he had parked on double lines. He knew that if he were to take the same risk however, he would receive a parking ticket; Leo was not here to bring him good fortune. The boy's absence slowly began to toll on Thomas, and his confidence also began to wane. "If only Leo were here with his good luck. Then I could really win and rub it in Eleanor's face", he said to himself whilst locking the car.

As he came outside Crown court he saw the building's roof like a pyramid and imagined his face melting like a crumpling papyrus scroll of a pharaoh's face bejewelled in sweat. The image of Eleanor standing beside her husband soon brought him back to his senses. He walked up the entrance door's steps and then greeted them with a sardonic "Good morning". Neither of them answered him and Eleanor folded her hands and turned away from him. Nicole, Thomas' lawyer, arrived a quarter of an hour after and apologised to her client.

"Sorry I got stuck in traffic."

Eleanor, Bradley, Nicole and Thomas entered the court room when one of the council representatives came to call them. Eleanor stilettoed down the court room's corridor shaking her hips, just the way Flora had taught her when they were younger. Thomas walked down to the table where he and his lawyer would sit with a high chin and straight shoulders, just like his Godmother had taught him too. The court room's appearance was just as bathetic as Thomas' hopeless case.

"Now I want us to be very focussed."

"Very what sorry judge?"

The judge was speaking so softly that Thomas could not hear him. He had started becoming deaf in the last years but had never started wearing a hearing aid. Hearing aids looked terrible. If Leonard or Stella saw him with one what would they think?

"Focussed."

"Sorry?"

"Focussed" Nicole nudged Thomas and whispered "Try and be quiet".

"Why is he speaking so softly? I can't hear a thing he's saying" Thomas whispered under his breath.

"Is there a problem with how I speak Mr? Haller?
"Haller."

"That's what I said Mr Haller."

"Now we don't have a problem at all" Nicole interjected and elbowed Thomas to make him shut up.

"Then we may proceed" the judge said. It had greatly annoyed Thomas to hear this judge speak so softly; for him to feel alienated out of the conversation. Having been scalded by his lawyer, Thomas put his head on the table in distress and began to moan inside of himself. It had not started well! He could not hear a word the judge was saying. Leo must have forgotten to send him his good fortune. Where were the positive thoughts he was supposed to send? It was thinking about Leo's negligence that made Thomas rescind back in his pessimism. "Leo probably doesn't care about me at all. He's probably already replaced me with some kid in the playground". If Leo had come with him to the trial; fortune would have dealt him another judge, one that he could hear and one that would look kindly upon his case.

For the rest half hour Bradley and Eleanor conveyed their points to the judge who came to be quite intrigued by this woman whose name was "Flora". He listened to both points equally but Thomas found he had given far more time to Eleanor and began to complain. The case had been dreadful so far. It was all Leo's fault. "There appears to me enough evidence" the judge was ignoring him by now, "to appoint this house to Eleanor. There is clearly a will here that cannot prove the contrary" and he began waving the paper condescendingly. "Except" interrupted Nicole, "that we have a witness to prove that Eleanor has been tampering with evidence. Thomas leaned over the desk to stare at

Eleanor to see if this shocked her, but she seemed unafflicted.

"And who would this be?" the judge began. It was right when the judge had begun to interrogate the prosecuting party about who their witness would be, that a type of rain began to fall upon them and a bell began to ring.

The judge began slamming his mallet in a panic and began to mumble something. He announced to both parties, "It would appear that this building may be on fire, I'm going to have to suspend this session here", still slamming the mallet. "This will have to be rescheduled in due time" he continued. And you", he pointed to Thomas, will have to bring along your witness". He dismissed the court, got up and began leaving the courtroom as fast he could.

"But!" Eleanor began.

Her frustrations were in vain. The case would have to be rescheduled, perhaps with another judge. Thomas looked at the other side of the court room and rejoiced in Eleanor's misery. Perhaps Leo had thought about him and brought him good luck after all.

No use to think about that now; he needed to evacuate this building whose fire-alarm was ringing to the tune of flames.

Chapter 31.

He returned home to tell Stella everything that had happened; how he had not been able to hear the judge speak and how the fire alarm had gone off in Crown Court. "You won't believe" he began saying just as she might have done. She listened attentively and was excited by his narrative; he had become much more sociable and affable since she had come to stay with him. The case would be rescheduled not too far from now.

"But it's important, that you be my witness Stella."

"Yes, don't worry. After all you've done for me" and she caressed Thomas under the chin. He had not seen her wear her lipstick in over two weeks but the touch of her skin on his was similarly rouge and chalk-like. When Thomas had told Stella about what had had happened, she had remarked, "It's quite strange for that to have happened".

"It is. Maybe it was meant to be, or maybe it was Monsieur". Thomas began to tell Stella about Monsieur; that folly of his. Stella, a graduate of theatre, liked the concept as soon as she heard it. "Maybe I can write about it" she began saying playfully. "Of course you can". Thomas had begun to inspire Stella in a multitude of manners, her poems' word choice had seen a flowering of obscure plant names and gardening terms. To inspire Stella, that appeared to be just as invaluable as Leonard not thinking that he was a coward.

Stella and Thomas conjectured about what "Monsieur Circumstance" might be like. Thomas was certain he was dressed in the Flaneur's attire. Monsieur had light side burns that scorched flagrantly down his cheeks, he had an elegant claw-hammer coat, but most of all Monsieur had a monocle. When Monsieur would stroll down the street with his hands in many people's affairs, he would wear his gold filled monocle in his left eye. For this reason he was sometimes short sighted and wrought disaster in people's lives. He had worn this monocle ever since his eye had been impaired in a brawl with time. They continued to discuss Monsieur and even began arguing when their conjectures did not coincide. "He has a spotted cravat", "No, he has a green square silk scarf".

"Does he drive a car?"

"No he walks."

"But if he does it's probably one of those luxurious cars, like a Rolls Royce."

The afternoon when Thomas had gone to court, the travel chest arrived. "I'll get it!" he said whilst descending the stairs. In these days where Stella had sprained her ankles, he had made that joke an innumerable amount of times. Luckily it was not the postman to deliver this package; Thomas could spare himself from seeing him another day. He ordered the delivery men who had driven their great lorry into his driveway to place the chest in the utility room.

They had dropped it to the floor; they lingered in the room expecting a tip, but Thomas pretended to not understand. He showed them to the door and shouted a few words of praise down the corridor to Stella about what he had ordered. As he went to inspect this travel chest that would form part of his show, Thomas remembered the theme that his work was going to treat.

The *all embracing art form*. He had lost sight of it entirely in these days he had spent with Stella and Leo. They had simplified life; made life more bearable.

When Leo returned from summer school Thomas hired the boy as his assistant chef. He had noticed Leo's gusto and resorted to winning him over by allowing him to cook. "Let's make something nice for your mother". Stella, who had felt herself a recluse in spending all her hours upstairs, asked Thomas to help her come down. He picked up Stella in his arms and deposited her by the divan so near the sliding-door, that she rested there as if she were still curled in limbo between garden and boudoir. With the help of Leo's extraordinary taste, Thomas prepared some lamb ribs with truffle-infused olive oil, but "without too much salt otherwise the flavour becomes too intense". Leo helped Thomas set the table and sauntered between both sides of the room as Thomas stirred the pan. At the dinner table Stella began telling them how she had almost completed her anthology and how she would soon try and publish it. "Do you know of anyone I could ask?" she said to Thomas. "No one".

After having eaten, Stella asked to be put back on the divan and Thomas and Leonard began playing with her as they held either end of her body. They threw her down on the divan and tried to frighten her. "Come on! Stop it!". Leonard became so boisterous that he wanted to show them how he had learnt to do a handstand but Stella said "Not here in the house", as if it were her own. Leo begged Thomas to come outside into the patio with him, which he did, and began skipping and jumping around the patio to flaunt his acrobatics. Stella remained inside the house watching them, with pen and notebook by her side. Leo's head spun just as much as the languid blue gyrations of the earth's sphere above them.

"Why don't you try" he said to Thomas.

"Oh I can't."

"Trust me you can."

"I love this house" –continuing to spin.

"It's almost like a mansion."

Thomas' home, with the great garden and the three floors, with the pantry that was always excessively full, was decadent and dazzling.

Every day they spent in it seemed to end more abruptly than the next.

When they returned inside they found Stella lulling a tune; all sad and pensive, just as if her name were Lady Yesterday.

Chapter 32.

Stella's casts came off at last. Twenty one days after Thomas had made her fall down the ladder, Stella's ankles returned to penduluming in the house with softness like to time. Thomas stood over her with a kitchen knife and spliced apart the plaster. Severed in two the encasing revealed her flesh that had turned a pale incarnadine. Stella moved her legs away from him, almost injuring them again, to not make him see that the plaster had begun to make fibres of her skin turn mouldy. "Don't look!" she said and soon after she rushed to the bathroom, limping with the sensation of walking again. He remained in the room confused about what he had done wrong.

The photography for Stella's "Blue Velvet Vision" anthology began. "Finally" she said, "we can start taking the photos for my anthology". She bit her lips and cowled her chin behind her hair, still ashamed of Thomas having seen her lurid ankles. She would never want someone to think that she was "unclassy". "Are you alright?". "Don't your ankles hurt?" "No I'm fine, really, I just want to get started". Stella tiptoed down to her room and went to get the cloak they had bought together for her photography. They sauntered down to the garden, Stella with the cloak and Thomas with the camera by his shoulder.

"Right… How shall we start?"

"I want to take at least twenty pictures."

Thomas had forgotten how commanding Stella was. She ordered him around the garden and scalded him when she thought they had not taken a picture correctly.

They laid out the cloak on the grass and Stella lay supine upon it. They had taken an apple from the kitchen and Stella placed it in her mouth as she laid down. It was a strange photograph, "but that's the effect I want" Stella said. They also took a picture by the shed, behind the spray of vines, just as Thomas had always desired. He could not have stumbled into a better opportunity to take pictures of Stella; when they would go and develop them, he would ask for a spare copy for himself. Then his picture book would be complete. He would have soon tired of listening to Stella's instructions had she not started to undress herself for the next picture. "Now one more controversial" she began. Stella wanted take a picture of the velvet cloak on her breasts, with her shoulders exposed. She asked him to turn around whilst she changed. He obeyed but furtively glanced behind him to see that under the sunshine her mole had turned a dark brown, as if it were an energised, sun-lit cacao.

Even if he could see nothing of Stella's nudity, he was surprised that she had shed her clothes in front of him. It was true that she had become more familiar with Thomas but above all Stella always looked to shatter convention in order to obtain the stardom she so craved. It was right when Thomas was leaning back and had put one knee on the grass to take the picture, that he was reminded of how old cameras in his godmother's time used to shatter their bulbs when they flashed. Those cameras had flash powder that exploded and shattered its receptacle of glass with a sound that was the snap! to a grand entrance. As he took the picture of Stella with the camera's flash, it appeared to him that he heard the light bulb's glass breaking to the splice of Stella's own beauty; and it was auroatic and refulgent with vanity.

Stella was trying to make a serious pose for the picture and he saw how infinitely unhappy she seemed, how the camera's flash that fell on and tapered her, also waxed her in sadness. Or maybe that was simply the effect she wanted. He looked at her before taking the second shot and yes, she was so infinitely unhappy, displeased, yet transmogrified to form this tight and voluptuous seriousness, whose only shame was the modesty of the coloured velvet cloak covering her breasts.

Thomas let the camera fall on his shoulder and moved closer to Stella and the cloak hiding her body. Stella often liked to discover the etymology of words; how and from where words came. She had told him that the word "velvet" had originally meant "shaggy hair". The velvet cloak draping down her tummy made him feel a sensation on the nape of his neck; the velvet the hairs of an abrasive brush against him –that polished a new seduction.

"Shall we go inside now?"

"Yes I'm actually getting quite cold."

They went inside the house and Thomas showed Stella the new trunk he had ordered for the show. They went into the utility room and kneeled down beside it. "I really like it, you see, you didn't really need my help at all". She was referring to how he had ordered the trunk without asking; she was in a mood where she sought victimhood in everything.

In the afternoon Thomas tried to encourage Stella for them to make an exciting dish, but this did little to raise her spirits. He found himself morphing to her sadness and after he had taken refuge in the studio, Stella came in to tell him she wanted to go home. "Come on, don't be like that" he said whilst trying to hug her and placing his hands on her hips. She pulled away and made an irate expression. "Please? Can you just take me home?". He would never want to take her home. He could risk not being alone again, now that company had come as a vice with its own poisons and pleasures. To cheer her up Thomas said, "Come on, let's take a walk. You need to put your ankles back in exercise". Of course Stella agreed. These personal exiles of hers, "maybe I just need to be alone for a bit", were phrases said just for the point of saying them. Stella did not want to be alone at all. She was more solitary than one might think. That was what Thomas had discovered in these days he had spent with Stella that was the illusion that must people did not care to notice; people were more solitary than what they might believe. Solitude made people animate their emptiness inside in other people, to give a name and a face to what they craved, to conjure up a milky white body that would be their milky panacea. Thomas had discovered that he was not the only one to fill this emptiness inside by fleshing it out in other people. Now he would become Stella's antidote or hypnosis.

They left the house together to promenade down Tilehouse road and to later pick up Leonard. "I want to take you beside the river wey", he was speaking whilst in front of her because the road had no pavement. "Just over here on the left". They turned and found themselves on the pavement of Pilgrim's Road, reconvening their shoulders side by side. Stella was telling Thomas how her ankles were quite in pain. Thomas, forgetting how much she hated medicine, made the error of saying, "I have some aspirin at home. Maybe we can go back and get some". "Never". They crossed the road over to Shalford Park and the space between the trees with the path to the river, throbbed just as much as he had ever seen it. They dirtied their shoes in the mud; the park behind them was desolate save for a few children that were playing and some dog-walkers.

"Have you ever had dogs?"

"Yes", revived from her mood swing.

"Four of them."

"Four?"

"Yes. We never took care of them. They're all buried in my backyard in Greece."

He took her hand in his. "Come on, let's go down here". They walked on the forest's path towards the river Wey. The path was narrow and straight like a corridor that led them down a majestic billiard hall with tan or maroon or perhaps orange pebbles like balls to be placed in billiard tables. Three quarters down the path he stopped her and said, "You see? These are your flowers". He plucked a stem of the astrantia midriff-high all around them and gave it to her. "What do you mean?" she said laughing. "These are called astrantia, just like you're called Stella". "Oh right I see". "Look at the bracts, they're just like stars".

"Are you sure you're not making it up? It says on the sign there that they're called meadow sweet."

They continued and left the marshes riddled with Stella's behind them. Stella stopped by the signboards that explained the wildlife; he continued onwards for he had read them many times before. They crossed the bridge. Thomas waited for Stella as she was lagging a few metres behind. "There's a throne of pebbles there and opposite there's a stream". "A throne?". "Yes, like a chair made of stones". These tendencies of his, to reveal what was here as if it were treasure, reminded her of her son Leonard. They continued down the dusty track, were persuaded by the atmospheric enchant of the River Wey and the green fluorescence emanated all around them. Thomas made Stella sit first on the chair of stones and then saw there was space also for him. They rested there in silence and then Stella got up to go down to the stream below them. "Shall we take a swim?" she said as she began removing her shoes.

"But it's only ankle high."

"So what?"

Thomas stood up from the bench smiling and looked down to tiptoe his way to the stream where Stella was. She had not gone in yet. "We have to go in together". She put the tip of her toenails, she had been painting them even if her ankles were sprained, and then shuddered. "It's ice-cold. But we're still going in". Thomas began to untie his shoelaces and then proposed that they stand on their shoes with bare feet and jump in directly so they wouldn't dirty their socks. They stood on top of their shoes "like fools" and then Stella jumped in. She began mumbling a few curses but then clapped her hands together. Thomas held out his hand and she helped him enter the stream. "I thought you didn't like swearing". "In fact I don't" and she smiled to mask her hypocrisy. Her aunt, a woman in Rhodes, said that the worst people were not those that wore masks; rather those that wore a mask underneath their face.

"You write poetry, you'll probably like this. Did you know that poetry is associated with walking?"

"No I didn't know that."

"The meter, feet and step of the poem are all terms to do with walking."

"But who cares!" she bent down and began splashing him. He put his arms around his face to protect himself, disappointed that this third-rate pearl of wisdom had not impressed her.

"Okay then. Let's play another game."

"Let's see who can stay in longest without shivering."

Thomas began smiling but then looked at her scornfully and accepted her challenge. They eyed one another, and eared and mouthed and handed and nosed –what was the other one?- both tried to not betray the cold they were feeling. The challenge also seemed to turn into a blinking contest.

"Let's say that we both win."

"Okay" she accepted. Out of instinct they hugged each other for warmth and Thomas noticed that Stella had fattened, no, not fattened, but become more curvaceous. Later he would look at her down the street and see the gluttonous sashay. He found himself clasping Stella to the point that she began to slip back, and hit her heel on a bucket that was in the water.

"What's this?"

"I think that's to increase or decrease the water level."

"We should make it our tradition to come here", Thomas was always one to seek out traditions.

"Yes I have an idea."

"Why don't we go inside this bucket one at a time. Then the other person holds our hands as we spin, like a two handed dance turn."

"And as we spin we wish for something."

He nodded enthusiastically and held her hands as she entered the bucket. He began spinning her round, at first their arms were caught in a tangle but then he made her swerve to the semi sphere of what she desired. "What did you wish for?" "Can't tell". He obviously hoped that she had wished something to do with him, but he knew that even that if they would be lovers, she would only wish for her happiness, regardless of whom it would entail. He knew what she was like. So almost out of vengeance, whilst he spun around the bucket and Stella held the tip of his fingers, he did not wish for something to do with her. He spun in this grand gyration and wished for the beatific mingling of the arts. His last show at Chelsea.

As soon as he had come out of the bucket, he found it difficult to reproach Stella for not having wished to be with him. They were here in this stream, with ripples of water pattering, and he considered that if rhyme was culturally associated with walking, meter, step and foot, now they bathed their feet in blank verse; it was not plagiarising other men, Paul and Daniel, no, it was their inimitable memory inscribed in water.

Thomas and Stella appeared outside Leo's school as if having been washed up from an urbane shore. Leo went to hug them both to join the society of wet people.

"What's for dinner?" he said as soon as they had turned the bend of the road.

"I was thinking of preparing" began Thomas.

"Actually" Stella interrupted, "Leo and I will be having dinner at home. But you're welcome to come."

"Aren't we going to Thomas'?"

"We've stayed at his far too much as it is."

"Stella... stay. I bought the Basque sausages for tonight; I can't eat all of them by myself."

Stella obliged. "Alright then" she said half-heartedly. Leonard ran in front of them and they had to hold him back because he was going much too fast. When Leo was out of earshot, and they had just passed the Weyside Café, Stella told Thomas an embarrassing anecdote about that ruin over the hills she had once visited as a student. At home Stella took over the kitchen and her assistant Leo also eclipsed any role he might have wished to have. He set out the table, then went to wait for dinner to be ready.

At the table Leo began eating and was monstrously enamoured by the Basque sausages he was crushing under his teeth. "Easy! You're eating like a little piglet".

Piglet! How could he have forgotten! This was another of Stella's favourite expressions. Whenever she caught or referred to someone eating too much, she would call them a "little piglet" and flare her nostril ridges. Thomas began to copy Leo, just so she could call him by the same name, which she did as soon as she saw the oil leaking from his mouth. He was relieved to have them here; to find solace in Stella insulting him, to enjoy the cuisine that he had helped to supervise. He tasted the chunks of apple Leonard had said to add in the sauce.

Stella was also in a much better mood than before. The fear of them leaving however, did not subside altogether. After they had talked together in the parlour, one went to the bathroom, the other to drink, and they separated. Stella went to her room and when he went upstairs to go to bed, he did not knock on her door. He put on his pyjamas with holes and let the lustre outside seep through, so that his sleeves became as prisms of light.

Before he was going to fall asleep Leonard came in his room to wish him goodnight, "We didn't say goodnight yet".

Thomas caressed him and fell back in his snore. When they were all sleeping, and darkness had drained the house to a livid black, Thomas trembled in the bed.

He got up half asleep and walked down the corridor; though he was not fully conscious, he guessed that it was much later than midnight. He walked until he arrived outside the guest room and opened it to feel their breathing. They were still here. As soon as he was made certain, he sleep-walked back, in-between dream and night, opening the garden doors downstairs; they were also called "arcadia doors". Into the dream sequence.

A rumour of parquet or parapet; the estate's gardener was coming from the patio, from a cusp, greater romantic mountain floor. In his entry from heaven to heathen was his employer; how had he called Stella? Ah yes, "Lady Yesterday" rolling her head back on the divan in a sensuous but garbled gasp, exhausted, looking towards the lawn parched to a fawn. "Thomas?

I'm thirsty" she said in the amalgamate room, kitchen and living room.

"But if you are to understand anything in this house, it's that we don't make matters of anything."

"Sorry? Would you like for me to get you a glass of water?"

"No. Don't you see? I'm waiting."

"For what?"

"I'm waiting until I become so extremely thirsty, that I will cherish every droplet, until I will find my own saliva quenching."

"Don't you think that's such a good idea?"

"I'm not sure I could do it Mrs…"

"You must mortify to intensify; that's common salt applied to any pleasure."

"Try it with the Lilies! Leave a Lily to thirst for ages, then watch when you give it but a drop, it will leap, like me, in joy. Take a photograph when you do that."

"Really? You're not going to drink for days?"

"No."

"Just so you can feel what's it like?"

"Yes, exactly."

Swish, swoosh. It's raining. Lady yesterday has been waiting hours; one can never tell time in sleep.

"Thomas! Thomas!"

"Yes?

"On second thought… Could you go fetch me that glass of water?"

Chapter 33.

Eleanor came to visit and sullied the floorboards of the home with scandal. That morning it was a Saturday and Thomas wanted to drive down to London to start setting up the apparatus for the show. For the first time in three weeks they separated. Thomas asked Stella to come with him to London but she said it was high time she went back home because "I'm paying the rent there and otherwise, what's the point?". Once he had heard that she would not come, he resorted to saying he would not go at all, which she dismissed by reassuring him that they would see each other on Monday, if he would need her help for the show. Of course he would.

Stella had been offered an interview for one of Ted's rivals in Shepherd's bush, near Hammersmith. "So you might move away?". "It's a possibility". He was frightened to see how easily Stella considered leaving. "I'm so bored of Guildford. Maybe it's time for a change". If she were to leave, what would happen to their work together? How easily could everything fall apart? He tried devising a way for Stella to stay longer with him, even if it would be just for a day. They had spoken in pyjamas on the stair-head and Thomas knew that Stella took a long time to get ready. He got changed whilst Stella was still having breakfast; he had woken up before her, and then went to her and said, "I'm going now".

"Wait. I haven't even gotten ready yet, I'm not ready to leave."

"Oh, I know. But that's okay, just close the door behind you alright? Or you can decide to stay and we see each other when I come back."

"But I told you I'm going home."

"Well if you reconsider you can stay here."

He looked at her and winked with burlesque sophistry. Unconvincing. She had brought her notebook to the breakfast table and was tearing out a page.

She had not been in good humour but Thomas hoped that she would stay in the house for the remainder of the day and wait for him. It seemed the only way for him to avoid coming back to an empty home. As she continued to eat her bread crackers with mortadella, Thomas went to the utility room to get the trunk and then leave for London. Entered the room and saw the trunk for his show on the floor. Even if returning to find Stella still here was his primary ambition of the day, the allure of that ideal, the *all embracing art form*, replaced whatever else he was thinking about with egotistical absolution.

The mixing of the arts. As he knelt down and opened the trunk, he considered the possibilities. To mix the arts would mean to distil symphony from pastels, to sculpt from violin horse-strings, to write not with hands, but genial moving feet from dance moves. It was impossibly seductive, just as much as the imagination would permit. Inside the open trunk, one could imagine all the objects of art to place inside.

The fumbling Thomas imagined himself taking a canvas on his shoulder as if it were a violin, and begin to rub the violin bow on the cotton of the canvas, to feel the tiny gold spots and scents of rosin explode under his nose hairs in a melody of monstrous, marvellous convolution. Only the long-lost hypothetical world of ideas could house the myth of such fascinating fervor, which sometimes hid, vanished, begot beauty, in another instance reappeared there, mimetised here, went beyond all times, digital, analogical and cast-away sundial, at the spumous crackle of dawn, at the russet hour, when a pessimistic poet full of self-loathing burnt clouds like papers on which he had inscribed wonderful words, not knowing that his contempt was serendipity for someone else who, in the comfort of his couch, looked on unburdened at the daedal finesses of the earth's chance being. Gesamtkunstwerk, the abstract spectacle which returned in wreaths and riddles the very complexity of the human mind, which had figmented for itself a body and a soul and voluble heart too, that wanted a say in the matter, at all times, this overloaded preference, one imagined, being the desire to mesh the subtle and the secret and the mauve of the world; mauve being man's first colour at birth, from which he would marl every other pleasure; with mauve lips and mauve sea-banks and mauver nights elided in semblance to the din of a lamp. The comely shape of this desire knowing no body, no gender, no organ, no answer, but knowing essence, soul, anima and anonymity; the amorphous bloom of a nothing, and the very clear failure to capture it, the world would swoon, and he with it, if but a morsel could be his. Behind bowers the myth dwelled and in front of artists the enigma mocked; if genius or fool or scientist could unpeel a shadow from the floor on which he had fallen in despair, then one might find the resolution adumbrated in block-shot scribbles like on the back of an adhesive label. Adieu and farewell, the creation would become his crypta. If –and there were not- there were ever a few who had wearied a form for the Gesamtkunstwerk, then perhaps it might be a door carved in the ceil of the sky, leaving at the last the primordial patheticalness of man's ape cave, closing the door shut, making all other crepitating chasing colours follow.

Perhaps in these three weeks he had forgotten the promise, the persuasion of these ideas that could enchant any man or woman. But his show at Chelsea would soon be and Stella and Leo would be by his side, he could have both; he could embrace all two or two thousand arts.

He left the house carrying this trunk, hoping that this plan to leave early would let Stella stay home until he returned. It would not work. Before leaving he went to say goodbye to Leonard, just as he had done in the evening, and found the boy grappling unto him. "In your travel chest for your show" he began suggesting, "You should put food". He smiled at him and pulled his hair behind his ear and promised he would consider. When he was loading the car he noticed another vehicle was parked down the road with the engine on, funambulating on a single yellow line as if on tight-rope.

Inside the home, known in the road as "Chantry-View", Stella was getting ready and was folding the sheets so Thomas could put them directly in the washing machine. She ordered Leo to help her and he was reluctant, for he soon wanted to return to Tommy's home.

Whilst Thomas was gone, Stella was able to put on her makeup undisturbed. When Thomas was home he would always scald her that she would get the blush on the carpet. She found this excruciating because it reminded her of the reason why she had left her home in Greece. She didn't want anyone to tell her what to do. She furtively applied the blush in the bedroom now he was gone and laughed at how pedantic he could be for no good reason. She took the brush and began scraping it around her face to set alight the capillaries profused in her cheek. As she was admiring herself in the hand mirror, manoeuvring in between ballistic trajectories of vanity, she dropped a gram of powder on the carpet. She put her hand on the carpet to try and remove it but this only made the stain worse. She intimated something to herself and then went to the bathroom to get a towel and clean the carpet. She scraped hard but it would not come out. She called over Leo to help her and the two found themselves scrubbing the carpet so hard, parts of the fabric began to come off. This was the only room of the upper floor with carpet. Why did this have to happen to her?

"This is why I don't like staying in other people's homes".

As soon as she had finished speaking the doorbell rang. Leo said "I'll get it" but she held his arm and asked him to continue scrubbing whilst she went to answer. Going to answer the door as if this were her own home, made the thought of her "future house" flash before her in fanciful, esoteric glimpses. She walked down the stairs and began to critique parts of the home and imagined how she would arrange it. "That won't do.

And that won't do either". Stella pulled down the latch of the door and found an old woman with fish eye earrings stare back at her.

"Oh, well.. Hello. Thomas isn't here if you're looking for him."

"It was actually you I was looking for."

Eleanor pulled up her hand over her bag and made her bag sway to one side.

"It's a pleasure to meet you Stella" she reached out her hand on which she noticed a ring that foliaged the fingers.

"And you are?"

"Eleanor."

Everything Thomas had told her about Eleanor scattered to project over this woman in front of her. He had said how she had become fat over the years, but she did not find the same to be true now; Eleanor appeared quite lean.

"Yes I know you must have heard everything about me from Thomas."

"No, actually not much" she lied.

Eleanor looked away and made her eyebrows twitch.

"Let me make it clear why I've come" and she began spreading apart her hands.

"I know that you're going to testify in court against me. I know that you saw me, you saw me break into this house to get back my mother's painting and" she was wagging a finger, "the letter she sent him".

"But you know" she continued saying, "that Thomas is just crazy".

"He's just an old man."

"And we… we can help each other".

"Look I don't know what you want."

"Let me finish."

"Don't show up at the court. Don't testify against me. If you don't, then we can come to an agreement."

"Look I've seen you with that boy. It can be tough, can't it?"

"If you think you can just come here and bribe me."

"Oh, I see" and Eleanor began spiralling around her finger.

"You've fallen for his little old man act."

"Well let me ask you something."

"Did Thomas ever tell you the reason why he fell out with my family?"

"No he didn't, but we didn't get to."

"But let me guess. You've told him all about your life haven't you?"

"Well.. Yes but-"

"Do you know why? Because he's selfish."

"I bet he hasn't told you either that my mother helped pay for this house where you're standing."

"He said he managed it all himself" it was one of the things Stella admired in Thomas.

"Of course he said that."

"Let me take down your bank details" she began lighting a cigarette, masking the lighter with her hand to protect it from the wind. She remembered how Thomas had been urging her to start smoking regularly.

"Look, I'm not going to accept."

"Let me just take down your bank details alright? Then you can decide what you want to do."

Chapter 34.

Thomas had not enjoyed a single moment since he had left the home; whatever sucrose satisfaction, whatever pride grafted from his work, could not outnumber the myriad follies of three! three, Stella, Leo and him, like the three that all society worshipped; the holy trinity, or if not that, the three-chord songs, arranged in bric a bracs and bars; all these that became austere ineffabilities, grim dispersions, now that they were gone. Oh it had been horrid in London. How he had missed Stella and Leo.

He had marinated long in traffic, had had to wait half an hour to find parking and had found out that he had not been allotted the space he wanted for the Chelsea show. He had also noticed how he was far behind in his work. The other gardeners had started already. A month and half before! Where they mad?

He found himself wrinkling together excuses, behind that forehead, excuses, all palatable excuses! He had had a woman, that was why he was behind, they had been working, but he had been bathing in streams in Guildford, had made the toothpaste for melancholy, because smiles, for a long time, had been lacking. Besides thinking about Stella and Leo, he had gone around the park where the other shows were held. Then envy, the aftertaste of pride, had corrupted him to the bone and the palate. There was one show he saw that was trying to recreate fast-food chain products which he found of ill taste. There were also the minimalist pieces he abhorred, especially now he was alone and had gone back to his complicated way of being. What would the jury think of his work? He would hurl everything at them, a single title he had in his career and yet that seemed nothing now. The essence of the *all embracing art* form would asphyxiate the jury and he would bring them to him with his noose of platinum to their knees.

Of what age were the men and women that would judge him? Young he guessed, very young; perhaps a mistake he had made was to put too much of his old-age into his work, his atavism, that would inevitably seem unpalatable to people like they. There was, of course, an inherent modernity in the all-embracing art form; other writers had termed it "the artwork of the future", that only futurity could smelt the abstract picture into a reality, be it with new machines or instruments or scientists. Of late, in a video, he had seen that a new outlandish computer software was capable of translating pictures into melodies. By sampling the moods of the colours through selective algorithms, it could match a drawing of horses to, say, songs that equestrians listened to on playback. Quantum computers then, machines that used quantum states of subatomic particles to store information, seemed the most prodigious spectacle of the group. That was precisely what quantum particles were; particles that could be in more than one state at a time, they could be music, whilst being paint-pigment or prose. Yes! Perhaps there would come a younger man far cleverer than he, that would give an answer modern and new and punchy, whilst still being, of course, virtuosic commandeer of language, science, philosophy.

But these other gardeners, they knew nothing. When he was driving back he was excited to tell Stella;

she was often one to criticise other poets just for self confidence. A friend of Thomas, who was published, she had ridiculed. Whenever she had criticised other people's work she had used the word "we", "we've done so much better", as if to imply that it was them against the world when it came to envy. He rejoiced in this "we", yes, he wanted to tell Stella how much better their work was, how superior her suggestions had been. Yet he found that whenever he spent time with Stella, or Leonard, he became profoundly quotidian, that he enjoyed the moments, but that if he were look back at himself, he would abhor how he had become: ordinary, peevish, romantic.

He had tried telephoning Stella before starting to drive but she had not answered. On the road back to Guildford, he had begun to lust after the dashboard; he remembered the foreign and more sensual word his godmother had used to describe it, "cruscotto", that made his suede fantasies crumble to the leather.

On the way back there was no traffic. Before getting out he passed his hand in the middle of the curved steering wheel, alike to the fall in-between Stella's back; the trapezium. He entered the house and said "I'm back!". No one was home. His plan had not worked. He found Stella's bed linen left by the washing machine. He telephoned to Stella immediately and she picked up this time. She was glad to hear everyone else's work was poor.

"So can you come? On Monday?"
"I can't actually. Sorry."
"Why? Why can't you come?"
"I have a job interview remember?"

"I'm actually going to be back very late."

"That will mean someone will need to take care of Leo."

"Yes but don't worry, I'll arrange something."

"No I can do it really... Please."

She consented. Over the telephone his voice had sounded similar to when he spoke out of her line of sight. Part of her liked it. The voice brooched itself to her ear and decorated the lobe with platinum and pleasure. They spoke a while longer on the telephone, but then Stella said she had to go; there was another call on the line.

He spent the rest of the weekend in agony and drove back to London. He just seemed to sift in-between these places, Guildford and London, without consciousness. The Chelsea competition would take place in the sixty six acres of the "Royal Hospital Chelsea"; a retirement home for the soldiers of the British army. Irony was not lost upon him. This venue for the last show of his career was a nursing home. He had never realised. Besides the Chelsea Flower Show the grounds also hosted old war memorials and parades. The grounds of the hospital were in the shape of an L with a portico made of marble and the rest of the building in brick. He had been allotted a space just by the side, by the windows of the retirement home where some pensioners had their rooms. If they would look out they would see him. Now he looked out to Monday, pirouetting over days, trampling on time.

He went to pick up Leo and all was similar to before, with the exception that Stella was not there. She had travelled down to Shepherd's bush and returned late in the evening. Thomas had taken Leo walking in the fields and then they had played chopsticks again together. Thomas was kind enough to go pick up Stella at the station when she returned from Hammersmith. "It's much too late to be walking back at that hour". Stella returned at midnight and Thomas arrived at the station with Chinese take-away. Stella kissed him on the cheek to thank him and then had told him about her interview. "It's absolutely amazing". She was telling them how the new place where she had been was a high-end shopping centre. "The only problem are the hours. They close at ten-o-clock". She had bought Thomas and Leo some presents. Stella always bought other people presents. She opened her bag as he was driving and gave him a "Limited edition skin wear" and a new jumper for her son. She had found Thomas' presence in her life, how he constantly called her, how he was beginning to depend so much on her, quite intrusive. For the moment she needed his help, now that she had received this opportunity to work in London. It had always been an ambition of hers. "How did the interview go?" Thomas asked again, for the second time.

"It went well. The only problem is the pay. But it's much higher up compared to where I was before. I think if they offer it to me I'll take it."

Stella did take the job. They even called to tell her that they would raise her initial hourly salary by fifty pence. Circumstance made Thomas soon become Leo's child-minder, "But only until I've moved to London" Stella was telling herself. They had given her a schedule that stated that she would have to stay late in the evenings until ten-o'clock. In those days Thomas had taken it upon himself to take care of Leonard whilst she was gone and to pick her up in the evenings. She had been extremely grateful at first and had bought him presents from the new shopping-centre where she worked.

In the days where Stella was gone until late, he could not work, neither could he go to London to arrange more details for his show. He had to take care of Leo; it was his responsibility. He resorted to taking him down to the betting shop and played all the lucky numbers he had compiled; the five and the fifteen, the nine. He won nothing. He bought some more scratch and win cards for Leo to open but he became reluctant to be part of his gambling and said "Can we just go home now?". Unlike Stella he meant home to be the same place where Thomas lived, behind the chantries. Guilt soon accosted Thomas. He took Leo sightseeing at the University of Surrey.

"You see it's important to do well. You should aspire, I mean, you should hope, to study here one day."

"Yes I've heard all about it."

They passed by the university's Cathedral and then by the different faculties' buildings. Stella had told both of them about this place where she had studied for four years. Thomas continued lecturing Leo about his future, hinting at the fact that he should not study theatre like his mother if he did not want to finish work at ten in the evening, three times a week.

Ten days later and it was August, his show was in a month, he was behind and Stella had not been helpful at all in her advice. Whenever she returned she was much too tired and Thomas actually found himself to be the one asked for advice. "What do you think about this one?". Stella was researching where to move in London for her new job.

"Could you help me sweetie? To do the move?"

He found himself in sweet subservience to Stella. He could bear the inconvenience of going to pick her up at the station, he could bear taking care of Leonard. What he could not bear however, what he scorned, was the solitude in between. The days where Stella would return early, when she would want to spend time by herself or with her son. Those days, they were principally Thursdays, Thomas dismembered himself in other places and activities. One evening he played a vinyl on the gramophone that was on display in the parlour. With the fitted disk on the table spinner, he let himself slide to the screech of the needle puncturing the black-squashed oval. In the gramophone horn he heard the blow of music that resembled the rustling of, say, "xerographic paper"; it was creased, crumpled and see-through just before the singer's voice came and embalmed in jazz blue.

Placing his ear close to the horn, he remembered what Stella had told him the first time she had come into his home. "It's strange that songs can have a masculine or feminine ending. That mixture. You put the idea in my head". There were virile and lithe-lady bodies, tummies and torsos, even in the invisible bodiless world of music.

The monotony of these days continued in a fashion that not even Stella's "Blue Velvet Vision" could graduate. All would have been dull, had not the trial against Eleanor come again on the Monday.

Chapter 35.

Almost a month had passed since the first session of the trial. During that time Stella had found a new job in Hammersmith and had signed the contract for an apartment near her work. "Are you sure you can afford it?" Thomas said when Stella had asked him to review the contract. "Yes, Yes, don't worry". He had not seen her since he had helped her move. In Guildford she had been living in Markenfeld's Road and he had been there to help move all her furniture and belongings. He had seen a cabinet she had made out of a restaurant's logo, with the flags they gave out for meals. He had not seen her since the move. "We'll keep in touch yes?" she had said. She had dieted recently and had become almost skeletal. "Yes! For the trial. Just six days before my birthday". In truth she had already given him enough presents for his next five birthdays. He longed for these two days he would spend with Stella. He would see her on Monday for the court case and he would see her on Sunday for his sixty-fifth birthday. She worked so intensely now that seeing her had become a rarity.

    For the first days where Stella had moved to London, he was glad that he could go to Chelsea and focus on his last show. He felt relieved that she was not so far away there, that she was nearby on the other side of town. He had been worried that her schedule might not allow her to come, but she would manage, he was certain. After all, she had promised him. The day before the trial he called Stella to remind her that she needed to come at "twelve in the morning. On time yes?". She had not answered so he had had to leave a voicemail.

The morning of the trial he awoke later than usual and risked being late. He went to have breakfast immediately, which he normally did after changing. In the kitchen he saw a piece of paper lying on the kitchen counter. It was torn from Stella's notebook. He wanted to read what was written inside but saw he was late and began estimating how long it would take him to change, to shave, to put on his shoes. When he was in the bathroom he looked in the glass and saw that his eyebrows were beginning to grow back; a hair protruded to announce the uncanny return. He took the tweezers and remembered when he had plucked out the piece of wood that had inserted itself as a minute ionic column inside Stella's bum cheek. That had been fun. But now there was only himself, only this syntactic HE did, HE went, HE came, this HE, HE, HE, HE, HE, HE as if to make the laugh of a histrionic villain.

When he was getting dressed, he considered how easily impressed Stella was when people she knew well wore clothes she had never seen before. He passed in-between his wardrobe dismissing dust, clothed by the clock, to put on a blazer Stella had never seen on him. He had also started applying gel in his hair and spread the substance copiously over his hair, to make it almost begin to sag, so that the avalanche glow at the highest peak of his locks became a dolomite dream. Driving, he passed by red twice and tooted the horn when he thought a car was going too slow. By tooting the horn first, he initiated the traffic jam's sonata.

When he arrived at Crown Court and passed by the building with the roof as a pyramid, he found it just as horrid as the first session. He paid for the parking reluctantly and when he saw Eleanor's car parked near his; he put his hands in his pockets to get his keys and damage it as best he could. This time, as he was walking to the entrance of Crown court, a man on a motorcycle passed him by and almost hit him. Thomas stumbled forward, dazed, and went to lean on a lamppost.

There was a procedure in every courtroom where witnesses and prosecutors entered and left the courtroom at different exits for the safety. The same was often done in stadiums.

How much did he want this house in his godmother's inheritance? Yes, it was true, there were other things he wanted now, there was the show looming and naturally there was Stella, there was Leonard. It was more a question of pride, apart from the house, there was also his godmother's painting that he had foregone. The orbit of these desires each attracted him within their field, but above all he found that at the height of vanity, he would prefer his work, or if not his work, woman. Stella!

"Thomas Haller."

The court representative was calling him, Eleanor and Bradley had already come in. Had there been a fire here? There had. He found parts of the courtroom's ceilings anguished to smoke stains. Altogether the room was still miserly, just as miserly as most of Guildford, despite its affluent reputation. They sat down by the same tables, by the same chairs and the same judge. Him again! Thomas tapped his knuckles on the table in frustration. He was judge "Atkinfield?" "Atkinson?" Atkinwhat?

"Apologies" the judge resumed as if a moment had passed, "for our interruption the last time we were here."

On Eleanor's behalf, there came only complaints. It was "absurd in the first place" that "the entire case hadn't ended there on the first session". The judge asked for the questionnaires he had ordered them to fill in last time. He took these in and started reading, then asked his assistant for a glass of water. A few moments later, he made a double motion with his hand and said, "Let the witness come in". Eleanor began snorting and looked over from her desk to condescend Thomas. He had not heard anything and was still looking blankly down to the floor, "Ah yes, the witness, Stella!".

The witnesses, as the judge had explained the first time they had come here, would enter through "That door" to their left and the judge's right. Thomas looked at the door and the guard standing behind it but it did not move. Readjusted his hair but Stella did not come in. "She's probably just late you know, stuck in traffic or something" he said aloud, as if they were not in a courtroom, but were adolescents loitering around by park benches.

"Will the witness please come in!" the judge repeated loudly.

The guard opened the door where Stella was supposed to emerge and disappeared to go see where she was.

"Does she know it's today?"

"Yes, I rang her yesterday evening to remind her."

Paranoid, paranoiac that Stella was unwell there in London, that she had not settled in well, that she had met another man, more successful than him. Was she also neglecting her son Leo? The possibility of this last was more excruciating than having to wait for Stella. He began fidgeting with the papers in front of him which annoyed the judge and prompted him to remain still. Eleanor was there on the other side, with her husband, just as he had seen them on the other side of the road many days ago. She held her hand up to her face with two slanted fingers that snippeted her cheeks in flesh-buns of white, with powder. Her eyes were tired, she removed her hand and then began resting her head by her husband's shoulder.

"Right" said the judge, "I think it's safe to say that" before the judge had finished, the guard opened the door for Stella to come in.

Perhaps too long since he'd seen Stella; he tried to make eye contact but she, who had started wearing her new brand's clothes, a canine-type of neck collar, did not look at him. He had not believed! He had not believed that she would come; for a moment he had guessed that she was reproaching him for something, that perhaps Leonard had told her about the gambling.

Naturally Thomas could not have known of the proposal that Eleanor had made Stella to testify against him, to not show up at all, nor could he imagine any other scenario.

A sterile plot; the mechanic plot of terrible style life gave to men and women: the price of an ending.

Chapter 36.

His failure came at the expense of not few, but many things; over a thousand pounds of lawyer expenses, dilating swirls of time that had magnified him further in his age, as an exuberant tonic, how many hours exactly? And a ripe exploded star. He had not expected it. Yes, Stella had told him about her past but she was an honest person. She had told him that she had fallen to many temptations, to applying pomade on a stranger's back and then almost sleeping with him, the night she had slept with someone else, but she was an honest person. Eleanor had thrown her a grimace, a cigarette and a pile of money, but he knew that it wasn't her fault.

When the case had finished and the judge had said "This case is closed. I hereby assign Flora's inheritance to Eleanor", they had been separated; they had left the courtroom at different exits. "I'm sorry but I did tell you" his lawyer had said, but he had not cared to listen at all, he had left marching out, trouncing the floor as if in full Broadway tap. He was glad Eleanor had been ushered to another exit, not least because she was wearing the fish-eye earrings again. There must have been a mistake, Stella must have gotten her story wrong. How could it be possible that she had testified against him? So utterly in denial, so unpersuadable, he arrived home and paced around the kitchen, "Just how? Stella? Why?" he saw the piece of paper torn from her notebook on the counter, he picked it up and then immediately put it back and decided he needed to speak to her. To ask her at least! What had happened?

The wire near the receiver dangled by him as a plasticized curl of her hair. No answer. Her phone was disconnected. He tried again but no answer. At last he resorted to leaving her another voice mail, "Please. Call me back as soon as possible".

It was now that whatever madness seemed impossible slowly began. For the next days Thomas spent every afternoon telephoning to Stella but the outcome was always the self-same. On the Thursday he received a telephone call; he was doing the washing up and went to answer. He still had the yellow rubber gloves on and felt vicious to pick up the telephone in this way. "No hard feelings eh?". It was Eleanor. She had telephoned him to "do the noble thing" because "Flora would have never wanted them to argue over this". That was easy for her to say now she had won. He tried holding back his disdain to not give her satisfaction. Eleanor lingered on the call and said:

"Say hi to Stella for me."

She hung up in his face. The desire to phone her back and ask her how she knew Stella personally, assailed him. But he had to resist, he could not, he could never give her that satisfaction. The superstitious Thomas could think about nothing else but the timing of this tragedy. His birthday was just three days away. How would he spend it?

He had realised before, just after showing up at Ted and getting Stella fired, that the answer to solitude had taken up many faces; it had been Flora's, Eleanor's and Stella's and now it was also Leonard's. He wanted to spend his sixty fifth birthday with Stella and Leo, they could talk about what happened; he was beginning to understand. Whatever had happened, oh that could be secondary! What was more important? His birthday; he didn't care about the house he convinced himself, if they would come see him for his birthday, then all would be forgiven.

She was honest, yes he knew it; she had actually never seen Eleanor break into the home, perhaps she had not felt to lie for him. She didn't want to lie that was it, and now she wasn't answering, well it was because of the late night shifts. His anger soon evaporated and he was made a white-haired ingredient left to simmer by the divan, telephoning to Stella:

"How are you? On my birthday, Stella, I will be at the River Wey, I will be there all day from nine to five so we can spend some time together. If you want to spend some time together I will be there, where it all began".

Where what had began? Could they really have called going down to the lake a tradition already? They had been there once, yes, perhaps it had been pleasant but they had been there only once. They had put their feet in the bucket and had spun each other round making wishes. Thomas did not know what Stella had wished; he had conjectured but could not be certain. He didn't have any means to know that Stella had wished to move away from Guildford as soon as possible, for a new life to begin. And his wish? Would the arts come together and fuse?

Despite what had happened he had not shed a single tear, yet. No, he was not so vulgar! Perhaps what he hated most was that he found himself as if at the end of a commercial novel; he only needed to look a few meters ahead to find the world end on a two dimensional page of paper, from which he would fall into desultory black space, out of creation he would fall.

The three days to his birthday passed with an excruciating monotony, then they were followed by excitement. His unhappiness and transgressions, they slipped away to new abstractions now Stella was gone. He returned to his picture book, his post stamps and then! he finally read that piece of paper torn from Stella's notebook.

Chapter 37.

It had been abrupt to read Stella's playlet, abrupt to travel down time across the époques; that was the idea she had tried to convey, that time was the name people gave to the invisible withering of the world.

Now he too seemed to transpire in-between times, to collate in-between hours so seamlessly, to his birthday! where Stella had not come, where he had waited with his feet in the stream for seven hours and had spun around in the bucket to make wishes every half hour. Her departure, it had been abrupt, there was no other way about it. She had come, untangled his life as a style, only to leave him with the bare plainness that remained, exploding the pace of his days which would otherwise be sluggish, far too long, far too unbearable. Stella had come into his life and made him admire the simplicity of living, yet now his life was simply simple without being pleasant at all; unimaginable that not even a connoisseur of horticulture like him could not put at rest the continual contempt of the world with a scent, or a type of plant or the soever sophistication.

But now perhaps, as we do it all again, as we return to when this story first began, we may look and judge him, Thomas Haller, differently for what he has done, for what he has not done, every Sunday since Stella left him. The first time! The first time we saw him, there in the beginning, when "our gardener was by the window of his home", and "he lifted the newest plant he had brought home from the market on to his desk". Yes, perhaps now, when we see him cut up with a "vertical and fabulous jerk" the Astrantia, and begin to devour the bracts and the flowers, we may understand the "ruby wedding", which makes him and flower marry in a chaste saliva mesh of violet.

You look at him and you think you know everything about him, and now perhaps, you truly do.

There was only one nuance remaining: the answer to the enigma he had begun to think about right before meeting Stella. The all-embracing art form. How could all of the arts come to mingle? He knew about failure: he knew what it had been like to watch someone exit his life so seamlessly. But he did not know the answer to this question[*]. He remembered Stella's words "the fusion of the arts will be liquid" and found his tongue wet with salivation.

On the twelfth of September, the day the Chelsea Flower show began, he understood. The night before he travelled down to the hospital ground where the show was taking place. The piece of paper with Stella's playlet; that had been the only mementos he had. It was perfect; perhaps Stella had done it on purpose. The page torn from her notebook would go in the trunk, together with the slabs of marble, the instruments and the illuminated paper engravings.

The grounds were closed. There was a guard at the gate that did not let him in at first, forcing him to cajole the young man with a small bribe. With a flashlight he had brought, Thomas crept to the space he had been allotted for his show; for a moment he considered damaging the other gardeners' pieces now that no one was here. No, that would be unsportsmanlike. Instead he

---

[*] Please return to the preface before reading the last page.

looked everywhere around him with the flashlight, at all the shows of the grounds, remembering one of the few lines he had coined in his life:

"There are as many flower types as there are types of melancholy."

At the place with his work, just by the side of the pavilion overlooking the hospital, he knelt down by the trunk and opened it. He put in Stella's play and yet was not satisfied. What was the *all-embracing art form*? What in the world did it look like? The following morning the judges came and found his answer. His answer to the world:

A SIXTY YEAR OLD MAN IN A TRUNK.

The liquid fusion of the arts?

IT WAS THE TEAR STREAMING DOWN HIS LEFT CHEEK.

The pensioners of the hospital looked out at him and there! as they all stared, he became as an imposter in a shine of grey!

THE END

Afterword

When one thinks about the *Gesamtkunstwerk*, a colour, normally the shade of incarnadine –a rubious sprite -hits the backdrop of the mind. What is this colour? I believe it is nothing other than the complexion of flesh. Why? A human being *is* the *Gesamtkunstwerk*. Art is nothing without its creator and an artist, despite self-loathing, doubt and disease, can create all the works of art imaginable, with his hands and his mind. A body, come to think of it, is already a work of art that combines everything; sound in the mouth, paint in the eyes, sculpture in the muscles, whorls of prose in a person's fingerprint. One need only think back to Wagner when he says: that what we require is "the disenchantment of the stone into the flesh and blood of man; out of immobility into motion, out of the monumental into the temporal". I take this to mean that man is the precipice of all art, that any creation, even if it comes from his highest self, will fall short from the original point.

Any fusion is liquid. Man's artistry culminates then in tears; he is most the fusion of which we speak, the gesamtkunstwerk, in moments of liquidity; when he drinks, sweats or swims.

Anyone who loves tragedy knows that failure forms part of a work of art. A tear is precisely this: a "not having made it".

The greatest artists are those who *become* the art they make. Their failure was necessary.

Made in the USA
Charleston, SC
20 September 2016